# GIDION'S HUNT

## GIDION KEEP, VAMPIRE HUNTER
### BOOK ONE

# BILL BLUME

**DIVERSIONBOOKS**

## Also by Bill Blume

*Gidion's Blood (Gidion Keep, Vampire Hunter: Book Two)*
*The Deadlands: And Other Stories*

Diversion Books
A Division of Diversion Publishing Corp.
443 Park Avenue South, Suite 1008
New York, New York 10016
www.DiversionBooks.com

This is a work of fiction. Names, characters, places and incidents either are the
product of the author's imagination or are used fictitiously. Any resemblance to
actual persons, living or dead, events or locales is entirely coincidental.

For more information, email info@diversionbooks.com

First Diversion Books edition August 2015.
Print ISBN: 978-1-68230-017-6
eBook ISBN: 978-1-62681-943-6

This book is dedicated to all the police officers and my fellow dispatchers who work the dark hours so the rest of the world can sleep a little safer.

# CHAPTER ONE

The most important defense a vampire hunter can have is anonymity. That was the warning Grandpa Murphy gave Gidion the night he showed him vampires were real. That night had resembled this one, only the drizzle had belonged to a spring shower, not a September rain.

Gidion was walking east on Cary Street when he saw a woman across the cobbled road. She stumbled out of the Siné Irish Pub. She was alone and slightly intoxicated, two things that might attract a hungry vampire.

Before the lady turned the corner onto Virginia Street, Gidion committed her description to heart: white female, long black hair, dark green top visible beneath a black raincoat, black high heels. He didn't get a good look at her face, but she seemed like a pretty lady, probably in her lower to mid-thirties. She wiped water from her eyes, and he didn't think the clouds had anything to do with those droplets. She disappeared around the corner of the white brick pub.

Gidion slipped his hand inside his hoodie to pat the red bat logo on his black t-shirt. Grandpa Murphy gave him the shirt, said red bats were considered good luck and warded against evil. Gidion's friends teased him for being superstitious, but when a guy is born on a Friday the 13th, he learns to take that stuff seriously. Dad swore he'd gotten that trait from his mother.

He jogged across Cary Street, stopping at the corner. He couldn't let the lady get too far ahead of him. There was a parking garage on that street. If she went inside, he'd have a hard time tracking her without being noticed. Parking garages were all concrete and echoes.

Fortunately, the lady in the raincoat walked past the parking garage. For someone who wasn't sober and dressed in shoes ill-designed for walking, "raincoat lady" was making good time. She'd already crossed Canal Street and was approaching the Canal Walk. He wondered if she lived in the condo building on the other side of the canal. If she did, then he wouldn't get to follow her much further, and there wouldn't be much point. He hadn't seen any hint of a vampire tracking her or anyone else all night.

She crossed the bridge over the Canal Walk. The tourist attraction that fed into the James River didn't draw many people at night, even though it was well-lit. Gidion maintained his distance, standing on the corner of Virginia and Canal. He checked his small supply of weapons, which included a small sword strapped to his back, hidden by his hoodie.

No one else seemed to be following the lady, and it looked pretty certain she was going for the apartment building. He was already contemplating going back to his patrol of Cary and Main Streets, when she took a sharp left onto the steps leading down to the Canal Walk. "Crap," he whispered. He walked as fast as he could without drawing attention to himself.

He ducked behind a black SUV as he saw someone dash out of the shadows at the far end of the corner on his side of the street. Gidion didn't get a good look, not enough to be sure it was the kind of predator he wanted. Vampires moved with more grace, but aside from fangs, which you could only see up close, they didn't exactly wear sparkling letters on their foreheads to advertise what they were. Last week, he'd interrupted a mugger in a parking lot just east of here, realizing the man was human before he might have killed him.

The traffic thundered overhead on the Downtown Expressway. Gidion looked down at the Canal Walk as he ran across the bridge. He didn't see raincoat lady, but he caught a glimpse of the man stalking her as he slipped around the lamplight illuminating the walk. The way he shifted about was too smooth, smoke floating on wind. Gidion made out enough to lock in the guy's appearance: white male, blond hair drawn back into a short ponytail, black jeans, black shirt, no jacket and no visible weapons. Most vampires didn't bother packing guns or knives, but some felt the need to be a bit more "gangsta" than others.

The sound of his footfalls on the wet, stone steps forced Gidion to slow his pace. He didn't dare take his eyes from the vampire. One misstep and he'd either end up falling on his face or tip off the bad guy that he was being hunted. That the jerk hadn't spotted him yet suggested a bit of good news-bad news. The vampire was probably so focused on his hunger, he was oblivious to everything but his dinner. That was the good news. The bad news? Hunger that fierce left a vampire in a really shitty mood, kind of like Gidion's dad before he'd had his coffee.

Gidion saw the vampire rush into the tunnel beneath the next bridge. That place made for a perfect ambush. Great for Gidion, but lousy for raincoat lady. No time left for caution. He sprinted and prayed the vampire's attention stayed on his dinner.

The vampire grabbed the woman by the hair and waist. She screamed, but only for a second. The vampire covered her mouth with his hand to muffle her cries as he dragged her behind a column.

They were too close for anything that would allow Gidion a killing shot. He needed them separated fast. Only one thing made a vampire run from a meal: losing the blood it already had.

An inhuman hiss echoed beneath the bridge as the vampire reared back his head and widened his jaw for the strike at her throat. Gidion lunged forward and grabbed him by the ponytail. The vampire's hiss cut off in surprise. Before the vampire could turn, Gidion slit open the front of its throat with a box cutter. The vampire released the woman, but Gidion didn't let go of him. Instead, he shoved the predator's head forward, pinning his chin against his chest. Grandpa Murphy said that forced out more blood than pulling back, kind of like squeezing juice out of an orange.

The vampire shoved Gidion back against the concrete column. Thank God these things didn't really possess superhuman strength, or that might have been enough for the vampire to finish him off. Gidion lost his grip on him as his entire back was flattened against the concrete. The vampire ran out the far side of the tunnel. Gidion saw the lady go for her cell phone. He swatted it from her hand into the canal and ran after his incomplete kill.

"What are you doing?" She thrust her hand towards the water without any real chance of retrieving the phone. Bad enough she'd screamed as loud as she had. Hopefully, no one had heard and called the police for her. It never failed. People always called 911 when they shouldn't. At least that's what Gidion's dad said.

The cut to the throat had started the job, but Gidion needed to finish this fast. The vampire ran down the sidewalk with a hand to his throat, trying to contain what was left of his false life. Gidion tackled him, forcing him to the right and onto the grass. He drove a knee into his kill's back, right on the spine with a loud crack of bone. That would make Grandpa Murphy proud.

He grabbed that short pony tail and yanked. "Where's the rest of your coven?" Gidion asked. "Where do they hide?"

"I don't have—" The vampire rasped, as if he might save some of the blood he was losing. "—a coven. Don't."

"Crap."

Gidion drew the short, wakizashi sword he carried on his back, beneath his hoodie. He delivered another knee strike to the back to make sure the vampire didn't get back up. Moving to the side, he slammed the sword's blade through the back of the vampire's throat, a clean decapitation.

He climbed off the grass and back onto the sidewalk. His hand shook as he wiped the sweat from his brow. Dammit, his heart was pounding worse than after a three-mile run. He used the back of the dead man's black shirt to wipe the blood from the sword and then slid the blade back into its wooden scabbard.

He crawled back from the grassy embankment and back onto the sidewalk. Christ, he was a mess. The entire bottom half of his black jeans was covered in mud. At least he'd avoided getting a lot of blood on his clothes this time. When he turned back towards the bridge, he was startled by the lady in the raincoat.

She stared at him, looking too horrified to speak. Her eyes met his and her face alighted with recognition. "Gidion Keep?"

"Oh, crap." He'd just saved his world history teacher, Ms. Aldgate. So much for anonymity.

# CHAPTER TWO

Gidion hadn't recognized Ms. Aldgate outside of the classroom. He'd never seen her without her hair pulled back, and she sure as hell didn't dress like that for school.

"What did you do?" she asked.

She stepped back as Gidion pulled out a black shopping bag he'd brought with him. "I saved your life." He displayed the vampire's fangs for her before he shoved the head in the bag.

"Don't call the police. Go home and don't waste any time getting to your car. Vampires sometimes hunt in packs, so he might not be alone." She stared at the bag. "Just get out of here."

He didn't know if she bought that lie about vampires hunting in packs; this guy had definitely been alone. If he hadn't, then the others would have moved in for the kill with him.

Gidion didn't stick around to find out what she thought. He pulled his hood up and ran east out of the Canal Walk. He'd parked in the lot near Bottom's Up Pizza. If he was lucky, Ms. Aldgate wouldn't call the cops, and he could retrieve the rest of the body before anyone else found it. Of course, if he was really lucky, maybe he could use this to score some extra credit in her class.

When he looked over his shoulder, he saw her running back the way they'd come. He kissed his fingertips and planted it on his shirt's red bat. He hoped his good luck charm worked better this time.

The red bat earned its keep long enough for Gidion to retrieve the rest of the vampire's body. He'd been extra careful gathering the body and loading it into the back of his grey Kia Soul. A black tarp hid the body bag. On top of that, he piled a baseball bat, football, helmet, running shoes, gym bag and a few other things that would leave anyone convinced the rest of the pile contained nothing but more sports gear.

Once he'd pulled onto the expressway, he pulled out his cell phone. "Grandpa, fire up the cremator," he said once he answered. "I've got one."

"You okay, boy? Seem pretty shook up." His voice sounded rougher than usual. Must have caught him in the middle of a smoke.

"Yeah, I'm good." He considered telling him about Ms. Aldgate, but he figured he didn't need to until he knew what she was gonna do. The fact he'd been able to get the body seemed like a good sign. He'd taken the head in case he hadn't been able to, just to make sure the body couldn't be "rezzed" by any of the vampire's friends. Not much danger of that, if his claim he didn't have a coven was true.

"I'll get things ready," Grandpa said. "Proud of ya, boy!"

"Thanks." Gidion heard his nerves rattle in his own voice and hung up before he did anything more to incriminate himself. The old sailor would interrogate him for certain when he reached the funeral home.

He tossed his phone onto the passenger seat and cranked up the stereo, blasting the White Rabbits' "Percussion Gun" after he cleared the toll booths. In less than ten minutes, he'd left downtown behind and was passing the train yards as he merged onto I-64. Traffic was almost non-existent after he took the ramp onto Staples Mill Road.

A few blocks from dropping off his night's catch, blue lights flashed in his rearview mirror.

"Oh, crap."

His stomach took a swan dive and his heart beat faster than the music in his car. Against every desire to plant the accelerator to the floor and make a run for it, he pulled his car into the lot of a near-empty shopping center and parked it. The cop's lights continued to flash. No red lights on the police car. That meant it must be Henrico County Police. Gidion looked down at the "good luck" bat on his shirt. "You know, now would be a great time to start working, because you've been doing a lousy job of it so far tonight."

He turned his music off and dug around in the glove compartment for that DMV card thingee. At least his driver's license, the car's inspection and tags were all current.

A flashlight shone through the rear window of the car. Gidion hoped the officer didn't see anything suspicious about all that crap piled back there. Jesus, he wasn't even speeding! Had Ms. Aldgate called the police after all? Surely, they couldn't have put out an all car bulletin on him this fast.

*Just act normal,* he told himself. Of course, wouldn't being a nervous wreck be normal for any teenager pulled over by a cop?

The officer tapped at the driver side window. He'd forgotten to roll it down. Great. He needed to calm down. He offered his best smile as the window slid down and then handed over his driver's license and registration without the officer having to ask.

"Thanks." The officer paused to glance at both and grunted as he looked back at Gidion. "You know why I pulled you over, Mr. Keep?"

*I really hope it doesn't have jack to do with the decapitated corpse in my trunk,* he thought to himself. "Um, not really."

"Well, you were going a little fast. You were doing 51 in a 45-mile-per-hour zone."

Okay, so he was speeding just a little. "Oh, uh, sorry. Didn't realize I was going that fast."

"Uh-huh." The officer looked at the driver's license again with this indifferent grunt. "You know the other reason I pulled you?"

"Um…" *Please don't let it be about the corpse in the trunk.*

The officer pointed the flashlight at the dashboard. "Here's a tip. Why don't you tell me what time it is?"

"It's, uh, one-thirteen. Oh."

"Yeah." The officer grunted. He sounded like he practiced his grunts a lot. He was quite good at them. "Do you realize that Henrico County has an eleven o'clock curfew for anyone seventeen and under? That means you either better be coming home from work or riding with an adult."

Technically, Gidion was on his way from work, but he couldn't exactly explain he was a vampire hunter to a police officer.

"Seems you live in Chesterfield County, so you're not heading in the right direction to be going home, kid." The officer flashed his light across the passenger seats. "And I don't see any adults in this car either." Gidion realized he actually did have an adult passenger, but since he was dead...still not helpful.

Just then the radio on the officer's belt crackled. "Radio to Car 161, switch to tac for a secure transmission."

Gidion groaned, because he knew that voice on the radio.

The officer arched an eyebrow at Gidion. He reached over to the transmitter clipped to his jacket. "10-4, Radio." He pointed at Gidion. "Sit tight."

"Yes, sir." Sitting tight was simple enough. His butt was so tight right now, he'd probably whistle if he farted. He fought the urge to look behind him at the trunk. He didn't want to give the officer any reason to look back there.

A grunt to his left let him know the officer was back.

"Well, Mr. Keep, I'm gonna let you go without a ticket. You wanna know why?"

Gidion just nodded. He already knew why.

"For starters, you weren't going that fast, but judging from the sound of your dad's voice just now, I think you're already in for it as it is." Just then, Gidion's phone beeped in his passenger seat to let him know he had a text message. "I'm guessing that's him right now."

Gidion picked up the cell phone. Yeah, that was Dad.

The officer transmitted over his radio. "Car 161 to Radio, show me clear with advice."

Dad answered the officer on the radio. "10-4, Car 161. He'll be getting a lot more advice in a few minutes. One-eighteen hours." Having a dad who worked as a police dispatcher just sucked sometimes.

"Sorry, kid." The officer laughed as he walked back to his patrol car.

Gidion opened his cell phone to read Dad's text. *'Get your ass here. NOW.'*

"I really need a new good luck shirt."

# CHAPTER THREE

Milligan's Funeral Home looked about as dead as one would expect at 1:30 in the morning. The building blended into the night with its grey brick exterior. The liveliest thing was Gidion's car turning into the parking lot and zipping around to the back. Gidion clicked the garage door opener clipped to his visor. Dim light spilled out as a large, metal door lifted.

Gidion threw his car into reverse and burrowed into the drop-off. The red glow of the taillights made Grandpa Murphy look like one of the permanent residents as he limped into the garage. Of course, Grandpa was a permanent resident since he owned the place.

"You drive worse than your dad."

Gidion left the car door open as he jumped out. Beneath the smell of his car's gas fumes, he smelled that blend of mint and tobacco he'd always associated with Grandpa. One day, he was going to tell him that gum only took the pipe smell from his breath, and it didn't even really do that.

"Sorry, Grandpa, we gotta make this one fast." He flung open the trunk.

"What? You can't make time to chat with your grandfather? You got a date or something?"

"Yeah, with Dad."

Gidion tossed all the sports gear into the backseat. He made sure to pull out the gym bag, though. He kept a change of clothes in it for just these occasions when his hunting got messy.

Grandpa lifted the black tarp to reveal the white body bag beneath. "Your dad, huh? What'd you do to piss him off?"

"Aside from breathing?" Gidion took the heavier end of

13

the body. They nodded their three-count and lifted it onto the waiting gurney.

"You bagged a thin one tonight, didn't you?"

"Yeah." He helped push the gurney inside. They'd gotten good at maneuvering this thing to the cremator room. This room definitely didn't fit with the rest of the place's subdued, earth-tone décor. Aside from the big grey behemoth cremator machine, the room was white walls and a black and grey linoleum floor.

"So, what happened?"

"Got pulled by a Henrico officer just down the road. I think Dad was working the radio, so I was instantly busted."

Grandpa grunted, which reminded Gidion of the traffic cop, only with a lot more smoke-induced texture. "How many times have I told you not to speed when you got a package?"

"Yeah, yeah, blame the White Rabbits."

"You're doing cocaine?" His eyeballs looked ready to pop out of his head.

"They're a rock group."

"Oh."

They nodded their three-count and lifted the body onto the cremator's conveyer. Gidion wiped his brow again. The cremator had the room pretty hot, but he'd been in here enough times now to know it wasn't preheated enough yet to toss in his catch.

"I thought the Beatles' name sounded stupid," Grandpa said. "What the hell kind of name for a rock band is 'White Rabbits'? They aren't a group of faggots, are they?"

Oh dear God. "Don't really know. I just like their music." Gidion was starting to think his visit with Dad might be a good thing after all.

"You learn anything from this bloodsucker?"

*Other than my world history teacher looks kind of hot?* Gidion decided not to say that one out loud, partly because the thought was sort of gross. "Nothing to help me find the local coven. He was just another stray." Gidion was already running out of the room, back to the garage. "Gotta run, Grandpa. Love ya!"

"Good luck, boy!"

Gidion jumped into his car. "Yeah, luck. Right."

He heard Grandpa shout something else he couldn't quite understand as his grey car jerked back into the night. No time to stick around and find out what he was going on about. Gidion made sure to close the garage door this time. Grandpa had been really cross the last time he'd forgotten, and he already had enough lectures penned onto his calendar thanks to that stupid traffic stop. At least the funeral home was on the way to the police station, so he hadn't lost too much time with his delivery.

He caught the light at the next intersection and veered onto Parham Road.

"Okay, okay, okay…Think fast, Gidion. You need an explanation for being out this way at night," he said in a sing-song voice. He had all of three blocks left to cook up his excuse. "I'm so screwed."

His excuse manufacturing time counted down as he passed the various public service buildings. The government center and the jail on his left warned he had just one block left. Parham Doctors Hospital on his right might as well have had a sign posted out front that said, 'We save lives, except for Gidion Keep's, because he's a goner.'

The brown brick Public Safety Building, which Henrico County's police and firefighters called home, was on his left. The place was more like three buildings. His dad worked in the nearest one, naturally. He pulled into the half-deserted parking lot and parked as far from the door as he could get.

He picked up his cell phone and sent a text message to let Dad know he was here. A response didn't take long. *Wait in your car. On the way.'*

If Dad was working the police radio, then he'd have to get someone to take it over so he could come outside. That gave him a little longer to create his explanation.

"This is so stupid." It wasn't like Dad didn't know about vampires. According to Grandpa, he'd also hunted them when he was Gidion's age and hunted up until Mom had died. That was more than a decade ago. Gidion had only been four, and he couldn't remember a lot about her now. He'd made the mistake of telling Dad that one time, his tenth birthday. Dad had looked like he was gonna cry.

Grandpa said if Dad ever found out what they were doing, he'd go ballistic. Gidion believed him.

The passenger door to the car opened and in came Dad. Damn, that didn't take nearly as long as he'd expected.

"Well, we've had a busy night," he said in his radio voice. Gidion wasn't sure where his dad had gotten a voice that deep, because it sure wasn't from Grandpa. Whenever Dad had yelled at him as a kid, he'd been so scared he'd shake. Things hadn't changed much now that he was a teenager.

"So do I really have to ask?" Dad said.

"Oh."

"Yes, 'oh'." The voice boomed inside the car. Dad wasn't much bigger than he was, but that voice almost squeezed Gidion out the window. "What are you doing out this late? For God's sake, the whole reason I'm on midnight shift is so I can free up my schedule for you during the day and evening. Do you think this is fun for me? Jesus, I expect better from you than—" Dad's voice trailed off as he looked down at Gidion's pants. "What the hell have you been doing? Your jeans are a mess."

Oh, crap. Suddenly, Gidion realized what Grandpa had been yelling on his way out of the garage. He'd forgotten to change clothes.

"Gidion Keep!" Dad glared at him. "What the hell have you been doing? Quit trying to cook up some stupid excuse. Answer me right this second."

Gidion panicked, eyes running in all directions when they settled on the pile of sports stuff in the backseat.

"Football," he said. "Seth, Pete, and I went to a park in the West End after the game and threw the ball around."

"Which park?"

"I don't know." He shrugged for good measure and then reminded himself not to ham it up too much.

"Short Pump?"

"I don't know. I guess. Seth picked it out. I just followed them there."

Dad scowled. "That explains your clothes, but then why were you on Staples Mill Road? That's nowhere near there."

It was moments like this that Gidion could totally believe Dad used to be a police officer. When Mom died, he'd transferred to Communications to work the 911 phones and the radios so he could have a more "consistent schedule." The older Gidion got, the more convinced he was that Dad resented being reduced to a civilian, that he missed being on the road.

"Dad, I was on the way home and realized I needed some gas. Only place I knew would be open was the Wawa up the road from here."

"Turn her on." Dad leaned over so he could see the gas gauge.

Gidion cranked the car back to life. Dear Lord, he hoped the car was as low as he'd made it sound. He'd been sitting near a quarter tank earlier, but if it wasn't riding near the "E" yet…

"All right," Dad said, satisfied by the placement of the hovering needle. "I can't believe you idiots were in a park this late. Are you boys that stupid? Do you have any idea what could have happened to you out there at this hour?" He shook his head. Gidion recognized the change in tone. He was safe for now. "You have enough money for gas?"

"Yeah, my paycheck from Grandpa went through today." This was part of Gidion's cover. He helped Grandpa at the funeral home on the weekends. He was looking forward to his next paycheck. Grandpa gave him a hundred dollar bonus for each vampire he killed. He was so gonna download some new tunes.

Dad cracked a smile and grabbed the top of Gidion's head the way he used to when Gidion was a kid to mess up his hair. "I suppose on the bright side, at least I got to see you tonight. Feel like I haven't seen you all week."

"I can think of better ways to see you."

"Yes, I agree." He laughed. "At least I'm off the rest of the weekend, and your grandpa will be over Sunday to watch the games with us."

"Cool."

Dad opened the door to get out. "You go straight home."

"After I get the gas, though, right?"

He sighed. "Yes, after you get some gas, but then you go straight home. Got it?"

"Yes, sir."

"You call me when you get home, and do it from the landline, not your cell phone."

"Okay." Dad wasn't stupid. He'd give him that. The caller ID would rat him out if he didn't call from the house. Looked like he was done hunting for the night.

"You working for your grandpa tomorrow?"

"Yeah, he's got me driving the hearse for two services." Gidion considered that easy money, but he had to wear a suit and tie. Those processions also went way too slow. Just once, he'd like to take off at sixty and totally freak out the folks trying to follow him.

"All right. Go home, and get some sleep. Love ya." Dad closed the door and hoofed it back to the Communications Center.

"Crap, that was close." He leaned back and let out a long breath. Thank God he'd noticed the football in the backseat, or he'd have been uber busted.

He wouldn't get to do anymore hunting this weekend with Dad home. So far, all he'd managed to bag were nomadic vampires, the ones without a coven. They'd all been guys, too. Grandpa said that was normal starting out. The most important thing was making sure the coven didn't find him first. That meant not telling anyone what he was doing. Even his friends didn't know. Grandpa would pop a lung if he found out about Ms. Aldgate. What the hell was he going to do about her?

# CHAPTER FOUR

Since he wasn't carrying a corpse in his trunk the next day, Gidion didn't worry about hanging so close to the speed limit as he rushed South on 288. Metric's latest album blasted from his stereo and competed with the wind rushing through his car's open windows. He was running late, thanks to Grandpa, who insisted on giving him the manila envelope which was catching some rays in his passenger seat.

Every Saturday afternoon, he and the guys met at Richmond Comix to pick up the new issues of their favorite series. Seth had already sent a text threatening to buy Gidion's copy of *Red Robin* for himself if he took much longer. His car felt like it lifted onto two wheels as he hooked a right into the shopping center along Midlothian Turnpike.

They'd started meeting here every Saturday back when they were in fifth grade. Back then, they rode their bikes here to spend their allowances. These days, they were each working with four wheels and their own paychecks. Gidion spotted Seth's dark green Mini Cooper, the "Green Machine." Pete's spray-paint black, beat-up Camaro had made it today, too. The Camaro worked so rarely, they'd nicknamed it "Death." They joked that Gidion's car didn't have enough personality to warrant a name, but he already called it the "Little Hearse" in his head. Only, he couldn't tell his friends why.

"Took you long enough, dude." Seth stood at the register near the back and thumbed through a copy of *Amazing Spider-Man*.

Pete didn't even look up from where he was hunting through the shelves in the far left corner of the long store. He just held up a hand in a half-hearted wave. Ever since school had started back, Pete's aloofness had received an upgrade which included wearing all his collars turned up and swearing off haircuts.

"The second funeral service ran over." He didn't understand why some preachers felt the need to go long on those things. They all just said the same stuff. Tragic loss, taken before his time, pray for the family, blah blah blah. While they were at it, they could at least throw in a suggestion to tip the driver who's sweating off half his body weight while he waited in the hearse.

Seth grimaced. "You'll never catch me riding in a car that carries dead people."

"Technically speaking, we're all dying, so every car carries 'dead people'." So spaketh Peter the philosopher. He wasn't exactly your "cute dolls and puppy dogs" kind of guy, not these days anyway. Gidion knew for a fact Pete still had a baby doll stashed in his closet which he used to pretend to breastfeed when he was five. In his defense, Pete had been competing with a younger sister for his parents' attention. Not much had changed, even though he was just way too scary tall for anyone to ignore.

"So what are you looking for over there, Pete?" Gidion asked as he stepped up to the counter. The guy working the register moved with the silent indifference of a zombie to pull Gidion's orders from his box.

"I'm looking for what every guy really wants in a comic book." He picked up an issue of *Red Sonja* with the heroine on the cover swinging a sword and wearing something slight enough that one good sneeze would require the cover to have a cover. "Well-drawn tits in spandex."

Seth arched his eyebrow as if doing his best Spock impression. "Isn't she wearing chain mail?"

Pete turned the comic book so he could look at it and shrugged. "Well, true, but really, we all know the spandex part is optional."

"I hear that."

Gidion shook his head as he handed over his debit card to the zombie behind the counter. "Remind me again why I let myself be seen in public with you two?"

"So you can borrow issues like that one when you get lonely."

Leave it to Seth to deliver the perfect comeback.

Pete wasn't one to let a smart remark pass without one of his own. "Well, we don't all have a nice pair of real tits to enjoy."

Gidion laughed. "Considering she's just a freshman, do they really qualify as——?"

"Hey! That's my woman you two are talking about."

Gidion looked at his watch. This must have been a record. They'd taken less than two minutes to invoke Seth's girlfriend, Andrea. That was pronounced Ahhhhn-drea, of course, because God forbid anyone mispronounce it—especially in her presence. She'd latched onto her "teddy bear" Seth less than a week after school started. For all of Gidion's quips, he envied Seth. He'd become the first in their triumvirate to land a real girlfriend. They'd agreed this past summer that any girls prior to car ownership didn't count. That meant the month Gidion was "going out" with Cathy Hollis in sixth grade was null and void.

The cashier rolled his eyes as he returned Gidion's debit card with his receipt.

Gidion looked over the thick stack of comics in his bag as they went outside. *Red Robin*, *Captain America*, *Avengers* and plenty more... He'd made off with a lot of fresh reading material.

"Hey, we should go to a movie tonight." This was the first Saturday night in months he wouldn't be hunting for fangs.

"No can do." Seth slapped himself on the leg with his rolled up *Spider-Man* issue. "I got plans."

"Wait." He just realized Seth wasn't carrying a bag. "That's all you got?"

"Dude, restaurants ain't cheap. You just wait and see." Less than a month dating and he was already the expert.

"What about you, Pete?"

"Uh, technically, I'm out, too." He shrugged and sat on Death's hood, which placed him eye level with Gidion. "Gotta go do something."

"Seriously? Since when did I become the only guy here without a social calendar?"

Seth and Pete exchanged this queer look.

"What?"

Seth pointed at him with his rolled up comic book. "Dude, you're the one who's been 'Mr. Mysterious and Busy' for months now."

"Oh." He winced as he remembered he needed to lock in his cover for last night. "Speaking of which, if anyone—as in any adults—asks, we were throwing a football around at Short Pump Park last night."

"Dude, I was making out with my woman, and no way I'm changing those details…not unless you wanna contribute to my dating fund."

Gidion looked at his bag of comics. After this haul, he barely had enough left for gas to make it through the next two weeks.

"Well, let's limit contact with my dad to hit-and-runs, okay? Just to avoid any lengthy Q-and-A." They looked unconvinced. "At least until after next week?"

Seth swatted him on the arm with his comic. "Relax, dude. We got your back."

"So what were you doing last night?" Pete asked.

"Uh…probably—"

"—better we don't know," Seth and Pete said in unison.

"Sorry, guys."

"You okay?" Seth said. "I mean, you aren't getting into drugs or gambling or something are you?"

"No!" Holy crap. He knew he'd been off in limbo a bit, but damn.

"Hey, drugs wouldn't be that bad a thing." Pete's voice started off all incensed, then trailed into a mutter. "Long as he shared." After a minute, Pete seemed to realize they were staring at him. "Just kidding." He put on this big smile which really didn't fit his face. Weird. Gidion had gotten to where he couldn't half tell when Pete was really joking.

Seth was the first to leave, which had become the norm of late.

"So, what are you doing tonight anyway?" Gidion asked.

"Just things." Pete dug through his bag of comics, and Gidion couldn't help but wonder if his friend was avoiding looking him in the eyes.

"And you guys were calling me all 'mysterious.' What's up? You got some dark secret like ballroom dancing lessons with your mom?"

That restored the eye contact, and twisted Pete's lips with disgust. "I am not dancing with my mother. I have some standards."

"So what are you doing?"

"What does it matter?" Pete got off the hood and tossed his bag of comics into his car.

Gidion felt as if he'd just had his head bit off. He'd hit a nerve without trying.

"Pete, you okay?"

He adjusted the upturned collar of his shirt, pulling it a little tighter. "Gid, I'm fine." He shrugged. "I've just been hanging out with some other people. Seth's got his girl, and you've been off doing whatever it is that isn't drugs or dating. I lost my job at the car shop, and the past month has just been all around shitty."

"Wait, when did you lose your job?"

Pete leaned on the top of the car and stared off. "Before the school year started."

Now Gidion felt like a real jerk. He hadn't even noticed. "What happened? I thought you liked it."

"Overslept a few times."

"Oh, that sucks." Gidion didn't really know what else to say to that. Even as bad as his luck could get, Pete seemed to have a black cloud permanently stuck above him. Seth and Gidion had both taken the fall for him a few times to help out in the past. "So if you haven't been working, what have you been doing?"

"Jesus, Gid, don't worry about it. It's not a big deal. I'm keeping busy, and I'm even getting a little cash on the side." He tapped the roof of his car. "Only reason I've been able to keep Death rolling."

"Well, I suppose that's good."

Pete glanced at Gidion's car. "Speaking of cars, how's No-Name over there doing?"

"Been running fine."

While Pete wasn't the most reliable guy for getting to work on time, he knew lots about fixing cars. He'd found Death in a scrapyard, bought it for a few hundred bucks and got it running. Pete already had oil stains under the tips of his fingernails and a permanent odor of grease before he had a driver's license. Heck, Dad even let Pete change the oil in his car.

"So what have you been doing?" Pete asked.

"Mainly hanging out with Grandpa and working out." Gidion supposed that wasn't a total lie, and providing a somewhat honest answer made him feel less like a hypocrite for pestering Pete about what he'd been up to.

A few minutes later, Death rattled its way out of the parking lot, leaving Gidion sitting by himself in the Little Hearse.

"This just sucks." He looked at the time on his dashboard's display, not even two o'clock yet. Dad was probably still asleep, giving him a few more hours to himself.

"Might as well work." He picked up the manila envelope Grandpa had given him just before leaving the funeral home. He opened it and dumped the contents onto the passenger seat, all the personal items from the guy who tried to chomp on Ms. Aldgate. Didn't look like much.

"A wallet." He flipped it open. The picture matched, but he was willing to bet the name didn't, Allen Pike. Then he picked up the only other thing to fall out of the envelope, a car key with a remote fob. "This is a first. Let's see what I can do with you."

He cranked up the Little Hearse and pulled it back onto Midlothian. It was time to go back downtown.

# CHAPTER FIVE

Ask any vampire with half a brain cell to choose between a Lamborghini Gallardo and a Buick LeSabre, and he'll choose the Buick every time.

Why?

Trunk space.

Sure, the Lamborghini will score him a few ladies to snack on along the way, but even the most high performance vehicle is eventually going to break down. If that happens on the most desolate stretch of an interstate a half hour before sunrise, then he'll need a place to hide.

Thanks to Grandpa Murphy, Gidion knew his kill from the night before had been driving a Ford. As soon as he reached downtown, he pulled out the key fob and pressed it whenever he came near a likely candidate.

He passed on the Fiestas, the SUVs and the pickups. After an hour of going up and down Cary and Main, he moved onto the more obscure parking locales. The clock was edging close to four by the time he checked a small lot near the Pipeline Overlook. The location provided a nice place for a vampire to bring a victim: lots of trees, limited foot traffic at night, noisy train tracks and even a view of the James River for those looking to add a little romance to dinner. Gidion spotted a light blue Crown Victoria in a space near the end of the lot, the front end partially over the grass. Grandpa called Crown Vics the car of choice for police and vampires alike. Soon as he pressed the lock button on the key fob, the car honked back at him.

"Yes!" He'd tried to hunt for some of his previous kills' cars, but this was the first time he'd gotten to do it with a key fob. That saved him a lot of legwork.

He pulled the Little Hearse into a space next to the vampire's car. This stretch of the Canal Walk had a little foot traffic this time of day, so he waited a few minutes to let enough folks cycle through so that no one would remember which car was his.

The fob came with a button to pop open the trunk, another useful feature for a vampire using his car as a mobile home. He stepped back a few feet and hit the button. Good thing, too. The vampire hadn't set up any booby traps, but the stench was enough to force him back a few more feet.

The daylight revealed a sleeping bag and several pillows. As he dared to move closer, he saw a bottle of Febreze up beside the spare tire. There was a product testimonial just begging to be made. "Febreze, the choice of nomadic vampires everywhere," he said. Behind the Febreze, there was a small duffel bag. That didn't contain much of use, just some clothes in desperate need of a washing and a few rolls of quarters, probably for laundromats. Making sure no one was looking, he slipped the quarter rolls into his pockets. Hey, it wasn't like the vampire needed the change anymore, and his car didn't run on pedal power.

He pushed the pillows aside and found something of real value.

"Cell phone." Guy was working with one of those touchscreen deals. Gidion had been harassing Dad to let him join the 21st century and get one of these. He was just lucky to have a cell with a keypad for texting, and he only got that because Dad had wanted one for himself, too.

Satisfied he'd found everything he was going to in the trunk, he searched the rest of the car's interior. Only things he found there were some very marked up road maps and two chargers for the cell phone, one for a regular outlet and another for the cigarette lighter.

The phone's battery had died. He closed up the Crown Vic and climbed back into his car. He plugged the phone into the cigarette lighter.

"Let's see who you've been talking to." He went straight for the text messages. The phone contained only one message from a number listed as "unavailable."

The message included a picture of a woman's face, one he knew, and the message warned that last night's attack was anything but random.

*Lillian Aldgate. Find her. Kill her.*
*Reward: admittance. —RICCVN*

*The Imperial March* started playing from his cell phone. Great. "Hey, Dad." Just great.

"Making sure you're alive." Dad still had that just-crawled-out-of-bed slur to his voice.

"Yeah, figured I'd just drive around and let you get some sleep."

"Thanks, but Page made more noise than you ever could have."

Gidion didn't doubt it. Their dog would bark if an ant farted across the street.

"You up for some dinner?" Dad asked.

Gidion's stomach, bitter that he'd forgotten about lunch, answered before his mouth could. "Sounds good to me."

"Head on home then. I should be ready by the time you get here. We can grab a burger, maybe even see a movie."

Gidion resisted the urge to bang his head on the steering wheel. "Sounds awesome. I'm on the way." Could his total lack of social status be any more confirmed than by hanging with his dad on a Saturday night?

He hung up and looked back at the picture of Ms. Aldgate. Was the message sent to just the one vampire, or was this sent as some text blast? Dozens of these fanged assassins could be after her, and he didn't have a way to warn her before Monday. What really had him scratching his head was why a vampire would put a hit on a high school teacher.

# CHAPTER SIX

Sundays were sacred in Gidion's home, but the only real prayer the Keeps engaged in involved their favorite football teams.

"What the hell are the Redskins doing?" Gidion's dad got up and went back into the kitchen, though whether to refill their salsa bowl or escape Washington's loss-in-progress against Dallas was tough to call.

"Looked like they were trying to run the ball on third and twelve." Gidion petted their dog Page on the chest. She liked to sit beside him on Sundays. Dad said it was because he dropped the most food on the floor.

"Idiots might as well have the cheerleaders on the field." Grandpa Murphy mimicked Dad's retreat, only going for the back porch to pull out his pipe. Dad didn't let him smoke it in the house. "They'd have a better chance of winning."

They'd decided to watch Washington and Dallas only because the other game was Buffalo and New England, two teams they refused to pull for.

Page looked up as Gidion stood. She didn't follow him. Instead, she sniffed around the sofa for anything snack worthy. She licked up a few crumbs of tortilla chips.

Grandpa was still filling his pipe as Gidion joined him outside. "Not even halftime, and those idiots are already losing twenty-one to nothing."

"At least Carolina is playing Cleveland later today." They always pulled for the Panthers, and the Browns sucked this year. Gidion closed the back door, giving him a moment to talk to Grandpa without Dad listening. "Hey, I need an excuse to get out of here."

"I know the game is going bad, but—"

"No, it's not that. I've got a lead I want to run down."

Grandpa smiled. "How much time you need?"

"Place isn't far from here, so probably less than an hour."

He lit his pipe and took a few puffs. The smell of sour apple smoke, Grandpa's smell, filled the porch. "I take it this is a recon trip and not a kill mission?"

Gidion nodded. One of grandpa's early lessons: never try to kill a vampire during the day. They wake up super-pissed.

"All right, boy. I've got something that'll work." He cracked open the back door. "Hey, son, I'm sending Gidion to the grocery store for some steaks."

"You cooking them, or am I?"

"Nah, I got this one. Anything's better than watching Washington get skinned. Might as well get one last weekend with the grill before the seasons turn on us." He pulled out his wallet and planted a wad of cash in Gidion's hand. "Get some charcoal, too."

"You got it, Grandpa."

Gidion didn't bother going back inside. He just ran to the front of the house and hopped in his car. Grandpa had taught him to leave all his gear loaded. Better not to ever get caught unprepared.

He flipped open his cell phone and pulled up the directions he'd saved for this trip. The phone recovered from the vampire contained a lot of contacts, but all the entries were names of cities instead of people. He'd seen one for Richmond. A quick reverse lookup online had given him an address to go along with the number. As luck would have it, the house wasn't far from here, just a few blocks away from his high school. He passed West Chester High, a group of two-story brown brick buildings connected by breezeways, and saw a few people using the tennis courts.

A few minutes later, he turned onto Tolliver Court. Two boys who looked like they were each seven years old were having a mock sword fight with branches in the middle of the road. He got out and pulled a small, pale blue, plastic tub from the back of the car. The tub contained a couple of magazines and a bunch of subscription forms. He carried the tub up to the front door of 10014, a rancher with tan vinyl siding. The front yard looked promising enough. A pile of leaves had formed around the base of a maple. If anyone was looking after this place, they weren't worried about yard work.

He knocked on the door a few times, but no one answered. The front porch included a window that looked into the living room. The curtains were pulled shut, but a small crack in them let him get a peek inside. He saw a few chairs and little else. That was promising.

Hardwood floors…another sign he'd hit pay dirt. Looked like there had been a rug. He could see the outline, but rugs weren't good for bloodstains. Hardwood was easier to clean by comparison. Still, very little could beat old-fashioned kitchen or bathroom linoleum. He looked for signs of blood or repeated cleanups, but no such luck. The lack of light inside didn't help.

Grandpa had told him about places like this. Many vampire covens set up safe houses for their nomadic brothers and sisters. They didn't want their fellow predators to know their true resting places. Safe houses also provided a somewhat neutral site to meet or a place to keep someone prisoner while they turned them. To hear Grandpa tell it, making a person into a bloodsucker wasn't that simple, and the process usually killed more people than it turned. It was crazy to think there could be a bunch of vampires sleeping inside this place.

"Who the hell are you?"

If Gidion hadn't been holding the tub of magazines, he'd have probably jumped a foot straight up. He turned to see a girl standing at the bottom of the stairs. She had jet black hair, all black clothes and a snarled mouth with lipstick dark enough to pass for dried blood. Underneath all the angst, she was pretty hot, though. She could probably make it into the top five of a Miss Teen Goth contest.

"Name's Gidion." He lifted his pale blue tub. "Selling some magazines to raise money for a field trip. You interested?"

"You miss the big 'no soliciting' sign at the entrance to the neighborhood, or are you just illiterate?"

Nice.

"It's a fundraiser. Didn't figure folks would mind. You live here?"

"No."

"Oh, well then I'll just knock a few more times." He stepped right back to the door and pounded his fist on it, making sure to give "Goth Chick" a big smile.

"She's not home." She said the "not" like it was a dagger meant to go between his ribs.

"She?"

"Ms. Eaton is out of town."

The reverse lookup he'd done had shown a name of Doris Eaton, so that matched.

"And you are?"

The way this girl crossed her arms, she must have been fighting the urge to rip his head off.

"I'm Stephanie."

"Stephanie Drake?" Holy crap! He knew this girl from school. Only, she'd never looked like this. Stephanie was the small, brown-haired girl who played the violin in orchestra. Pretty cute, too, or rather, she used to be. He hadn't seen her at school since the new year started, and now he understood why. She was still there, and he had seen her, just didn't recognize her.

"Gidion." She said the name as if digging through her memory and then smiled, but not in a way that made her look any happier about him being there. "Oh, yeah. You're the weird boy who was in my English class last year."

She was calling him weird? "Yeah, Mrs. Pulley's class." He walked down the steps to stand beside her. She was about his height. One thing he'd liked about Stephanie, she was one of the few girls who hadn't gotten taller than him when everyone else sprouted in middle school. He was still playing catch-up. "You know when Ms. Eaton might be back home?"

"Not anytime soon. Why do you care?"

He answered her by holding up his tub again. "Suppose I could leave a flier."

"You're wasting your time. I'll just throw it away." She beat him to the next question. "She asked me to keep an eye on her house while she's away. Pick up her mail. All that fun stuff."

"Suppose you have a point." After all, he was willing to bet Ms. Eaton wasn't ever coming back. Either she was sporting a set of fangs or dead.

The real question was where Stephanie fit into this. She wasn't a vampire, but if this was a safe house, then she was working for them. He didn't see any bite marks on her throat, though. According to Grandpa, there were lots of places for a vampire to snack on someone, places that didn't require a lady to wear scarves to hide the telltale marks. Then again, as unlikely as it seemed to Gidion, she might not know the things she was working for were vampires.

"You think your parents would be interested in buying some magazines?"

She laughed. "I think my dad would call the cops."

"Good to know." At least he had his excuse to just leave. He headed for his car. "See you at school, Stephanie."

"Yeah, sure."

She didn't follow, just waited at the foot of the front steps. He bet anything she was going to check the place over the second his car disappeared around the corner. He was tempted to do a U-turn just to catch her in the act, but he decided against it. Bad enough he'd been spotted scoping out the place, but far worse that the one who caught him knew him by name. Grandpa said the best defense a vampire hunter could have was anonymity, and in one weekend, he'd been recognized twice while hunting. He really needed to do something about this streak of bad luck.

# CHAPTER SEVEN

The smell of charcoal and charred meat overpowered Grandpa's pipe on the back porch.

"Feeders." Grandpa took out his pipe and spit over the railing into the grass. "Traitors to their own race. Hookers have more decency and self-respect."

Gidion petted Page on the head as he looked over his shoulder at the back door. He hoped Dad wouldn't pop out with an update on the Redskins' imminent loss to Dallas. They'd both have a hell of a lot to explain if he overheard any of this.

"So what do I do about this girl? It's not like I can cut her head off and bring her in for the cremator."

Grandpa grunted in a way that almost asked, 'Why not?'

"You do whatever it takes to stay alive, boy."

He tried to form the mental image of taking his wakizashi sword to Stephanie's throat, and even with her whole goth look, he just couldn't do it. It was hard to hold the image of how she was now. He kept thinking of the shy girl with the brown hair.

Grandpa snapped him back from his thoughts. "She pretty?"

"What?"

"I'll take that as a 'yes'." He shook his head as he pressed a calloused finger into one of the steaks, checking to see if it was ready. "Don't get distracted, boy. That'll get you killed."

"Yeah, well I don't want to end up in jail either."

Grandpa pointed at him with the cooking tongs, a motion that held Page rapt and drew an irritated whimper when the motion didn't drop any scraps. "Keep your head on straight, and you won't need to worry about that." He flipped the steak he'd checked. "Don't go thinking you can save this girl. Doesn't work like that. Once a feeder gets hooked, they're as good as dead."

"You're talking like she's some kind of drug addict."

Grandpa nodded. "'bout the same, only it's kind of a dual addiction. That's how feeders work. They get off on the vampires drinking from them, and in return, the vampires give them a small taste of their taint. Blood for blood. Forms a connection, one that gets stronger with time."

"So that's why they're called feeders, because that's all their relationship is about?"

That got a laugh out of Grandpa. "Not much of a relationship, but yeah. You treat that flea bag of yours better."

Page shuffled in place as she sensed she was being talked about, probably hoping they were discussing whether to give her a bite of steak.

"So what do I do about this girl? Taking her head is not an option. Pretty girls go missing, and the media goes nuts. They'll eventually piece together enough of what happened, and I'll end up in a place where I don't wanna lean over to pick up the soap."

"You kill the vampire she belongs to." Grandpa laughed. "Do that and you'll be the least of that girl's problems."

Gidion didn't like the sound of that. "What's that supposed to mean?"

"Girl doesn't kill herself, she'll just find another vampire to hook herself to."

Before Gidion could say anything else, the back door opened. Dad came out with a plate for the steaks and something partially-wrapped in tin foil.

"Smelling good, Dad. Got enough heat left for the rest of this?"

"Depends on what you've got."

Gidion stepped out of the way.

"Diced up some red potatoes and got some corn on the cob." Gidion got on his tiptoes to see that Dad had put some olive oil, sea salt and pepper on the potatoes. They were going all out. He needed to do daytime recon more often.

Grandpa did another check of the steak with his knuckles. "Oh, yeah, that's ready. Gidion, hold that plate for me while I make some room on here for the rest of this."

Dad smiled at Gidion as he took the plate. Football Sundays were always the best. The games gave them something safe to talk about. It was too bad they didn't have games every day.

Gidion had recognized years ago that this was a bit of group denial. Every so often, reality would peek through. He could see it when Grandpa walked back inside and found the kitchen table set.

"We're not eating in the den?"

"It's still more than a half hour before the Carolina game kicks off," Dad said. "Figured we'd be civilized today."

Grandpa grumped in silence as he took the spot with his back to the wall. A portrait of mom in her wedding dress was hung there. Grandpa wouldn't ever say it with Gidion in the room, but he knew the old man didn't like looking at her picture there, didn't understand why Dad refused to take it down.

Mom was the one topic considered off-limits when Grandpa was in the house. As Dad once told him, "Your grandpa never liked her, and any talk with him about her just isn't going to end well."

Truth was, they didn't talk about Mom either. She just hung on the wall. Some days, he couldn't decide if they were pretending she was or wasn't there.

# CHAPTER EIGHT

By the time Monday rolled around, Gidion was almost glad to be back at school. He'd avoided the D building on campus, which housed the social studies department. His world history class wasn't until after lunch, and he didn't want to face Ms. Aldgate any sooner than he had to.

"I gotta go to the library before lunch is over," Gidion said between bites of his usual lunch, Peanut Butter Twix and a can of Mountain Dew.

"The library?" Seth asked as he took a break from kissing Andrea. Gidion hoped Pete would get here soon.

West Chester High had a nice campus, the buildings were arranged like a tic-tac-toe board with a large courtyard for the center. Within the courtyard, there were a few circular benches, bordered by raised bushes. Ever since the start of their freshmen year, they'd staked out the same spot in one of those circles. With Andrea and Seth making out, Gidion was starting to feel like the one invading their lunch spot. Where the hell was Pete? He needed some backup here—fast.

"Wait, we don't have a paper due today or something do we?" Andrea asked. She was in his class with Ms. Aldgate.

"No, I just need to use one of the computers, something with Internet access. My luck has been crap lately. I need to get a rabbit's foot."

"I think I saw some of those on a keychain rack at a drug store near here." Even though she was offering the tip, Andrea looked at him as if he was a freak for wanting one.

"Were they real rabbit's feet?"

"They were light blue and pink," she said.

"I don't think those will do me any good. I need the real thing."

"A real rabbit's foot?" She cringed. "That's disgusting."

Seth laughed. "That's our Gidion."

"Dude, I gotta turn this streak around. I got pulled over Friday night by a cop while my dad was working the radio. What are the odds of that? I was instantly busted."

"Ouch, that is bad. Did he ground you?"

"No, shockingly."

Andrea felt the need to jump back into the conversation. "Wait, you didn't get punished? Did you get a ticket?"

"Well, no."

Andrea pushed her hair out of her eyes which were narrowed with confusion. "You didn't get punished or get a ticket. How is that bad luck?"

"Just trust me on this. I need a rabbit's foot or something. Can you get a rabbit's foot on eBay?" For that matter, would the library computers even let him access eBay? He'd already searched online last night while he was at home, but he hadn't found what he needed. "And what about lucky coins? I mean, what makes a coin lucky, and where do I even find one?"

Seth was about to answer, but then looked around. "Hey, where's Pete?"

"Beats me." He was tempted to point out it was amazing just how much a guy could notice when he takes more than a five-second break from sucking down his girlfriend's carbon dioxide output. "I haven't seen him all day."

"You won't miss him when you do," Andrea said.

Seth looked as perplexed as Gidion. "Hun, what do you mean by that?"

"Have a look for yourselves." She pointed towards the breezeway. Pete was walking their way.

"Holy crap," Seth whispered.

"Hey, guys." Pete plopped down between Gidion and Seth. Andrea had been right. No missing him, not with him wearing a big, black dog collar, complete with silver studs. He was wearing a matching pair on his wrists.

"Does the entire set come with a leash?" Gidion asked.

"Funny, Gid. Real funny."

"Okay," Seth said, "seriously, what's up with the dog collar?"

Pete shrugged and looked at the ground as he unwrapped his chicken sandwich. "Figured it looked bad ass."

"You look like you're waiting on someone to take you for a walk." Gidion tried to make that sound like a joke, but seeing Pete like this was freaking him out. He'd always been the strangest out of the three of them, but this was out there even for him.

"Whatever." He didn't look up, just ate his sandwich.

"Speaking of going for walks, I need to run by my locker." Andrea stood and held out her arm waiting for her "teddy bear" to escort her.

"That's my cue guys." Seth stood, and the lovebirds wandered off, arm-in-arm.

"I think Seth should be the one wearing that collar." Gidion laughed but stopped as soon as he realized Pete didn't share in the joke. They just sat there and ate their lunch.

After he'd finished his candy bar, Gidion considered heading for the library, but he hated to just bail on his friend. "Are you okay? I mean, you've just been kind of off lately."

"I'm fine." Funny how he said that in a way that made "fine" sound more like "total crap."

"So what'd you do this weekend? Anything good?"

"Went dancing."

"You? Really?" Gidion couldn't quite see that. His friend's lanky body just didn't look like it could possibly dance in any fashion that wouldn't resemble a full-body seizure. He was more impressed than anything else. He wouldn't have the courage to dance in public, and he wouldn't have thought Pete any different. "So where'd you go?"

Another shrug. Pete wouldn't look up to meet him in the eyes either.

"Oh, did you wanna borrow some of the issues I got this

weekend? *Red Robin* was really good." He knew better than to offer an issue of *Captain America*.

"What? Oh, no. Thanks."

This was just painfully pathetic. Gidion decided to cut his losses. "Hey, I gotta run by the library before fifth period. Trying to find a real rabbit's foot online."

Pete nodded. He'd already finished his chicken sandwich, but his jaw was working like he was still chewing it. What was wrong with him?

"Gid, where are you going for your field trip?"

"What?"

"Heard you were going on a field trip, was wondering where you were going?"

"Where did you—?" Everything inside him went cold as he realized only one person could have told Pete that, goth girl Stephanie. No wonder Pete couldn't look him in the eyes. At least he had the decency to feel guilty about spying on him.

Everything about Pete and the changes Gidion had seen in him suddenly clicked. The upturned collars on his shirts and now the stupid dog collar weren't about looking "bad ass." He was hiding the marks of what he'd become. He really was on a leash, and Gidion knew exactly what was holding it.

"You can tell Stephanie it's actually a mission trip…to Mexico. People just tend to get a little weird if they think it's something to do with religion, so I just call it a 'field trip'." The improvised lie felt tight in his throat.

"Oh."

Gidion and Pete didn't say another word. Pete kept his eyes focused on the ground. Gidion fought down the urge to beat the snot out of him with his bookbag. He couldn't even manage a grunt for a "good-bye" as he headed for the library. Just looking at Pete made him nauseous.

He was the great vampire hunter, so good at what he did that he'd totally missed one of his best friends had become a feeder.

# CHAPTER NINE

Gidion kept his watch in sync with the school bell, so he cut it to the last possible second for his world history class. Ms. Aldgate stared at him as he sat down. He wondered if the next fifty minutes were going to be as long and awkward for her as he knew it would be for him.

"We're going to continue our discussion on the Reformation." She stood from behind her desk and walked over to the dry erase board. She'd already written "The Reformation" onto the white surface in big black letters. "Can anyone name me some of the causes?" She picked up a marker and started her list with a "1" that was so well-written, it could have come out of a computer.

"Gidion." She looked right at him.

"What? I mean, um." Holy crap, she was calling on him right off the bat? Maybe this wasn't as awkward for her. Fabulous. As he struggled to form an answer, he saw Seth's girlfriend Andrea looking at him. The look on her face seemed to say, 'Sucks to be you.'

He heard that Winnie the Pooh voice in his head going, 'think, think, think,' and an answer came to him. "Uh, corruption in the church?"

"Yes."

He could imagine the game show "ding ding ding" celebrating his correct answer. Thank God! Andrea smiled at him and mouthed something he interpreted as 'Nice one!'

That was the only time Ms. Aldgate called on him. As the class discussion moved onto Martin Luther, his Ninety-Five Theses and Henry VIII, he realized what Ms. Aldgate had really been doing. She was making it very clear she was not going to be intimidated by him and certainly not on her turf. He didn't think that was a good sign, one that made his fifty-minute class seem more like two hours.

"I want everyone to finish reading chapter eight in your books before tomorrow. You'll take a ten question quiz at the start of class, and it will not be multiple-choice."

The warning received a round of groans. Gidion was the only one letting out a relieved sigh as the class stood to leave. He wanted out of here, but Ms. Aldgate stopped him before he could make a break for the door.

"Gidion," she said, "I want to see you for a few minutes after class."

A few minutes? They only had five minutes between classes.

Andrea whispered to him as she slid her book into her backpack. "What did you do to tick her off?"

"No idea." He didn't look at her as he lied. He just packed his bag, so he could get out of there as fast as possible whenever he got the chance to run.

Andrea and the others rushed from the room. He stood by his desk and watched the door, as if he might wish his way out before Ms. Aldgate could say anything.

"I've got P.E. for sixth period." He hoped that would sway her to let him leave, but she closed the door to her room.

He'd never really analyzed the way Ms. Aldgate had decorated her class, but now that he was desperate not to look her in the eyes, he studied the room. He remembered her once saying, "Making sense of history requires you to find the order in chaos." She used every available bit of space on her wall to post maps and timelines. Other teachers covered their walls, too, but most of them only turned their rooms into educational junkyards. Everything on Ms. Aldgate's wall earned its place. Her desk contained the only hint of whimsy with a pencil holder in the shape of an elephant's foot and a small potted cactus. She didn't tolerate anything that didn't make sense, so she probably wasn't taking well to being hunted down and nearly killed by a mythological monster on a Friday night.

"I don't have a class during sixth period," she said as she sat on the front edge of her desk. "I'll write your P.E. teacher a note."

He gave himself a silent pep talk. He'd known this was coming, even from the moment they'd recognized each other at the Canal Walk.

"I don't have a cell phone because of you," she said.

Seriously? "You're alive because of me."

"There's also a man dead because of you." He'd heard her take this tone in class when one of his classmates had made the mistake of playing the smartass.

"For starters, he wasn't a man. He was a vampire," Gidion said. "And he wasn't alive even before I took off his head."

She paled at the mention of the beheading.

"I'm assuming you didn't call the police." He'd spent his inactive moments of the weekend worrying whether a cop would show up to cuff him in front of Dad.

"No, I haven't called them, not yet. I'm going to have to."

"You gotta be kidding."

She rolled her eyes. "I have to call them, because the phone company won't replace my cell phone until I've reported what happened to the one you knocked into the river."

"Does that mean you aren't going to tell them about me or the vampire?"

She rubbed her thumb over her fingers as she considered her answer. "That depends on what you tell me. It's not that I'm not grateful, Gidion, but I need to know what you were doing there."

He wanted to sit, but Ms. Aldgate had enough of a height advantage as it was.

"I hunt vampires. Downtown makes for a great hunting ground...for them and me. Richmond is an important 'rest stop' for vampires traveling along the I-95 corridor." He stared at her, trying to gauge her reactions. "Had you ever seen one before that night?"

Her foot tapped at the floor, the Berber carpet muting the noise. Something about it reminded him of his dog, the way Page panicked at approaching storms. "I'm still not convinced what I saw that night was a vampire."

Figures. Grandpa had warned him about this. This was the greatest defense a vampire possessed, the denial of their existence by their prey. Give a person enough time, and they could rewrite their entire life. Who wanted to live in a world where anyone they passed on the street at night might sprout fangs and rip out their throat? In a way, it would be easier to grant Ms. Aldgate her denial, but that same scenario could end with him in a jail cell and her dead.

"Do your parents know what you're doing?" she asked.

"My mom is dead." His hands clenched into tight fists.

She looked down. "Sorry." Her voice lowered. "What about your father?"

"Dad doesn't know. I'd rather keep it that way."

The school bell rang. Had it really only been five minutes? Great, he was officially late for his next class.

"Gidion, what you're doing is dangerous. What if that man hadn't been a vampire?"

"I'm careful. I've been trained to hunt them. I knew what he was before he even grabbed you."

She didn't say anything to that, so he decided to press with his own questions. "Can you think of any reason a vampire would want you dead?"

"You mean other than for my blood?" She then muttered, "I can't believe I just said that."

"That attack on you wasn't random." He wasn't sure this was the smartest move, but he didn't see much advantage to leaving her in the dark.

"Why would you say that?"

"I found some of the vampire's belongings. He had a cell phone. In it, I found a text." He reached into his bag and pulled out the phone. He turned it on and displayed the text for her to read.

She muttered a "Dear God" as she read the message. Not every day you get to read that someone wants you dead. All things considered, she took the news pretty well. Come to think of it, lots of kids had probably wanted her dead over the years. Likely came with being a teacher.

"Who is 'R-I-C-C-V-N'?"

"I think it's just an abbreviation for 'Richmond Coven.' For some reason, the local coven wants you dead."

"But why?" She held the phone so he could see her picture in the message. "I didn't even know they existed until the other night. What could I possibly have done to make an entire group of these monsters want me dead?"

"I was hoping you'd tell me. I can think of lots of reasons, but most of them require you having known vampires existed before that night." He'd spent the weekend considering that, but he'd come up empty. "I don't see how you could threaten their secrecy. Is it possible someone you know could have been turned into one or might know about them?"

She laughed. He heard the fear in her voice, the way it shook. "My father worked in a car plant outside of Birmingham. All of my family still lives there. I don't see how they could possibly be a threat to any vampires, certainly not here in Richmond."

"And no one you know has disappeared under mysterious circumstances, no one with a grudge?"

She shook her head. "This is insane."

"You can't think of anything that's recently happened that might—?"

"No. I haven't a clue. I'm a teacher." She looked at the message on the phone. "What is this reward? 'Admittance'?"

"The vampire who came after you wasn't part of the Richmond Coven." This role-reversal, him teaching his teacher, was just freaking him out. "He was a nomadic vampire. Dude was living out of his trunk. Most covens keep their numbers small to avoid being noticed. Nomadic vampires who overstay their welcome get run out of town or killed by their own kind."

Here came the really weird part, the one where he told his teacher what to do. "I don't want to panic you, but I don't have a way to know if that hit was sent to just this vampire or if the message was a text blast."

"Text blast?"

"A text blast is when a message is sent to a group of phones. This might not have been a personal message to that vampire."

She crossed her arms. "I have to take this to the police."

"That's a bad idea." He could see her ready to protest, and cut her off. "They might believe that someone wants you dead, but how do you explain the phone? You can't tell them it's a vampire's without them writing you off as crazy. Even if they just investigate this as any other threat, they're going to ask where you got the phone. That means telling them about the attack at the Canal Walk, and that doesn't end well for me or you."

"Gidion, you protected me that night."

"And now I need you to protect me. You can't go to the police. Assuming they even believe you, they'll probably wonder why you waited until days later to go to them. Just think about it."

"What am I supposed to do? Sit in my house with the doors locked and hope they don't break down my door and kill me?" Her arms were all over the place, as if to provide each word out of her mouth with a special emphasis.

"Actually, I was wondering if you had anyone you could stay with for a few days. I've already used the information I've gotten from that phone to locate a house used by these vampires. Give me time to find them and finish the job."

"How much time? I don't have any family in town, Gidion. I've friends, but how do I explain needing to stay with them?"

"I don't know. Tell them you're fumigating your house or something, and you need to let it air out because you have bad allergies or asthma. The point is that you need to take measures to stay safe."

She slammed her fist on her desk. He'd never seen one of his teacher's like this. The idea these adults had a life outside of the classroom just didn't compute in his brain. She paced in front of the desk, rubbing her forehead.

"Aren't vampires unable to enter a house unless they're invited?" she asked.

"Sorry, that's just a load of crap. Most aren't any stronger than a normal person. They just heal faster, and they aren't hampered by a conscience when it's time to kill. And before you ask, the whole garlic and silver thing is bunk, too. The good news is that they can't get into your house any more easily than anyone else."

She stared at him, still looking irritated, as if he'd just told her his dog had eaten his homework. That "good news" probably wasn't much comfort.

"Do you own a gun?" he asked.

"No." She sounded insulted. "Will a gun kill them?"

"Not really. You need a powerful caliber to do enough damage just to slow them down, that or aim well enough to target a major artery. Your best defense is to make them lose enough blood that they haven't got any choice but to run. Go to a hardware store, and get yourself a box cutter."

"A box cutter?"

"I'm a big fan of those. They're easy to conceal in a pocket and safer than carrying a knife, but don't go cheap. Get the ones that have a grip on them. You're gonna sweat in an attack, and you don't want it to slip out of your hand when you need it." He'd have shown her his, but he knew better than to carry any of his gear while on campus. "Go for the throat or wrists. You can cut the inside of their thighs, but it's tough to get to a major artery down there with just a razor. That works better with a knife. Cut them until they let go and run for it."

She sat on the desk again while he said that, and her grip had tightened on the wood top enough to turn her knuckles as pale as her face.

"I'm a schoolteacher, not some backwoods hunter. I've never fired a gun, much less held one."

"Another argument for the box cutter." He opened his book bag and pulled out a sheet of paper to write on. "Here's my cell number. If you think of anything or see anything, call or text me."

She glared at him. "I don't have a cell to text with."

Oh, yeah. He'd forgotten about that.

"Sorry. Call Henrico Police and ask for the Telephone Reporting

Unit to report your phone stolen."

She shook her head, the change in the conversation catching her unprepared. "Why them? I was inside the city, shouldn't I call Richmond Police?"

"Call Henrico and you can make a report over the phone about your cell getting stolen." He'd heard Dad mention "TRU" enough whenever he was talking shop. "You'll get a report number you can give the phone company, but best of all, you'll get to talk to a civilian instead of an officer. Just say your cell disappeared while you were at Short Pump Town Center or somewhere else in Henrico County, not the city. Don't make up a description of anyone who took it. Just say you didn't see it happen."

Her eyes narrowed as she processed the advice. "Why is that better than meeting with an officer?"

"Cops deal with liars all the time. My dad used to be a cop and now works in a 911 center. He says most people use the same kinds of lies when they try to hide something from police." She didn't look convinced. "It's like students trying to make up an excuse for not having their homework. How many times have you heard the same bullshit lines from different students?"

"Good point." She smirked. "But mind your language."

"Sorry. Just call them. You'll get a police report for your phone without a lot of questions, and they won't assign it to an investigator since you won't give them anything worth investigating."

She surprised him with a smile. "Suppose this explains why you always look like you're going to fall asleep in my class, and I just thought you weren't interested."

"Sorry about that. I don't usually stay out later than two on the weeknights." He shrugged. "Not much point. Places close too early to make it worth hunting, for me or the vampires."

They went silent, and after a moment, Gidion realized they were waiting for each other to say something.

"I need my teacher's pass from you," he said.

She hopped back to her feet and went around her desk. "I'd appreciate it if you kept me updated."

"I will, and one last thing." He looked away from her, zipping shut his backpack. "Don't tell anyone else about this. Definitely don't trust any students, even if they claim to be a friend of mine." He thought about that stupid dog collar on Pete's neck. "Especially if they say that."

"Here." She handed the hall pass to him, and he shoved it into his front pocket.

He wished he could go hunting right now, but he had to wait. At least Dad went back to work tonight, and that meant he'd be able to do the same.

# CHAPTER TEN

Surveillance sounds simple enough. Sit in a car and watch. Unfortunately, that's not how it works, especially when it's a one-man job, there's the small matter of bathroom breaks. In a suburban setting, there's also the problem of the nosey neighbor. All it takes is one person with too much time on their hands, and the police show up. Even if they don't flash the blue lights, it's a safe bet everyone… including the person being watched…will know someone is there who shouldn't be.

With that in mind, Gidion opted against a visit back to the safe house. Stephanie would be watching, and she was already suspicious of him. If she spotted him a second time, then she'd know his being there wasn't just coincidence. Better to sit on that info until he needed to use it.

The sun was setting as the Little Hearse pulled off the Downtown Expressway. He wasn't holding out much hope for hunting on a Monday night. Most Mondays, he didn't even bother with a trip downtown. If nothing else, he hoped the walk would help him clear his mind, help him figure out his next move. He needed a way to find where the Richmond Coven was making its nest. He'd been trying that for a while now, but with Ms. Aldgate's life at stake, that goal had become a lot more urgent.

He drove until he found a space down near the Bottom's Up restaurant. The weather had turned colder, which was good for Gidion. That made his dark grey hoodie a lot less suspicious as he strolled through the Shockoe Bottom area of downtown.

The crowd turned out larger this night than he'd expected. As he walked around the corner onto East Franklin Street, he spotted a group of teenagers dressed in all black going into the Old World nightclub. That wouldn't normally grab his interest, but his eyes were drawn to the tallest guy and his dog collar.

It was Pete.

Pete didn't see him, and none of the others with him even glanced in Gidion's direction as they went inside. Old World was a brick building which had been converted into a dance club a few years ago. The sign out front had "Old World" in white letters in a blue rectangle with a red circle behind it. Nothing about the place had registered on his radar anymore than the rest of the clubs, but to see what he assumed to be a group of feeders entering it changed everything.

He was about to step inside when the bouncer pushed him back. "No kids allowed. Beat it." Dang, this guy had to be at least a foot taller than him, twice as wide and all muscle.

"What are you talking about?"

"No one under twenty-one. Now, get lost."

"Are you kidding me? You just let a whole group of teenagers in there."

The bouncer reached for him, but Gidion stepped back. He held up his hands. No point in arguing with Mr. No Neck.

"Gidion?"

He looked through the open door. Stephanie smiled at him. She was still all gothed out, but this time, she was in a dress...a really short dress.

"Is he a friend of yours?" As aggressive and intimidating as the bouncer had been with Gidion, he sounded even more submissive to Stephanie.

"Well, I don't know." She stepped out enough for the light from a street lamp to make her pale skin glow. "Are we friends, Gidion?"

He wasn't sure how to answer that, and the show of her legs, which looked a lot longer in that dress, didn't help his brain form an answer any faster.

"Sorry." He shook his head to right his thoughts. "I mean, I saw Pete go inside. Just wanted to say 'Hi' to him was all."

She laughed. "Do you want me to invite you in?"

Gidion glanced at the bouncer. The guy was looking at the two of them, perhaps trying to figure out which way this was gonna go. He was suddenly very aware that his car was a good three blocks from here. If he ran for it, there was no knowing if he could get there before this bouncer, Stephanie or someone in her group caught up to him. Of course, going inside wouldn't exactly improve his odds of flight, if he tried to make a break for it. Then there was the thought of Pete. Maybe he could get him to leave, talk some sense into him or at least learn something useful from him.

He smiled at Stephanie. "Coming in would be nice."

She extended her hand. "Then come inside."

The bouncer stepped aside as Gidion took the offered hand. Grandpa would probably hit him in the back of the head for this, but he couldn't just walk away, not with Pete in there.

Stephanie slipped her arm around his as they walked inside. If anyone was paying attention, they might mistake the two of them for a couple on a date.

He studied the place as best he could. The club included one of those light-up dance floors and strobe lights mounted high on the walls throughout the place. Despite all the lights, the place was damn dark. The only reason anyone could see the bar was the mirror behind it reflecting all those lights and a long, blue neon line running across the front of the bar. Good luck having a quiet conversation in this place, too. The bass was cranked well above good sense. He recognized the music playing as Apocalyptica. A vampire could drag someone into a booth, drain them dry and no one would ever hear a scream.

Gidion stiffened as Stephanie leaned closer to him, her lips far too close to his throat for his liking, even if she wasn't a vampire. "I'm starting to think you're following me, Gidion."

She had to scream her words for him to hear her, but that didn't rob the statement of its subtle accusation. He needed to play this right.

"Guess I'm just lucky." He went for his best James Bond smile, hoping she'd believe he was really flirting with her. "You look really hot in that dress."

"Thank you, but you look dressed for track practice." Hard to tell if she was just teasing or making another accusation.

"So, how is it you can get past Mr. No Neck at the door?"

She laughed. "That's good. I'll have to start calling him that."

"So how do you get him to let you in?"

She stopped walking, the dance floor behind her. The lights cast her in a rainbow-edged silhouette. "Guess I'm just lucky."

He didn't need to see her face to know he'd probably overplayed his hand by pressing that question.

"You're cute, Gidion, but you seem too much of a goody-two-shoes to be club-hopping on a school night."

He shrugged, hoping it came across nonchalant. "Funny, up until this school year, I'd have sworn the same thing about you."

"Guess neither of us is what we seem." Definitely nothing subtle in that statement.

"So where's Pete? If it's all the same, I'd just like to say 'Hi' to him and get out of here."

She slid closer, her body pressed against his, arms slipping around his neck. No girl had ever made a move that forward with him. He wasn't sure how to react, even if his body was pretty sure how it wanted to respond, and as close as she was, she could probably feel it.

"Why not take off the lame hoodie and play with me? Pete will come by soon enough."

His voice cracked as he tried to answer, and cleared his throat for the second try. "Didn't realize you and he were such good friends these days."

She laughed. "Pete? My friend? Please. He's more like a decoration, a very tall gargoyle."

He knew he should say something to defend Pete, but that was hard to do with her hips up against his.

"I wouldn't mind making you a friend, though." She leaned in close as if to kiss him. "That reminds me. You never answered me at the door. Are we friends?"

Her arms slid from around his neck and then beneath his arms to reach behind him. Dammit, she was frisking him! He broke free of her hold and stepped back before she could find anything. She'd most likely felt the box cutter in his hoodie's front pocket when she'd pressed her body against his. Maybe she'd just assume that was his car keys. Right.

"I don't think we know each other well enough yet to be that friendly." The desire for her didn't vanish when he'd pulled away. He took a breath to get his wits back and hoped he didn't need to run anytime in the next minute or two. "I'll just go see Pete and be on my way. Thanks for getting me in the door."

The shadows didn't hide her glare as he slipped into the crowd. He needed to find Pete fast and get the hell out of here. Old World didn't look very big from the front, but it made up for its lack of width with plenty of depth. The further he got into the place the darker it got. The smell of cigarette smoke and sweat grew thicker in the back. Light poured in to his right. He turned to see a door closing, but not before he spotted a set of stairs that led up. Did the vampires own this place? Most likely, given Stephanie's pull with the bouncer. The vampires might even live upstairs, but he didn't think that was likely. Health inspectors would probably check out the entire place.

Gidion had looked all through the back. He earned a few dirty looks from folks making out in the back booths. As he worked his way back towards the front, he saw Stephanie. She didn't see him, and he moved fast to keep it that way. She was yelling something at two gothed out guys he'd seen walk in with Pete. They could pass for No Neck's illegitimate sons, Thing One and Thing Two.

He reached the far side of the dance floor and spotted Pete leaning against the wall by himself. Pete checked his watch three times before Gidion shifted through all the bodies to reach him.

"Pete!" Gidion's first few tries to get his friend's attention failed. Only once he'd gotten within reach did Pete notice him.

"Gidion, what are you doing here?" His eyes about popped out of his head. He didn't stay focused on Gidion. He looked around the room instead.

"I saw you come in. Dude, let's get out of here."

Pete didn't seem to hear him. Having a conversation was even harder this close to the dance floor, which cast his friend's face in alternating shades of red, blue and yellow.

"How did you get in?"

"Stephanie got me past the bouncer. Now, let's go."

That brought Pete's popped-out eyes back towards him. "She knows you're here?"

"Yeah, I think she already regrets that decision, so let's go." He grabbed Pete's arm. His body was shaking and his skin clammy. "Are you okay?"

"Just get out of here. I'm gonna be a while."

"Pete, you're in some crappy shape. Let's get you out of here."

Pete jerked his arm free. "I'm in crappy shape? Are you dim? I'm not the one who's gonna get killed here. Get lost, Gid!"

The argument ended there. Someone grabbed him by his hoodie and tossed him onto the dance floor. He slid across the glass surface on his back. That ticked off quite a few people. He knocked over one lady as his foot caught her leg. He looked back where he'd been standing and saw Thing One and Thing Two walking towards him.

"Just great," Gidion muttered to himself.

"You walking out, or do we have to throw you out?" one of the "Things" said. He hadn't really decided which was One or Two.

Gidion scrambled to his feet, making a quick check of his weapons. He couldn't use most of them against other humans, but he needed to make sure he hadn't dropped any of them. "All right." He held up his hands and stepped back.

"Pete, let's go!"

Pete didn't move. He just stared at Gidion.

Thing One and Two were almost on top of him, and he spotted Mr. No Neck heading his way, too. The Thing who'd spoken tried to grab Gidion, but he dodged the attempt. "Pete!" Stupid idiot wouldn't go. Gidion opted not to press his luck. He slipped into the crowd and got past No Neck.

Stephanie stood by the door and smiled at him as he walked past. "Bye, Gidion."

He looked back inside. No Neck was far enough away for him to stop for a moment. "Nothing better happen to Pete," he said to Stephanie.

"You're worried about him?" She laughed. "If you were smart, you'd worry about yourself and run."

He didn't run, but he walked fast enough to make sure none of Stephanie's friends caught up with him.

"See you at school, Gidion." Stephanie's taunt chased him as he turned the corner. He wouldn't do anymore hunting downtown, not tonight. No, he had a better idea about where to go next and ran the rest of the way back to his car.

# CHAPTER ELEVEN

The Little Hearse's engine growled as Gidion turned into Stephanie's neighborhood. He parked on Winstead Road which was two blocks from her cul-de-sac and a road she wouldn't have any reason to turn onto when she drove home. Even if surveillance on the vampires' safe house wasn't practical, that didn't mean he couldn't get anything of use from the place.

He made sure his car was legally parked, so if a nosey neighbor called the police, the most an officer could do would be to look at it and then leave. A cop couldn't question him about the car if he wasn't with it.

Gidion kept his hood down as he walked the two blocks to Tolliver Court. He didn't care if anyone called the police about the car, but he didn't want people to call about some strange guy in a hoodie. Besides, the one person he knew would recognize him was too busy holding court at Old World, and as long as she was there, then no one was watching the safe house.

As he walked onto Tolliver Court, he saw the front porch light was off. That didn't surprise him. Why would a vampire care about scaring off burglars? For them, that would be like someone spontaneously delivering pizza and then not having to pay for it.

His main goal was to find the key to get inside. This was the big flaw in the vampire safe house. Nomadic vampires needed a way to get in without breaking into the place. They could put spare keys in plastic bags and bury them just beside the front steps, but that might look a bit weird if people kept digging through the front yard. If they took too long finding the key, that just gave Mr. or Mrs. Nosey Neighbor another opportunity to pester their local police dispatcher.

Besides, Gidion didn't see any patches of earth that looked like they had been dug through often.

The vampires could hide a key in some kind of lawn decoration, but this house didn't have one that he could see. Nor was there a plant on the front deck where a key might be hidden in the planting soil. Putting a key in the bottom of a vertical mailbox at the front door might work, too, but this house didn't have one of those. He didn't see any combination lockboxes, either, but those would require a guest to know the combination.

Of course, they could just leave the front door unlocked. Gidion grabbed the doorknob, turned it and pushed the door open. He listened for any beeps, the kind that might indicate an alarm system, but he didn't hear anything. He checked the door frame and didn't see any sensors. Not surprising really. That would require any guests to know the code for the alarm system, and that also added the risk of police coming here. Not exactly ideal for vampires who couldn't explain what they were doing in Ms. Doris Eaton's house. He considered just closing the door and going home. At least he now knew there weren't any tricks to getting in this place. Still, there might be something here which could lead him to the Richmond Coven's real lair, and there was no telling when he might get a chance like this again with Stephanie living next door.

He listened for any movement, but he didn't hear any. He pulled out his box cutter and went inside.

The place reeked of Clorox. He wondered how many times Stephanie had cleaned the bloodstains from a messy eater. A basket with what looked like pamphlets in it sat on a table in the foyer. He picked up one. Not really a pamphlet, more like a list of house rules. Rule number one was, 'No blood on the carpet.' Given the hardwood floor in the living room and hallway, he wondered if this was a generic list or if it meant some of the back rooms had carpet.

He loved number two, 'You kill it; you dispose of it. Our maid cleans the mess, but guests are required to take their leftovers with them.' He folded it in half and slipped it in his back pocket to read later. He couldn't wait to show this to Grandpa. He'd laugh himself into a coughing fit.

He'd looked at it close enough to see it didn't include any contact information. Did they even have any kept anywhere in here? That would be nice, but he wouldn't bet on it.

The living room to his right was empty, so he moved forward and glanced down the hallway to the left. He noticed a door with a set of steps that led downstairs. The kitchen was further forward and to his right. He decided to check on the kitchen first. Going down into the basement just felt like a bad idea, and he didn't want to stay too long, lest someone show up while he was here.

Enough moonlight was spilling through the window over the kitchen sink for him to see a few notes stuck on the refrigerator with Hello Kitty magnets. Just too weird.

He heard a whimper to his right. The sound scared the hell out of him, but what he saw didn't make things better. A girl with long blond hair was tied to a chair at the kitchen table. Her mouth was gagged and her eyeballs looked ready jump out and tag him.

He walked over to her and signaled for her to stay quiet. He hoped whoever brought her here had run out.

"Who the hell are you?" The question came from some guy behind him. So much for the guy having run out.

Gidion needed to think fast. He slipped his box cutter back into his jacket before he turned around. A guy with fangs was standing there in red-and-white polka dot boxers. He must have been taking off his clothes in another room so he wouldn't get his dinner's blood on them. A practical vampire…how refreshing. He had to be a nomadic vampire. If he wasn't, then he would have instantly known Gidion didn't belong here and attacked. That was one of those unwritten vampire rules for nomads: don't snack on the local vampire's hired help.

Gidion needed to get close enough to attack without making the vampire get alarmed. Best thing to do was just act like he belonged here.

"I'm David. Stephanie sent me to check on the place while she's out. Dude, did you even read the rules?" He pulled out the house rules list from his back pocket and did his best not to look like he was uncomfortable as he held them up for the vampire to see.

"I read the rules," the vampire said. "Feeders aren't supposed to come in here at night."

"Well, you obviously didn't read rule eight." Gidion snapped the words out the way Dad had the other night in the car. "You're gonna mess up the furniture with those ropes tied like that! And you better get rid of her body when you're done, because I am not cleaning up that kind of mess. That's rule number two, in case you forgot."

He was almost close enough.

The vampire growled. "There's nothing in there about the furniture in the kitchen."

"Rule number eight, dude!" Gidion shoved the paper right in front of the guy's face, totally obscuring his field of vision.

Gidion drew his box cutter and went for the throat. The vampire reacted too fast. Gidion missed the neck, but he caught the guy's left wrist as he tried to block the strike. Not as good as the carotid artery, and it was a strike across instead of down, not near as deadly.

He pressed the advantage and charged. He thrust his left forearm against the vampire's chest and shoved him back into the oven. A pot clattered to the floor. Gidion thrust his forearm up to the throat and into the lower jaw. He heard the crunch of bone as the vampire's mouth was slammed shut by that move.

Gidion followed with the box cutter, going for the throat again. The guy grabbed a frying pan off the counter and swung it at his head. He blocked it with his right forearm. The pain rang deep into his bones and the box cutter fell to the floor. Gidion retreated.

The vampire threw the frying pan at him. He dodged to the right and reached behind his back for his sword. Not all the feeling had returned to his arm, but at least it wasn't fractured. He'd done that to his arm several times when he was younger, so he knew the difference.

His hand grabbed hold of the sword as the vampire hissed.

"I'm sorry." Gidion held his other hand up as he pretended to plead. "Please don't hurt me."

The vampire laughed. "Oh, you'll hurt." He leaped forward. He moved damn fast, but not faster than Gidion could draw his sword. The guy realized his mistake too late. The blade slit across his stomach as Gidion sidestepped his attack.

A second strike went deep into the right thigh, sending him to the floor. Gidion planted his foot on his back, knocking the wind out of him and then sliced off his head before he could recover.

Gidion staggered back from the body. He sat in a chair next to the girl who was still tied up. She jerked about screaming through her restraints.

"Give me a minute for my breath to catch up." He massaged his forearm. Dammit, that frying pan hurt like hell. Might not have broken anything, but that was gonna turn into one really nasty bruise.

He looked back up at the girl. "He the only one here?"

She nodded.

"Thank God. You hurt?"

She shook her head and gave him an evil look as she shook her chair about, silently demanding to be ungagged and cut loose.

He stood and put away his sword before picking up his box cutter. He used that to cut the ropes, starting with the ones binding her wrists. She took care of the gag herself once her hands were free.

"Thank you," she said. "That guy. He was a—I mean—he…"

He was working on the ropes tying her ankles to the chair's legs. "We can talk about that later. For now, you can help me with the body."

"Help you with—with him?" She looked at Gidion like he'd just asked her to stick her hand into a pot of boiling water.

He ignored her question and cut the last of her bonds. "What's your name?"

"Tamara."

She looked close to his age, probably a little older and pretty, too. Didn't recognize her from school. No telling if she was even from around here. For all he knew, vamp-dude could have grabbed her from somewhere in California and driven her all the way here. "Well, Tamara, I hope you're a lot stronger than you look, because I think this guy is gonna be pretty heavy."

"Oh, God. I think I'm going to be sick." She ran for the sink and puked.

He had a bad feeling things just got a whole lot more complicated.

# CHAPTER TWELVE

People don't appreciate how difficult it is to dispose of a dead body. Downtown, Gidion favored the "drunk-friend-carry" approach, but in a suburban setting, a couple of drunk people walking down the street brings the police. If someone needs to frequently dispose of dead bodies in a residential area, a house needs one of two things: either a very tall fence around the property (which the safe house didn't have) or a garage. As most any homeowner will attest, a garage hides a world of sins.

He considered driving his car here to load the body, but that didn't give him much time. After a quick search of the house, Gidion found what he needed most in the basement: the keys to the vampire's car. He was amused to see it was another Ford Crown Victoria. This one was grey.

"Tamara, take the other arm," he said as he lifted the headless, half-naked body by the right arm and flung it over his shoulders.

"Oh, God," she said as she took the other side.

He'd already warned her that they needed to hurry. There was no telling how long it would take Stephanie to get home, although he was betting it wouldn't be anytime soon. It wasn't even past 10:30 yet, but that didn't mean another vampire wouldn't drop in to spend the night. About the only thing he had going for him was that Tamara was still too freaked to ask a lot of questions. She might have even been scared of him. He wasn't sure.

They made it into the garage and loaded the body into the trunk. "Just get in the car, and I'll get the head." She didn't argue. She looked like she was on autopilot as she climbed into the car. That wouldn't last much longer, but he needed enough time to get the head and the rest of the vamp's belongings.

After a quick run through the house, he decided he had everything he needed and tossed it into the trunk of the car. He hit the button to open the garage door. He drove out just enough to clear the garage and then ran back in to hit the button to shut the door.

"You buckled?" he asked as he climbed into the driver's seat. She didn't answer. Her gaze was locked straight ahead and her hand was braced against the dashboard. He just looked before he pulled out onto the street and drove out of the cul-de-sac.

Lord, he hoped this car wasn't stolen. Odds favored that if it was, the owner wasn't left alive to report it. "I'm parked a few blocks from here." He stopped as he looked at her. If her skin was any greener, she could have passed for half-plant. He'd planned to have her follow him in his car, but there was no way she was driving in this condition. "Tell you what. We'll deal with my car later. Word of advice," he reached over in a slow motion to grab her by the wrist and pull her hand away from the dashboard, "avoid touching any surfaces in here with your fingers. We're gonna have to wipe it down later."

She swallowed, trying to pull herself together. "Where are we going?"

"Gotta dispose of the body. If everything goes the way I've got it planned, the vampires who own that house will assume he just left after he killed you and that the blood in the kitchen is yours."

"There are more of those—things?"

"Yeah." He just realized this was his fourth kill. He was tempted to tell her, but then again, his kills still hanging in the single digits probably wouldn't sound as impressive to her.

"Give me a minute." He pulled out his cell and waved it as an explanation. Grandpa picked up on the second ring. "Grandpa, I've got one. Get the fire going."

"Damn, it's not even eleven o'clock, kid. Nice job."

"Uh, yeah, I'll explain all that when I get there. I'm about a half hour out."

That received a brief silence. "A half hour? Where are you coming from?"

"The safe house."

"Are you out of your mind!"

He could tell by the look on Tamara's face that she'd heard that. He flashed her a smile before he answered Grandpa. "Yeah, long story. Just be warned, I'm not in my car. Had to borrow the vampire's, a grey Crown Vic."

"Gidion…"

Oh, boy. He was really gonna flip at this next part. "And I'm not alone. I've got a girl with me."

"Oh, good God." Grandpa let fly a few curses before he said anything of substance. "And you're bringing her here? Are you even sure you can trust this girl?"

"I'm sure, Grandpa." Yeah, right. "See you in thirty." He hung up before Grandpa could say anything else.

Neither he nor Tamara said anything until he'd reached Route 288. He made damn sure to stay under the speed limit. This wasn't his car, so he didn't want anything getting him pulled over.

"Are you okay?" he asked.

"I will be," she said. "Thank you, David."

"David?" Why was she—? Then he remembered. "Oh, sorry. My name's Gidion. I just said that to the vampire in case he got away. Didn't want him to tell his friends what my name was."

"How did you know I was there?" she asked.

"I didn't. I'm a vampire hunter. That's a safe house that I recently found. Wasn't expecting anyone to be in there yet. They usually don't find their meals that early in the night." She rubbed her temples with her fingertips. Probably better to steer the conversation to more normal waters. "You from around here?"

"Yeah. You?"

He nodded. "Richmond, born and raised. How old are you?"

"Seventeen," she said. "I'm a senior."

"Where?"

"Midlothian Springs High."

He laughed. "We're rivals. I go to West Chester. Our teams play this Friday."

That at least garnered a smile. All things considered, she was handling this pretty well. It's not every day a vampire tries to kill you and someone cuts its head off.

"Do you mind if I borrow your phone?" she said. "I need to call my parents."

"That's not a good idea," he said, "not yet. We need to get our stories straight. First things first, tell me how you ended up in that house with Mr. Fangs-and-Polka-Dots."

"It's still Monday, right?" she said.

He nodded.

"I was walking back to my car when that guy walked up to me. He asked me for directions to the mall. Next thing I knew, he'd grabbed me and tossed me into his trunk. Don't remember much after that. I think he hit me." She rubbed the back of her neck. He looked and saw a nice bruise there. Yeah, he'd knocked her out or at least made her dizzy enough to keep quiet until he'd gotten her to the safe house.

"Where were you when he grabbed you?" he asked.

"Where? Oh, um, it was my guitar lesson."

"And that is where?" He'd heard Dad make this complaint about 911 callers. Ask them where they were, and they'd say something like "Richmond" or "the West End," as if that really told a dispatcher where to send help.

"Richmond Music Center," she said.

"You take lessons there every Monday night?"

"Yeah."

"All right, we need to give you some kind of cover for being out this late."

She looked confused. "Wait, aren't we going to tell the police?"

Great, this conversation again. "That's really not an option. Do you have a boyfriend?"

"That's really none of your damn business."

He sighed. This wasn't going as smoothly as he'd expected.

"Tamara, we need a way to explain you being out late. If you have a boyfriend, that's going to limit certain options."

"I can't just tell my parents the truth?"

"Oh, sure. 'Sorry, Mom and Dad, I got abducted and nearly eaten by a vampire. I didn't mean to stay out so late.' Yeah, that'll work."

"Oh."

"So, back to my previous question. Do you have a boyfriend?"

"Recently broke up."

"Perfect. I mean, um, sorry." Jeez, he really had no skills with girls. "Look, this might be totally out of character for you, but probably best to tell your folks you met a cute guy, decided to hang out with him and lost track of time."

"So, in addition to nearly getting killed, I'm going to get grounded," she said. "That's just perfect."

"Sorry, and it's gonna need to be plenty later. We gotta get you cleaned up before you go home."

"Just where are we going?" she asked.

"You ever see those vampire movies where the vampire gets killed and the body goes all 'poof' into ashes?" He saw her nod. "Yeah, doesn't work like that. Fortunately, my grandpa owns a funeral home with a cremator."

"Oh." She must have decided that was more than she really wanted to know, because she immediately changed the topic. "What grade are you in?"

He was tempted to lie that he was a junior, but figured she wouldn't believe that. "Sophomore."

"I'm a senior." She said that with the typical, I'm-a-senior-so-that-makes-me-superior tone. "My folks are supposed to believe I spent tonight out—with you?"

Nice. "Recently broke up, huh?"

"Sorry." The way she smiled at him, he could tell she meant it. "I do appreciate you saving me. I really do. I just…" The smile cracked as tears ran down her face again. She turned away to look out the passenger door window. "Sorry, I'm not usually like this."

This was the first time he'd spent more than two minutes

with a vampire's intended victim right after the attack. He'd never considered what this time must be like, and he thought about Ms. Aldgate. For her, this wasn't even finished. At least once he got Tamara cleaned up, back to her car and home, this would be done.

"It's okay." He reached over to give her a reassuring pat on the arm, but he stopped short. That just seemed a little too forward. "We can't speed right now, but once we get this guy dropped off, I'll be able to drive faster."

They spent the rest of the drive in silence until they reached the funeral home. Gidion called Grandpa on his cell to let him know they were there and to open the back door. He sounded pissed. He decided to use Tamara as an excuse to get out of here fast.

"Tamara, this is Grandpa Murphy."

She waved and smiled at him, but her eyes went all over the place. Most people never got to go inside a funeral home by the back.

"Good to meet you, darlin'," Grandpa said.

Gidion popped open the trunk and whispered to him. "She could use an ice pack. You got any handy?"

"Yeah, got a few in the break room."

"Tamara, there's a small kitchen, first door on the right. Get an ice pack from the freezer for your head and neck."

"Thanks." She walked past them. He noticed she did her best not to look inside the trunk.

"We're gonna have a long talk about this, kid." Grandpa lowered his voice as she walked out of the garage. "Maybe not tonight, but this kind of thing can't happen again. You got it."

They did a three count and lifted the body onto the gurney. Hurt his arm, too. He made a mental note to also get himself an ice pack.

"Sorry, but I couldn't just leave her there, and I sure as hell wasn't going to drive anywhere but straight here in a borrowed car with a body in the trunk."

"You just better hope that girl doesn't talk."

They pushed the gurney to the cremator room. With any luck, the most talking she'd do would go a long way to improving his reputation. Spending a night out late with a senior girl…Oh, yeah. Didn't get much better than that. Of course, with her going to another school, what were the odds of anyone at West Chester even hearing about it? Damn.

"Do I wanna know how you bagged this guy in his boxers? Nice ones, by the way."

"Probably not." Gidion placed the head on the conveyer, between the body's legs.

"Where's your car?" Grandpa asked.

"Left it parked a few blocks from the safe house," Gidion said. "Didn't want to risk transferring a body from one car to the other in the middle of the 'burbs. Gonna pick it up and dump off the vampire's car after I've gotten Tamara back to hers."

"There's blood all over that girl's shirt. If she goes home looking like that—"

"Relax, Grandpa." They paused for another three-count lift onto the cremator's conveyer. "I'm gonna run her by my house so she can clean up."

"Your place?" Grandpa grunted what he thought about that. "Hope you're thinking with your brain and not your third leg."

"Just trust me."

"Uh huh." Grandpa's voice was thick with sarcasm. "I'm sure that she's a fine-looking catch has nothing to do with your generosity."

"Hadn't really noticed."

"Sure."

Gidion decided not to argue that point, mainly because he knew he was full of crap. He tossed the vampire's clothes on top of the body.

"You already search this guy's stuff?" Grandpa asked.

"Yeah, didn't find much, but I scored another cell phone and his wallet. These nomadic vampires like to travel light, don't they?"

"Wouldn't you?"

Gidion rubbed his right arm. Damn, that vampire did a number on it with the frying pan.

"You get hurt?" Grandpa asked.

"Right arm got hit pretty hard, but I'll be fine."

Grandpa checked the temperature gauge on the cremator. "Still warming up," he said to himself, then looked back at Gidion. "Take tomorrow night off. Your dad working a double again tomorrow?"

"Yeah, he's going in at four."

"Dinner at my place. Come by at six, and don't be late."

"I'll see you later, Grandpa. Love ya."

"G'night, boy."

Gidion found Tamara still sitting in the break room. She hadn't bothered with the lights, just settled on the moonlight coming in through the window. She had an ice pack planted on the back of her neck. He grabbed an ice pack from the freezer for himself.

"How are you holding up?" he asked.

"This," she pointed to the back of her head, "I'll get over. Just dreading when I call my parents. They're probably already worried, and they're gonna flip when I tell them I was out all this time with a boy."

"Let's hurry then. We're gonna run by my house. You can wash the blood out of your hair when we get there, and I'll see if I can get your shirt clean."

She eyed him suspiciously as he said that. "Uh huh."

He wasn't sure why she was giving him the evil eye, but then he realized he'd essentially told her he planned to take her to his place and get her shirt off. Hunting vampires was a lot easier than talking to girls.

# CHAPTER THIRTEEN

Gidion was relieved to see his dad hadn't come home from work early. He parked the Crown Vic on the side street. Page barked like crazy until they got inside. Tamara looked as scared of his dog as she had of the vampire.

"Sorry, I'm more of a cat person." She had resorted to an awkward shuffle to slowly get by his dog. By this point, Page had stopped barking and was sniffing Tamara in all the inappropriate places.

"Page! Quit that!" He grabbed her by the collar. "Sorry." The dog resisted at first, but finally gave in as Gidion dragged her into Dad's room and closed the door.

He led Tamara to the bathroom. He'd given some thought to how to get her shirt without coming across like some pervert.

"I'll give you one of my hoodies." God knows, he owned enough of them. He hid most of them in his old toy chest which lived in his closet these days. Bloodstains were the main reason for why he owned so many. "Here you go."

"You really have a thing for grey hoodies, don't you?" she said with a smirk.

"I once read that grey is harder to see at night than black." He shrugged. "Not sure if that's true, though."

"Weird." She took the hoodie from him.

"Um, your strip. I mean shirt! Your shirt!" Oh, dear Lord. He was an idiot. "I mean…just drop your shirt and jeans outside the bathroom door, and I'll do what I can about the bloodstains while you shower."

Going by the expression on her face, she was either really amused or seriously pissed with him. "You've never been on a date, have you?"

"Uh, no." He was too embarrassed to lie and just went downstairs to the kitchen.

He scrubbed the sink clean and then heard a soft thud to his right. Tamara's green shirt and blue jeans had landed at the base of the stairs in a small pile.

"Figured I'd save you the climb." Tamara's voice came from upstairs.

"Oh, thanks." He walked over to pick them up and looked up the stairs in time to see her looking down at him. She was leaning out of the bathroom door. He couldn't see much of her, but he could see a bright green bra strap going over her left shoulder. She laughed at him, the dumbstruck look on his face, just before she disappeared back into the bathroom.

"I have a senior girl in her underwear in my bathroom," he whispered to himself. "Wow." Then he heard the shower start running, and he knew his stupid grin must have been as wide as his face. He now had a naked senior girl taking a shower in his bathroom. "Wow."

He forced himself to tune out the sound of the shower, the way the water got softer or louder as she moved around in there. He needed to hurry, but the sight of her in that green bra kept distracting him. Damn. She was really hot.

By the time the shower turned off, he was soaking his hoodie in the sink. He heard a loud whirring sound from the bathroom and realized that must have been a hair dryer. He didn't realize they even had one.

"Hey, I hope you don't mind," Tamara said as she walked into the kitchen a few minutes later.

"Mind?" What was she talking about?

"I went digging through your room for some pants."

That's when he realized she was wearing some of his sweatpants. "Oh! No, I mean, yeah, that's cool. Sorry, I was so focused on, um." He stopped himself short of saying he'd been focused on her breasts. "The shirt. Just didn't, um. You know."

Oh, God, he was making an absolute idiot out of himself.

She leaned against the counter, and looked at the sink. "My shirt and jeans in there?"

"No, I already finished with those. Tossed them in the dryer. Did the best I could. The jeans will probably be fine, but I think the shirt's done for. It'll be good enough to get you home, as long as your parents don't look too close at it."

"Thanks for trying." She leaned closer and touched the water. "Cold water?"

"Yeah, works better when you're dealing with blood stains. Hot water just cooks the stain into the fabric." Thank God. Something he could talk about without going all tongue-tied.

"Neat."

He smiled at her and noticed the hoodie she was wearing wasn't zipped up all the way, a hint of that green bra visible. Was she flirting with him or just messing with him…or maybe both? If she wasn't flirting, then this was just cruel and unusual punishment.

"You can keep that." He pointed at the hoodie and wiped his brow. Damn, she had him sweating. "Might help hide the bloodstains."

"Thanks." She canted her head. "You must be a big Batman fan, huh?"

"What? Oh, the shirt." He'd forgotten he was wearing his shirt with the red bat logo on it. "More of a Red Robin fan than Batman, but this is a good luck charm. The Chinese consider red bats good luck." He wanted to bang his head against the wall. 'More of a Red Robin fan,' he repeated in his head. Could he possibly kill his chances with this girl any more than by showing off what a comic book geek he was?

"I like it." Her smile looked sincere enough.

"Got an extra one, if you want it."

"Considering the night I've had, suppose a little extra good luck wouldn't hurt. My dad always keeps a rabbit's foot on his desk."

"Really? Any idea where he got it? I've been wanting to get one." He'd seen a few on eBay, but he wasn't sure he trusted those to be the real thing.

"No idea. As far as I know, he's always had it." She looked away from him after she said that. "Where are your parents?"

"Dad works the midnight shift in Henrico County's 911 Center."

"What about your mom?"

"Died when I was little."

She winced. "Sorry."

"It's okay."

"That her?" She pointed towards the wedding portrait hanging near the kitchen table.

"Yeah."

"She was really pretty. You look a lot like her."

He nodded. Dad had always said he could see a lot of Mom in his face, especially the shape of his nose. He sometimes worried that looking at him hurt Dad, reminded him of losing Mom.

"So why do you do this?" Tamara asked. "I mean, you hunt vampires?"

"It's a Keep family tradition. Oh, that's my last name, Keep. Not sure how far back it goes, but the Keeps have hunted vampires for a long time."

"So your grandfather and dad also hunt vampires?"

"Used to. Grandpa quit when my dad was ten or thereabouts. Ruined his leg falling off a bridge. After that, he trained Dad to do it. Dad quit right after Mom died, and then Grandpa trained me."

"How do you know a bad vampire from a good one? I mean, how do you know which ones to kill?"

Gidion laughed. "I just kill the ones with fangs."

"They don't all have fangs?"

"Yeah, they all have fangs. That's the point." He grinned at her. "Sorry, just a little vampire hunter humor."

To his relief, she smiled at his quip.

"But how can you be sure one isn't good? I mean, the guy who had me tied up when you showed up, pretty obvious, but what about one you just happen to see walking down the street?"

"Look, this isn't like *Twilight*, and they aren't searching for the reincarnation of lost loves or any of that stupid crap. We're their food. It's that simple."

"And that automatically makes them all bad?"

He couldn't fathom that she needed to be convinced of this, not after nearly being killed by one of these things. Then again, this was probably part of that whole denial thing, the hope that things weren't really as bad as they were.

"Let's put it this way. If chickens had the sense and the ability to defend themselves, do you think they'd worry about which humans are good or bad?"

"Ew." She looked like she was going to be sick again. "I don't think I'll ever be able to eat chicken again."

"Sorry."

She shrugged. "Hey, I asked."

The dryer buzzed, sparing them anymore vampire-hunting small talk. Her clothes weren't completely dry, but they were close enough to get her past her parents.

She called home as he drove her to her car. Richmond Music Center was less than ten minutes from where he lived. In the silence of the car, he could hear her mom shriek over the phone. He felt sorry for her. She really was going to catch hell from her parents for this, and she didn't deserve it. Tamara kept the phone call short. She wiped her eyes, but she didn't cry. Maybe she was tougher than she looked.

The shopping center parking lot was empty except for a dark green Lexus.

"That's your car?" The damn thing looked brand new. Kids going to Midlothian Springs High School had a rep for coming from rich families. She wasn't exactly bucking that trend.

"Yeah, that's mine." She sighed. "Probably won't get to drive it for the rest of the week, except to school and back home."

"Sorry about that."

"I don't blame you. I blame that stupid—thing."

Gidion got out first and checked her car and scanned the parking lot for any sign of movement. The closest hiding places were far enough away to where he decided they were safe. Still, he didn't trust the night anymore.

"You got my cell number?" he asked as he opened the door for her to get out.

She nodded.

"Text me when you get home, and by home, I mean inside the house."

"That might not be so simple," she said. "They might take my phone from me."

"Then email me, if you can."

She held up the sheet of paper onto which he'd written all his contact info. "Got it." Then she shoved the paper into her front pocket.

"Gidion, thanks for saving me." She opened her car door but didn't climb in right away.

"No problem."

He was scanning the parking lot again. Right as he looked back at her, she caught him by surprise. She grabbed him by the arms, leaned in and kissed him. Holy shit! It wasn't some peck on the cheek either. This was right on the lips. Every hair on his head stood straight as if he'd been shocked by lightning.

His legs were shaking and his head all dizzy as she pulled back. She climbed into her car and smiled up at him. "For the record," she said, "when I tell my parents I spent the night out with a really nice, cute guy, I won't be lying."

He just smiled as she closed the car door and drove off. Once the car had disappeared onto Midlothian Turnpike, Gidion jumped and spun a full three-sixty. "Oh, HELL yeah! Whoo!"

He hummed to himself as he wiped down the interior of the Crown Vic and put on some gloves before he drove out of the parking lot. Holy crap! She'd kissed him. Hell, she'd called him cute!

Then it hit him.

"Aw, man." He couldn't tell anyone about it. How would he explain that he'd even been with her tonight, a senior girl from an entirely different high school? That just sucked. "If only I'd gotten a rabbit's foot before tonight."

Despite that downer note, he was still humming to himself as he pulled up to his car. He circled the block once just to make sure no one was waiting for him. Given where he'd left his car, he didn't think it was likely Stephanie would have noticed it. He parked the Crown Vic right behind it and dashed from the vampire's car into his.

His phone beeped once he was almost home. It was a text from Tamara. *Home safe. Thanks again! I'll B @ the game Friday. Hope U will 2*

"She wants to see me again." He pumped his fist into the air. "Hell yeah!"

He was dancing as he walked back into his house. The dancing stopped as he heard Page scratching at Dad's door and whimpering to be let out.

"Oh, crap!" He'd forgotten about her. "Sorry, girl." She gave him a dirty look after he opened the door and went straight to the bathroom and then the kitchen as she sniffed out all the places Tamara had gone in the house.

While his dog engaged in her investigation, Gidion delved back into his. He pulled out the vampire's cell phone and checked out the call history and contacts.

"Let's see who you've been calling, Mr. Polka Dots." This guy's contact list was a lot shorter than the other vamp's had been. Guy wasn't worried about proper spelling either. The name for the Richmond safe house was entered as "rIckmond." Most of the other contact names were about as bad. He pulled out the cell phone from the other vampire and compared some of the phone numbers. Both of these guys seemed to favor the East Coast, but Mr. Polka Dots had a few random numbers in there, too, like Detroit and Chicago… or rather "Destroidt and Chickaggo."

"Someone's spelling skills really sucked."

He went to the text messages after that. He didn't see any sent messages. Either the phone wasn't set to store those, or the guy had recently cleared it. The received ones were interesting. Gidion didn't recognize the number this guy had been texting with, but he'd received a few messages tonight from the same person. The most recent one wasn't illuminating. Just a simple, *'Good.'* Before that was, *'Make sure she suffers. A LOT!'* Was that about Tamara? He looked at the time, and the texts were traded just about the time he'd gone inside the safe house.

The next text was much older, more than a week old, and from a different number. *'Sounds good. Have fun with the girl. I'll take the woman.'* Gidion didn't recognize the number, but Polka Dots had saved it in his contacts with the name "Pike."

"Pike." He pulled out the wallet from the first vampire. The name on the driver's license was Allen Pike. He pressed a button for Polka Dot's phone to dial "Pike." A heartbeat later, the first vampire's phone lit up and played some cheesy ringtone, "The Girl from Ipanema."

He hung up.

"Oh, that's not good." That meant Polka Dots and Pike were coordinating their attacks.

Gidion went back to Polka Dot's cell. He saw a text from a restricted number with a picture attached. It was the same text about Gidion's teacher, the one with Ms. Aldgate's picture. Was it too much to hope these were the only two vampires to get that message? "I hate it when I'm right," he said, remembering his fear that the message had been a text blast.

Unlike Pike's phone, there was a second text message with a picture. He opened it, but this wasn't Ms. Aldgate's picture.

*Tamara Gardner. Find her. Kill her.*
*Reward: admittance. –RICCVN*

"What the hell?" The Richmond Coven wanted her dead, too? First a teacher, and now a student from an entirely different school. He couldn't figure out why the vampires would consider either one a threat. Neither even knew vampires existed prior to their attacks. What was it that connected them? How many people were these vampires targeting? He needed to find out before another vampire came after Tamara, his teacher, or both of them and figure out a way to end this.

# CHAPTER FOURTEEN

If Gidion had his way, the nimrod who decided 7:25 a.m. was a good time to start school would be dragged into the streets and run over by a bus. Coming from a long line of nighthawks, he wasn't a morning person, and on a day like this, he had too much to get done before he was truly awake.

He started with a call to Pete on his way to school, but the call went straight to voicemail. The text message he sent next went unanswered. He timed his next text message just ten minutes before school started. By that time, he was standing in the science building, next to the door to Pete's first class. The text wasn't for Pete, though. That one went to Tamara, *'Call me after school. It's important.'* He would've told her more than that, but he wasn't sure if she still had her phone or if her parents had taken it from her. He also hoped that if she had the phone, her parents wouldn't be around her to see he'd texted her.

She answered less than a minute later. *'Everything okay?'*

*'Not urgent, but found out something important about last night you need to know.'*

*'Ok. Mysterious…Can't wait.'*

She included a smiley face at the end. That was just too cool. He looked up and saw this guy with a dopey looking grin and then realized it was his reflection in the window of a classroom door. The teacher, one he didn't recognize, gave him this evil eye. He wondered why until he realized he had three minutes left to get to class.

Where the hell was Pete? He had to worry about that later. For now, he needed to get halfway across campus for his Algebra III class.

He kept an eye out for Pete between classes, but he didn't see him. The text he'd sent Pete went unanswered, but that wasn't surprising. The teachers at West Chester were militant about confiscating cell phones if they even suspected students were texting in class, and the five minute breaks between classes didn't really allow for much of a conversation, text or otherwise. Lunch confirmed for him that Pete hadn't shown up at school.

"No, haven't seen him all day." Seth took a bite of his sandwich and then offered Andrea a bite of it.

"Has he said anything to you about what's going on with him?" Gidion asked.

Andrea placed a chip in Seth's mouth before he could answer. Lord, these two were way over the top.

"Thanks," he said as he chewed the chip. "I don't know what's going on with him lately. I figured you probably had a better idea. You've both been really MIA, you more than him. Thought you two had been hanging out since Andrea and I have been going out a lot."

"Hey, are we going to the movies this weekend?" she asked Seth, as if Gidion wasn't there.

"Sure," Seth said.

"When did he start hanging out with Stephanie Drake?"

"Wait." Andrea covered Seth's mouth before he could answer. "Pete's dating Stephanie Drake? I heard she broke up with Dillon Masters over the summer, but not that she was going out with anyone else yet. Heard the breakup was really ugly, too."

Gidion needed a wall to smack his head against. On second thought, better to smack Andrea's head against it.

"No, Pete and Stephanie are not dating. He's been hanging out with her crowd, though."

Seth pried his girlfriend's hand off his face. "Wow, I didn't have a clue. When did that happen?"

Maybe he should smack Seth's head against a wall, too. "Dude, that's what I was asking you."

"Oh." Seth shrugged. "Sorry, no clue, man."

"Hey, if Seth and Stephanie are dating, maybe we could do a

double-date kind of thing," Andrea said.

Good God! Was Gidion the only one left in this place who lived in the real freaking world? "They are not dating." He waved his hands around in a mock version of sign language, purposefully sticking his hands right in front of her face.

"I said 'if'." She rolled her eyes. "If you had a girl, could make it a triple-date. That would be so brilliant."

Gidion wanted to snap back that he'd been making out with a senior girl last night, but "making out" was really overstating it, and it wasn't like he could explain how he'd met her.

"Look, I gotta run." Retreat seemed a better option than sitting here while Andrea tried to shove as much estrogen into their lives as possible. He bet she was gonna drag Seth to a chick flick this weekend.

He'd deal with Pete after school. For now, he could check on Ms. Aldgate.

Gidion found her classroom empty. Fabulous. At least the door was open, so she couldn't have gone far. He dropped his backpack on the floor by his desk and pulled out his stuff for class. God, this had to be an all-time low for him, arriving for class a solid half hour early.

He was busy reading chapter eight in his history book when he heard Ms. Aldgate talking to someone in the hallway.

"A formal complaint? They don't really expect me to change their child's grade, do they?"

"At least these parents care how their child does. How many parents can you say that about?" He didn't recognize the man's voice until he saw Principal Vermel stop outside the classroom door. Most folks liked to call him "Principal Vermin" behind his back. That poor excuse for a beard didn't do much for him either. Neither did his height, or rather the lack thereof, not that Gidion could throw stones.

"Other than that, how are you doing, Lillian?"

"The usual."

"You look nice today."

Oh, how gross. Was "the Vermin" flirting with Ms. Aldgate? Jeez, he was a good six inches shorter than her. A Chihuahua had a better chance of humping a Great Dane.

"Ms. Aldgate?" Gidion waved to her from his desk as she and the Vermin looked over at him. The principal had that hand-in-the-cookie-jar look. "I had a question about that chapter you had us read last night."

"Of course, I'll be right there." She smiled at him and then turned back to the Vermin. "If you'll excuse me."

"Yes, yes...I'll, uh, keep you informed."

"Thank you."

The Vermin scurried away. Ms. Aldgate shook her head as she walked back into the classroom.

"So, what was your question about chapter eight, Gidion?"

"Oh, nothing. Just figured you needed an excuse to get rid of Mr. Vermi—uh, Vermel."

She smirked. "Yes, we call him that, too. So what do you want, Gidion? You don't typically show up early for class. You make an art out of sitting down right as the bell rings."

"I like to maximize my time between classes." Was that so wrong?

She looked back at the door. "So am I to assume this is about...?"

"Yeah." He pulled out the driver's license he'd taken off of Mr. Polka Dots. "Wanted to see if you recognized this guy."

"Andy Blake?" She shook her head. "I don't recall ever seeing him. Should I?"

"Wasn't thinking you would, but figured it was worth a check."

"He must be a vampire with a fake name like that," she said.

"How are you so sure of that?" He figured the name was an alias, but she just sounded so certain.

"Isn't it obvious? *Andy* Blake?" She stared at him a second as if that explained everything. "You know. Anita Blake? Laurell K. Hamilton?"

He shook his head. "Sorry, no clue what you're talking about. Is this something I should know?"

"Given what most of her books are like and your age, probably not."

"What about the name Tamara Gardner?"

That just received a shrug. "Sorry," she said. "Are these two connected to the attack on me?"

"Well, 'Andy' attacked Tamara Gardner last night. She's a senior at Midlothian Springs and a very good kisser." He figured he might as well brag about it to her since she was the only one with whom he could. "Anyway, she had a hit put on her by the Richmond Coven. He was coordinating with the vampire who attacked you at the Canal Walk."

He pulled out Mr. Polka Dot's cell phone and showed her the text with Tamara's picture.

"Pretty hot, isn't she?"

She sighed. "Gidion."

"Sorry, but I haven't gotten to tell anyone else considering how I met her. Anyway, does she look familiar to you?"

She took the phone from him and looked at the picture. "No." She closed it and handed it back to him. "What is it you're thinking here? That there's a connection between me and this girl?"

"These vampires received the texts about the hits on you and Tamara at the same time. Something connects the two of you."

"I don't recognize that girl, and there's not really any reason for me to. The only school I've taught at in Richmond is West Chester. This is my seventh year here."

Gidion put the phone back into his backpack. "How did you end up in Richmond anyway?"

"My ex-husband got a job here," she said. "We were still married at the time."

"What's his name?"

"You think he might be tied into this somehow?" The way she eyed him as she crossed her arms made her opinion pretty clear. "Or are you just being nosey?"

"Something connects you with Tamara," he said. "I've got to figure out what that is. Does your ex still live in Richmond?"

"Sadly." Her voice trailed off.

"What?" Something had clicked for her, and God knows, he needed a lead to run with.

"I saw him the night I was attacked."

He suddenly remembered when he'd seen her walk out of Siné that night. "Ohhhh…Did you two have a fight?" That would explain why she'd been crying.

Her body stiffened. "I'd rather not talk about it."

He pulled out his notebook and a pencil. "I need to get some info on your ex." When it became clear she wasn't intending to answer that, he looked up at her. "Just so I can make sure he's not connected to this."

"I'm rather certain he's not."

"Let me do what I do, and you can go from 'rather certain' to 'without a doubt'."

The last time he'd seen her mouth form a line that hard was when one of his classmates had made the mistake of going three days in a row without doing his homework.

"Oh, before I forget, you ever go to Old World?" he asked. "It's a dance club."

"No, but I've heard of it."

"Good, probably best if you to stay clear of it. I think it's somehow connected to the Richmond Coven."

"After the other night, I plan to stay clear of downtown altogether."

Yeah, that probably was best, but he decided not to say that. "So, let's talk about your ex…" He wondered what the chances were the guy had paid a visit to Old World.

# CHAPTER FIFTEEN

When Gidion, Pete and Seth became friends, it didn't take long to figure out whose house was best to go to—Gidion's. Dad might not rank high in the "cool" department, but at least domestic disputes weren't a daily occurrence.

Seth's parents eventually divorced a few years ago, but the "Unhappy-Lives-Here" vibe had never lifted from the Parson home. That said, it was still a better option than Pete's place. The only love Pete's parents had was a passion for hating each other and a refusal to use birth control. Pete had two older brothers and a younger sister. One brother was with the Army somewhere in Afghanistan. No one knew where the oldest brother was, but the top-running bets had Roddy Addams rotting in a prison or a ditch.

This house was karma's bitch, complete with a Rottweiler in the backyard that Pete's dad loved more than his kids. Place probably came with a few garden snakes, too, just without a garden, more like a miniature grass jungle.

"Welcome to the Addams Family's Technicolor cousins," Gidion said as he parked the Little Hearse on the street. He checked his phone. Still no call or text from Tamara. He really had way too many people to chase after these days. Hopefully, she wouldn't try to reach him while he was here. He'd driven straight to Pete's after school.

He knocked on the door. Good news was that it looked like both of Pete's parents weren't here. The only car in the driveway was Pete's. No answer. He didn't even hear anyone moving around in there.

"Yo!" He walked over to the left corner of the house, just under

Pete's window. "Pete! Yo, dude!"

That was effective—not.

"Oh, the hell with this." He went back to the front door. Sure enough, it was unlocked. He pushed open the door. The den/living room had DVD cases on the floor. Place was pretty much status quo for the Addams.

"Pete, it's Gidion!" Nada. He stepped over a shirt in the hallway, probably belonged to Pete's dad by the looks of it.

The door to Pete's room was cracked open. He could see his friend sprawled on the bed. He was dressed the same as last night, just minus the dog collar. "Pete?" At least he was still breathing. Either he was snoring or wheezing.

He went in the room and stopped as he saw the bite marks low on Pete's throat. The dog collar and upturned shirt collars had warned him they would be there, but that didn't mean he'd been ready to see it. Seeing him like this, was it any wonder why he'd lost his job at the car shop? No wonder he'd "overslept" enough times to get fired.

After the shock cleared, Gidion kicked the side of the bed.

"Pete! Wake up!"

Pete's head rolled over. His eyes opened and then narrowed. "Gid?" He placed a hand on his forehead. "Oh, man. Head hurts."

Gidion resisted the urge to slap him and really make his head hurt. "You're looking pale, Pete."

"Rough night." He turned away, as he sat up.

"Yeah, I hear it's a real bitch donating blood."

Pete's back stiffened. "What do you know about it?"

"Enough to know you're in a crapload of trouble, pal."

"Me?" He laughed at him like he was an idiot. "I don't know what you think you know, but—"

"Vampires, Pete. You're some vampire's bitch. That's what I know."

"Vampires?" Pete laughed. The idiot was trying to bluff his way out of this, but his reaction had come too late. "What have you been smoking?"

Gidion saw two half-empty glasses of water sitting on the nightstand. "You wanna know how this really works?" He picked up the glasses and poured the water back and forth. "This is how it goes. You're the small glass, and this is the vampire." He raised the bigger glass. "Right now, seems all fine and dandy. Thing is…he's taking a lot of your blood, and you're only getting a little in return."

"She." Pete glared up at him.

"If you found a leech on your leg, would you really worry whether it was a boy or a girl?" He emptied out the last of the small glass into the larger one. "Gee, looks like your glass is empty."

"You don't know shit about it."

"I know it's only a matter of time before they kill you."

"The only person who's gonna get me killed is you." Pete stood. In all the time Gidion had known him, this was the first time Pete's height scared him. Then Pete collapsed back onto the bed, his legs unable to support his weight. "Why the hell do you think I'm so wiped out? They bled me until I passed out and only gave me two lousy, fucking drops in return." Tears ran down his face. "They did it because you followed me into the club last night."

"So they own the club?"

"I don't know!" He sobbed. "It's just where they like us to meet them."

Gidion's phone rang. Dammit, it was Tamara. "Pete, I've got to take this call. I'll get you something to drink." Something that wouldn't be red and didn't sound like it was Sesame Street's letter of the day, he thought to himself.

Pete flopped onto his side on the bed. Gidion hoped he wasn't passing out again.

He answered his phone. "Hey."

"I call at a bad time?" Tamara asked.

"Kind of, but don't worry about that." He went into the kitchen and opened the fridge. Damn, there was some scary looking stuff in there. "Long story short, that attack on you wasn't random, and you're still in danger."

"What? How can you be so sure?"

"I'm not in a safe place to talk." He looked over his shoulder to make sure Pete wasn't there trying to listen, not that he was likely to crawl out of his bedroom anytime soon. "Any chance I can call you later tonight?"

"Probably better if I call you. My parents didn't take my phone, but they weren't exactly thrilled last night either."

"Sorry about that." He pulled out a can of Coke from the fridge. The sugar content and caffeine would probably help Pete a little. "In the meantime, don't go out alone, not even during the daylight."

She laughed. "No danger of that. They grounded me. If I wasn't in the band, I don't think they'd even let me go to the game this Friday night."

"My Cavaliers are gonna stomp your Vikings." He couldn't resist a little trash talk. Football was more sacred than vampire hunting.

"Oh, please. We've beaten you for five years straight."

He laughed. "Call me later, and be careful. Okay?"

"Trust me." She sighed. "I'm not going anywhere tonight."

He hung up, and took the soda to Pete.

"You still alive in here?" Gidion asked.

Pete sat up. He resembled a puppet with half his strings cut.

"I know these vampires are putting hits out on humans, a teacher at our school and a student at another. Why?"

Pete took the Coke and sipped it. "I don't know anything about that."

"You're telling me you've been hanging out with these monsters for months, and you don't know anything?"

"You don't get it, Gid. I'm a guy, so I'm nothing in their world."

You're nothing but a blood bag, he thought to himself. "What do you know?"

"I know only what Stephanie tells me."

"She the one who got you into this?"

He shook his head. Gidion didn't get the feeling Pete was going to discuss that without him pressing a lot harder. How he got in didn't matter as much as getting him out.

"Where do I find them, Pete? Where do they sleep?"

"I don't know."

"Bullshit!"

"I don't know!"

He'd known Pete since they were little. He considered Pete one of the worst liars he'd ever met. He believed him, but he didn't want to.

"I can't help you unless you help me."

"I don't need your help."

He laughed. "Oh, really? That can of Coke didn't teleport from the kitchen into your hand, pal. I'll bet you can't even walk to the bathroom without help."

"The only reason I'm like this is because of you!"

"Pete, they're using you. You think I'm the one to blame? You're smarter than this."

He glared up at him, ready to pounce. Gidion fought down the instinct to go for his box cutter, but he did shift his position in the room to be closer to a baseball bat that was propped against a dresser.

"They punished me because of you," Pete said. "I'd be just fine if you hadn't gone into the nightclub."

"Last I checked, Stephanie invited me in there. Sounds more like she's pissed because I turned her down when she made a pass at me."

"You and Stephanie?"

Good God. The idiot was latching onto the least important details. It was like they were speaking in different languages.

"Yeah, she's turned into a real bitch."

Even running on fumes, Pete still launched up from the bed at Gidion.

"Shit!" He balked on the bat, just couldn't bring himself to turn his friend into batting practice. His back slammed into the closet door. Pete pulled back for a punch. Gidion slammed his fists into Pete's chest, sending him onto the bed. All the adrenaline in the world didn't change that Pete was running on empty.

"They're targeting people, a girl and a teacher," Gidion said. "I need to find these vampires and end this."

"What part of 'I don't know' was tough to understand?" He picked up the can of Coke he'd dropped. Half of it had spilled onto the floor.

"Does Stephanie know?"

"Get out." Pete sounded ready for another run at him. What was it? Was he carrying a torch for that witch? He was tempted to tell him what she'd called him at "Old World," but he wondered if Pete would even believe it.

"Listen, Pete. You can help me save a life—two lives."

"Only thing you're gonna do is get me killed."

"Once I kill those vampires, you've got nothing to worry about."

"Stephanie already thinks you know more than you've let on."

No shock there. Gidion suspected as much, and that begged one question. "What is she planning to do about it?"

"They're gonna be watching you." He looked towards his window. "Might already be doing it."

"Great." This time of day, it would have to be another feeder. He just hoped the feeder spying on him wasn't the one in this room. "Let's get our story straight then. I came here accusing you of doing drugs. You denied, and I called you a lousy lying piece of crap before I stormed out of here."

"You really think they'll believe that?"

"Let's hope so, because your life is riding on it."

Pete looked up at him. "You realize all it takes for me to save my ass is to just tell them you know about them."

Gidion felt a chill go down his back. Jesus, would Pete do that to him? The second the fear passed, anger kicked in. He stepped closer and got right in his face.

"And don't forget that all it would take for me to get you killed is telling them you were the one who let me know about them."

"I won't tell them." He held up his hands. "I promise. I wasn't serious."

"I am." Gidion didn't pull back. "Now answer my question. Does Stephanie know where the vampires sleep? Does she know where their home is?"

"I don't know." He held up his hands to stave off Gidion's protest. "But if any of them do, then she would."

"She's the top feeder, huh?"

He nodded. "The women always call the shots."

"How many vampires?"

Pete narrowed his eyes and grit his teeth. He'd seen him wear this same face the last time he had to choose between the latest issues of *Red Sonja* or *Witchblade*.

"At least five, maybe six or seven." He shook his head. "It's hard to say. They don't all show up every time, and they sometimes have guests."

"Who's the coven leader?"

"Elizabeth." No hesitation in that answer.

"When do you next see them?"

"I don't know. Stephanie sends us a text when they want us. If we don't go right away, they short us." Even without screaming, Pete's voice shrieked on that last detail.

"Like they did to you last night?"

Pete nodded.

"The next time you get summoned," Gidion said, "you text me when and where you're going. Make sure you delete it from your sent messages. Don't need them checking your phone and seeing you contacted me."

"Do you have any idea what they'd do to me if they found out!"

Gidion knew damn well what they'd do, and "shorting" him was the least of his worries if that happened.

"Make sure they don't. As far as they're concerned, I think you're doing drugs and that Stephanie and her goons are the ones selling them to you."

Pete placed the can of Coke on his nightstand, pushing the pile of comics and empty glasses aside to make room for it.

"I'm sorry, Gid." He sobbed, his chest heaving as he spoke. "I didn't think anything bad would happen—not like this."

"If things turn worse, you call me. I'll do what I can to protect you. Just stick to our story, and text me the next time they contact you with a time and place to meet."

"What are you gonna do?"

"Follow them back to their home." Gidion put a hand on Pete's shoulder. "Get some rest, pal."

Pete didn't stand to walk him out. Gidion hadn't really expected him to.

As soon as he walked out the front door, any question as to whether he was already being followed was answered. A blue pickup was parked in front of the house across the street. He recognized the driver from last night at Old World. It was one of the two who'd come after him on the dance floor, Thing One and Thing Two. This one had a purple, vertically-challenged Mohawk. He'd make this dude Thing One.

Gidion had planned to play off that he couldn't see his tail, but their eyes met. He decided to make the most of it. Going straight for the Little Hearse's trunk, Gidion reached inside and pulled out a black aluminum bat from the pile of "sports camouflage" in there.

"You!" Gidion didn't bother closing the trunk. He marched straight at the pickup and pointed the bat at Thing One. "Are you the one selling him drugs?" he shouted as loud as he could. He reared back with the bat. Thing One scrambled to crank the truck. "Get out of here!"

The truck screeched from its spot, but not before Gidion smashed a hole in the driver side window. The pickup went onto two wheels as it turned the corner and disappeared from view on its way out of the neighborhood.

Gidion hoped he was convincing. As long as the vampires believed he only suspected Pete had a drug problem, the better his chances were of staying alive long enough to kill them. They weren't done spying on him, though. They'd just send someone else instead of Thing One, and that one probably wouldn't be so easy to spot.

# CHAPTER SIXTEEN

Page was barking as if fire demons were charging the front door. She didn't like it when the neighborhood kids got home from school.

"You're home late." Dad was in the bathroom, "shaping" his beard. He never bothered with shaving cream. He just wet his face and got rid of the hair on the bottom of his jaw and down to his throat. After that, he'd get his cheeks. Dad was a perfectionist about his beard, really about most everything he did.

Gidion dropped his book bag by the bedroom door. "Yeah, went by Pete's on the way home. You working a double?"

"Yeah, going in at four." That gave Dad about twenty minutes before he had to roll out the door. "You got a lot of homework?"

"Not too bad. Mostly reading. Got most of my math done at lunch." After Ms. Aldgate had given him what information she could on her ex, he spent most of lunch in the library doing homework. Who would have guessed that Seth's dating life would improve Gidion's study habits?

"So, how's Pete doing these days?" He rinsed the razor and put it in the cabinet.

"Varying degrees of shitty."

"Hey, mind the language." He smiled at him as he walked past him and into his bedroom.

Gidion scowled. "You're the one I stole the saying from."

"Only reason I didn't smack you for it." He was teasing him. "So what fresh hell is brewing in Pete's world?"

"He's just being stupid."

That earned an interesting look from Dad. "That's not exactly what I'd call 'fresh hell' for Pete."

"What's that supposed to mean?"

"Never cared for Pete. The boy's an idiot."

Not that Dad had ever suggested he liked Pete or Seth, but he'd never flat out stated a dislike for one of them.

"He's not an idiot, Dad."

Dad stole a glance at the clock and sighed. "Sorry, I know it's not a nice thing to say about one of your friends, but Pete's always had a bad habit of making bad choices. Always worried me to see you hang out with him."

"I'm not stupid."

"I know. It's why I never tried to forbid you from playing with him. Kind of put faith in time to do it for me." He put on a blue dress shirt and buttoned it. "Are you okay? You're not in some kind of trouble are you?"

*Aside from a coven of vampires who are sure to want me dead the minute they realize I'm hunting them?* Yeah, he was just peachy.

"Gidion, are you all right?"

"I'm fine," he said. "Just trying to help Pete is all."

"Help Pete?" Dad sat on the bed and laughed as he pulled out his loafers. "Make me a promise."

"What kind of promise?"

"I don't want to pay for a window you didn't break this time."

"Jeez, you knew?" Back when they were in elementary school, they'd been playing wall ball on the back of Pete's house. Pete threw the ball through a window. About ten seconds after the glass fell to pieces, Pete did the same. His parents weren't home, but his dad had threatened to beat the snot out of him if he caught him bouncing that tennis ball off the back of the house again. He hadn't warned Seth or Gidion about that. Gidion had taken the fall for him. Gidion's dad might threaten to smack him, but the worst he'd ever done was plant him back into a chair or drag him by the arm across a room. When Pete's dad threatened to beat his kids, bones broke.

"Of course, I knew." Dad sounded insulted.

"But if you knew, then why'd you ground me for a week after that?"

"Do you have any idea how much that window cost? I swear, I think his dad tried to make me buy the most expensive one he could find. Stupid thing was probably worth more than that pigsty of a house." He laughed. "Hell, yes, I punished your ass. Wasn't punishing you for breaking that window. That was for lying and making me your accomplice to cover for Pete."

Man, Gidion never suspected Dad had known. That made him a lot more nervous about his vampire hunting. If Dad could read him that easily back then, what were the odds he didn't suspect what he'd been doing these past few months?

"Oh, um, Grandpa invited me over for dinner tonight." More like ordered.

"Sorry to hear that." Dad smiled at him, then walked over to his dresser to retrieve his ID card, wallet, keys and various other going-to-work necessities. "You need any money to pick up dinner on the way to his house?"

"No, I'm probably good. Suspect he'll order pizza for me to pick up."

Dad nodded. Grandpa didn't cook, and when he did, the results weren't pretty. He subscribed to the Southern tradition of cooking vegetables to the point of oblivion.

"Gotta go." Dad patted him on the shoulder. He smiled, the grin widening as he looked at him. "You know. Funny thing was, as ticked as I was with you about that window, I was proud of you, too. You stood by your friend, even as scared as you were. Just remember as you two get older, you've got to let him pay his way for his mistakes. That's part of growing up."

"Are you saying I was wrong to do that?"

Dad didn't answer right away. "I don't know. People learn a lot more from their mistakes than having the right way handed to them. I follow that rule whenever I train someone to do my job at work, but it's different when it's someone you love. I've stepped in for you more times than I should have, and it gets harder not to step in as you get older."

"You don't trust me?"

"It's not that. The difference is that the risks get greater as you get older."

He wasn't hurting for risk these days. Four lives to worry about, including his.

"Have fun over at Grandpa's," he said. "Text me when you get home."

"All right, Dad."

Dad diverted to the kitchen to grab something from the freezer for dinner before he rushed out the front door. So far, he'd dodged Dad's suspicions, but after this conversation, he wondered just how far he could go before Dad figured it out...and shut him down.

# CHAPTER SEVENTEEN

Grandpa owned a small house inside the city. The place only had one bedroom and had suffered through enough remodels to qualify for a multiple personality disorder. Thanks to Grandpa, the mental issues probably included paranoia. The front door didn't just have a bolt, but included a large metal bar that could be dropped in front of it. He also kept a variety of swords on the wall. The wakizashi Gidion used had once had a place on the wall next to the bedroom door.

Gidion dropped a box of meat lover's pizza on the kitchen table. Grandpa was under the kitchen sink battling a drip that refused to die.

"Nimrods who owned this place before me must have relied on idiots to update the plumbing. Not a damn pipe in this place is the right length or fits right."

"What do you want to drink, Grandpa?" Gidion stepped around his elder to pull two glasses from the cabinet.

"Grab me a beer, kid." He growled like a dog defending his turf. "Damn idiots. Sure as hell weren't in the Navy. I can tell you that much."

Gidion knew for a fact that Grandpa had already replaced all the plumbing underneath that sink—twice, but he wasn't dumb enough to point that out. Grandpa was already in a mood to chew out his happy ass. No point adding an accelerant to that fire.

"You want a Killian's or a Bass Ale?" Gidion asked as he looked at the selection in the fridge. Grandpa might have been all American, but when it came to his beers, he was a snot. Domestic beer didn't live in a Keep house. Dad lived by the same philosophy.

"Get me a Killian's," he said as he crawled out from underneath the sink. "And give me a hand here."

Gidion held out his hand and pulled him to his feet. He didn't weigh as much as he used to. It was weird to watch Grandpa get smaller as he got bigger.

Grandpa turned on the hot water and canted his head to look beneath the sink. He grunted his approval of his handiwork. Gidion wondered how long it would last.

"So, we've got a lot to talk about, don't we?" Grandpa pulled out two paper plates and set them on the kitchen table.

More than you know, Gidion thought to himself. "Look, about Tamara…"

"Yeah, yeah." Grandpa waved him off. "Listen, I know you couldn't just leave her there, but you can't be bringing every pretty puss to the funeral home. When they've seen your face, they've already learned too much."

That last line was one of Grandpa's favorites. He'd grilled that into him during the past few months.

"I couldn't just drop her off at home without cleaning her up first."

Grandpa laughed like that was the funniest thing he'd heard all year.

"Well, it's true." Gidion sat a little straighter as he mounted his defense. "Dropping her off at home looking like she'd been beaten and bloodied would cause too many questions."

"And her showing up after midnight didn't cause a bunch of questions?"

Gidion didn't answer that. Dammit. He chomped a large piece of pizza to keep his mouth too busy to implicate himself even more. Grandpa was right. It wasn't like he would've gone to all that trouble if she hadn't been some pretty girl.

"For what it's worth," Gidion said once he'd finished his bite of pizza, "she kissed me when I dropped her off at her car."

"That's the Keep blood in ya, boy!" He pounded his fist on his chest. "Damn proud of ya."

"Yeah, about that whole 'when they've seen your face, they

already know too much' stuff." He put down his slice of pizza and traced a finger around the rim of his glass of iced tea. "We need to talk about the other night."

"Thought we were doing that."

"Um, yeah, I'm not talking about last night. I'm talking about the other night when I killed the vampire down at the Canal Walk." He cleared his throat, not that it made his confession any easier to say. "The lady I saved that night walked away knowing a lot more than my face."

"What?"

"Grandpa, the lady I saved recognized me. She's my world history teacher."

Cue the explosion. After a few words unfit for public consumption, some of which Gidion assumed to be foreign curses or Grandpa just having a seizure, he explained the whole mess. He told him about the hits the vampires had on his teacher and Tamara, the lack of any obvious connection between them and the worst news of all: Pete.

"You're risking disaster with that boy." Grandpa downed what was left of his beer. "You can't trust him. All they gotta do is give him a drop of blood and he'll slit your throat for them if they ask."

"I've got Pete under control, Grandpa. Just trust me."

"The fact you think you can control a feeder is sign enough you've lost all control of this mess, boy. They own him."

This after Dad's bashing of Pete bit too deep into the wound. "Listen, I know Pete. He won't roll on me. We've had each other's backs since we were kids."

Grandpa laughed. "Boy, you're developing into a fine young man, but you aren't there yet."

"Look, Pete might be the key to taking out the entire coven. They punished him. He's bitter about it, too. All it takes is for him to lead me to the vampires and then I track them home at the end of the night. Soon as that happens, I just wait for sunrise," he slapped his hand on the table, "and it's game over."

"What? You think you can waltz into their lair and kill at your leisure?" Grandpa shook his head. "We've been over this, boy. You don't ever attack a vampire when it's asleep. They wake up as pissed off as a feral cat in heat."

"They can wake up as pissed as they like. Won't save them when a fire burns their house down around them. If the flames don't get them, then the sunlight will."

That got Grandpa to stop the smart remarks. He nodded. "That could work, but not if Pete outs you before you can follow them to their lair."

"He won't turn on me."

"You can't trust him. The boy is hooked on their blood. People who get a taste for what's in those beasts' veins never recover. They're dead on their feet and just don't know it."

Gidion knew better than to debate this. Grandpa and Dad both got like this. Whenever they "knew something," they wouldn't budge. Didn't matter even when he was right.

"There's something else I want to talk about," Gidion said as he started eating his pizza again.

"What's that?"

"Dad."

Grandpa leaned back in his chair. "If you're worried he knows what you're doing, then stop."

"No, I'm sure he doesn't know yet. If he did, he'd crawl down your throat until he reached daylight, wouldn't he?"

Something between a groan and a growl whispered from Grandpa's throat.

"Yeah, that's what I thought," Gidion said.

Grandpa eyed him about the same way he'd glared at the bum pipes beneath the sink. "It's not like I haven't warned you about your dad's reaction if he found out."

"No, but Dad's not an idiot. He did this, and I'm guessing you trained him the same way you trained me. What's to stop him from piecing it together?"

That only made Grandpa laugh. "You think I did this without his approval?"

"Wait. He knows?"

Grandpa shook his head. "No, he knows I've given you the training…well, some of it. As far as he's concerned, you've been taught how to fight, vampire hunter style, minus all the killing moves and the knowledge they exist."

"You're telling me he bought that?" Even Gidion wouldn't have been fooled by that.

"Your dad hunted longer than I did. You've been lucky so far, making every kill you've gone for. Take it from one who's been there. You aren't gonna bat a thousand. A few get away, and some hold a grudge enough to come back for another try when you're older and weaker. They've got time on their side."

Gidion glanced at the front door, the metal bar that could slide into place. Then he considered the walls, all the swords on display, none kept in a scabbard, making them easy to draw at a moment's need. The place was arranged for a last stand. Grandpa could take two steps in any direction and arm himself. Was this what his house would look like if he lived to be in his seventies?

"So, what you're saying is that you conned Dad into going along with my training in case any vamps came after me as payback against him or you."

Grandpa nodded. "You got it."

"He really bought that?"

"He watches you a lot closer than you think," Grandpa said. "Mind your steps."

"Yeah, I'll do that." He thought about the conversation about Pete's window. How had Dad managed not to suspect anything yet? Hell, maybe he had.

"How's your arm doing?"

Gidion held up his right arm and gripped it with his left hand. "Sore, but I'll be fine for hunting tomorrow." The forearm hurt more than anything else. Moving wasn't painful, but lifting stuff sure wasn't pleasant, like the bones in there were tender or something. Still, better his arm than his head.

"You might should take off tomorrow, too," Grandpa said

around a mouthful of pizza. "You're good, a real natural, but don't get cocky. Getting cocky…"

"'…gets you killed'," Gidion said. "Yeah, I know. Don't worry. I'll be careful. If I don't feel up for it, I'll stay home."

"Gidion, when the vampires get close to your scent, the best thing to do is lie low. You seem determined to run straight at 'em."

"If I hide in a hole, then Ms. Aldgate and Tamara are gonna die. They aren't after them for a quick snack. Someone in the coven wants them dead. I gotta find out why and keep that from happening. Besides, while I trust Pete to keep his mouth shut for now, it's only a matter of time before he slips up or I do. Soon as they figure out what I know, it's open season on Gidion Keep."

"Damn," Grandpa stood and walked into the den to pick up his pipe. "You can't save everyone, kid. There comes a time where you gotta accept that."

"I'll worry about it when I have to. For now, I'm just trying to keep myself and as many others as I can alive."

"Well, take a few days to let that arm get all healed before you try anything. Got it?"

Gidion nodded. "I'll be careful. Promise."

Of course, if Pete sent a text tonight that the vampires had summoned him, then he wasn't going to sit on his butt. He probably only had one shot at tracking Pete to find the vampires. Couldn't pass on that. Pete was his surefire way to end this and save everyone, including himself.

# CHAPTER EIGHTEEN

The sun had already set and the clocks in the house were fast approaching nine o'clock by the time Gidion made it back home. He'd finished his homework before going to Grandpa's, so he didn't need to deal with that. Instead, he went for the bathtub. According to Dad, Mom had been big into herbal remedies. Her favorite cure-all was lavender oil.

Trouble sleeping? Rub a few drops of lavender oil on your temples.

Headache? Lavender oil on the forehead.

Bug bite? Put a drop of lavender oil on it.

Hell, he'd seen Dad add lavender oil to mouthwash to help knock out a bad mouth ulcer.

Way his arm was giving him hell, Gidion opted for a hot bath with thirteen drops of lavender oil added. Taking notes in class had hurt like hell. He hoped Ms. Aldgate realized every detail she made him write hurt her chances for survival.

Page strolled into the narrow bathroom and sprawled across the bathmat. She wasn't being social, merely cowardly. A thunderstorm had made its way into the area. So far, they'd only gotten thunder here. The rain was to the north, but thunder scared the bejesus out of his dog. The way she panicked at the hint of bad weather, Gidion suspected a fortune-telling cat at the pound had warned Page she would die by lightning.

Gidion's eyes narrowed, looking over the top edge of a Kyle Mills thriller novel at his dog. "You know, it's a lot easier to read without your panicked panting for a soundtrack."

The expression on Page's face didn't alter a hair. He didn't care how keen dog's ears were, she probably couldn't hear him over that panting. He turned up the speaker he'd plugged his iPod into, playing Metric's latest album. Fortunately, he had the volume on his phone's ringer loud enough to hear it over Page and the music.

"Yes!" It was Tamara, finally.

"Hey there," she said, her voice close to a whisper. He turned down his music to hear her better.

"I take it this call is being made on the QT." He sat up, shifting so he could keep his sore arm in the water while he held the phone with his other hand.

She laughed. "Gidion, I'm in the closet. Seriously."

"I'm a little less hidden, but then my dad isn't home." He shifted, because one of the safety gripper strip thingees was digging into his butt.

"Wait," Tamara said, "are you taking a bath?"

He winced. Crap. "Uh, yeah. Arm's still sore from the way that vampire smacked my arm with a frying pan, so I'm giving it a good soak."

She made this weird, excited cooing sound.

"Sorry," he said.

"Oh no." She had a laugh in her voice. "No need to apologize. Just don't splash the water too much, or you'll drive me insane over here."

Holy hell, she was getting turned on by the idea of him in the tub. Yes! Grandpa never mentioned vampire hunting came with these kinds of benefits.

"I'll do my best." He went silent for a moment. Why had he asked her to call him again? "Oh! Yeah. I mean, I needed to let you know what I found out after you got home last night."

"Just what is going on?"

"After you got home, I went through that vampire's stuff. He'd gotten a text more than a week ago, a text about you. For some reason, the Richmond Coven wants you dead."

"Wait, you mean there might be more of those things coming after me?" Her voice got louder, and then she quickly lowered it, probably remembering she wasn't supposed to be on the phone. "Why? That's just nuts."

"You didn't know vampires existed before last night?"

"I've never ruled out the possibility," she said, "but I was kind of holding out hope they'd be more sparkly."

"Yeah, not so much. What about friends who've gone missing recently?"

"Thank God, no."

"Have you ever heard of Lillian Aldgate?" No answer to that. "She's a history teacher at my high school."

"Sorry, no. Why?"

"The coven put out a hit on her at the same time as you." He'd really hoped Tamara might know his teacher somehow. He needed to know what the common element was. There might be no ending this otherwise. "What about Charles Finley?"

"No, who's he?"

"My teacher's ex-husband."

"Her ex? Is he a vampire?"

"No, but she ran into him downtown a few minutes before a vampire attacked her." He wiped some drops of water from his eyebrows before they could slide down into his eyes. "Look, until I've shut this down, don't go anywhere alone. Either you go out with both of your parents or a large group. Vampires value their secrecy, so they won't compromise that even to kill you."

"Since I'm grounded, consider that done."

"If you notice any unfamiliar cars parked near your house, let me know. Note anything you can about it: license plates, color, make, model, the works. Oh, and if you own a box cutter, keep it with you at all times."

"A box cutter?"

He gave her the same box cutter speech he'd given his teacher.

"Gidion, I don't have a box cutter, and it's not like I can ask my parents to go with me to a hardware store to get one."

"Good point." He thought on that. "You're definitely at the game Friday night?"

"I'm in the school marching band, so yeah, I get to go despite being grounded. Are you going to be there, or are you going to be out playing Batman?"

She was comparing him with Batman? Awesome!

"I'll be there. I can bring you one of mine."

"Just how many do you have?"

"I really have no—" He jumped as Page leaped up and ran down to the den. She started barking as if Satan had just pissed on the front lawn. "Tamara, I gotta go."

"You all right?"

"Yeah, I'll text you in a moment." He hung up and scrambled out of the tub.

Page would bark if a flea farted across the street, but she had different levels of barking. Most of the time, she worked with a "kids-irritate-me" bark. Door-to-door salesmen received a more aggressive greeting from Page, because they had dared to invade her territory. Whatever just set her off had her flipping out. He made a cursory run of the towel over his body and then wrapped it around his waist. He turned off the music coming from his iPod and picked up the box cutter he'd left on top of the toilet.

He heard Page scratch and slam her body against the front door. Holy crap, she wanted a piece of something out there. She didn't get this bent even when a stray dog tried to mark her territory. Whatever had her ticked, at least it was outside. He went to his room and threw on some underwear and then some dark grey sweats. One of Grandpa's rules was to avoid fighting in the buff. Not only did clothing offer a layer of protection, but unless a person made a habit of it, it wasn't easy to fight with certain body parts dangling about.

Gidion kept the lights off in the house. He went down to the den. Page's barking and whining hurt his ears, but he didn't try to shut her up. She was doing her job, and she wasn't worth the poop that came out her hind end if she didn't warn him of trouble.

He kept low and looked out the window. A silver Lincoln Town Car was parked across the street. He kept a record of every car he saw parked near his house. He knew this wasn't one of the regulars.

Gidion sat in a chair by the windows. Even if anyone was watching him, they weren't likely to see him move around inside as long as his lights were off. The staring match had begun, only in this game, the challenge wasn't to see who blinked first. It was a question of who saw the other's shadow move first. He couldn't tell if anyone was in the Lincoln. The way Page was going off, you'd think someone was at the front door, but a look through the peephole had confirmed no one was there. He kept the front porch light on all night.

After fifteen minutes, he finally saw movement. At least one person was in the Lincoln. "Gotcha." Tough to tell anything else, but that was enough. Given it was night, had he rated a vampire for a tail instead of a feeder?

He couldn't just go out to the car and attack the guy. For all he knew, the dude wasn't even here for him. He might be dropping off someone at the house across the street. Even if he was with the vampires, attacking him only tipped Gidion's hand. He couldn't solve this problem with a box cutter or a sword. Fortunately, he owned a more effective weapon for this.

Gidion moved back from the window and pulled out his cell phone. He knelt a little lower to keep the light of the phone from giving him away and dialed.

A woman's voice answered his call. "Chesterfield Communications."

"Yes, I've got a suspicious car parked in front of my house."

"What's the address, sir?"

"I think it's in front of 9631 Capricorn Drive. It's a silver Lincoln Town Car. There's a guy sitting inside, and he's been there for about an hour now." Okay, so he fudged the time, but he didn't want the lady rolling her eyes if he only said it had been fifteen minutes.

"Do you see any weapons or any sign he might be intoxicated?" the dispatcher asked.

"Not that I can see."

"Did you want to talk to the officer when he gets out there?"

"No."

"Your name?"

"Tim Drake."

"All right, Mr. Drake. We'll get someone out that way. If anything changes before they get there, just give us a call back."

"Thanks."

He turned the phone off. A minute later, a text appeared from Tamara. Crap. He'd forgotten his promise to text her. He sent her a message letting her know he was all right and gave her the description of the car in front of his house. He also gave her some advice on what to do if she saw a suspicious car in front of her house during the next few days and couldn't reach him.

There are a few important details to making a complaint to the police about a suspicious dude in a car. First off, never exaggerate too much. Yeah, he could claim the guy had a gun or a knife. The cops would get there a lot quicker, but they'd also be more likely to call him back or try to figure out where he lived and confront him about making a false report. Cops don't like being bullshitted. Second, he didn't give his address. A well-meaning cop might come to his door when he responded, and that would out him as the one who called. No, he gave the address across the street from him. The false name? Well, in Gidion's case, Dad monitored the Chesterfield Police radios when he was at work. If the Chesterfield dispatcher gave out the name of the caller, Dad would freak the minute he heard his name. Knowing Dad, he'd probably notice the mention of the street name and call or text to check on him. That was fine, because that would let Gidion know when the call had been assigned to an officer.

His phone beeped a few minutes later to let him know he'd gotten another text. There was Dad, right on cue.

*Heard the dispatcher give out a call near our house. Everything okay?*

Page had calmed a bit by this point, reduced to low growls and pacing circles by the front door. *'All good here,'* Gidion texted back. *What's up?'*

*'Suspicious car call.'*

*'Nope, all good.'*

A few minutes later, Dad sent a message to tell him good night.

Gidion got ready for the cops after that. He pulled out a tripod and set it up right in front of the window. Then he put Dad's digital camera on it. From there, it was back to the waiting game.

The first Chesterfield Police car arrived five minutes later and parked so that the front of his car was almost kissing the Lincoln's fender. The cop lit up the inside of the Lincoln using a small searchlight mounted just above the mirror on the driver side door. The guy in the front seat covered his eyes with his forearm. The light made the dude's pale skin look white as chalk. Definitely a bloodsucker, and he looked pissed.

"Smile nice for the police officer, fang face," Gidion said. A second officer arrived less than a minute later, parking right behind the Lincoln, trapping it there.

Gidion turned on the digital camera and made sure the flash was turned off. Otherwise, he'd only get a picture of his reflection in the window. Didn't need the extra light at this point anyway. The lack of a flash was why he had the tripod. Pictures taken without a flash could end up blurry if the camera wasn't perfectly still, and he wanted a nice picture of his friend across the street.

"Say, 'cheese,' jerk."

The cops went so far as to make the guy get out of his car. Even better for him. The most he'd hoped for was a picture of him in the car.

In the movies, this was where the vampire would kill the cops and then slip away. Fortunately, reality didn't work that way. Kill a cop, and all a person would accomplish is bringing down a lot of hell. Police are a tight-knit group. Hurt or kill one, and every other officer, even the ones who don't like the one hurt, would crack open every skull it might take to find the jerk responsible. Vampires didn't mess with cops, unless the cop in question figured out he wasn't dealing with something human. Vampires didn't jeopardize their secrecy.

Gidion took a few pictures, making sure the camera was set on the highest resolution. Would be nice if the cops held up the guy's driver's license for him, but even with the highest resolution setting, he wasn't likely to make out anything useful from this distance. He got a good look at his new friend, though. Gidion pulled out a notepad and wrote down every detail he could: white male, short black hair, beard, tall—real tall. The guy wore a black leather, aviator jacket with one of those furry collars.

The cops stayed out there close to fifteen minutes. They didn't arrest vampire dude. Sitting in a parked car in a place a person doesn't live isn't illegal—rude, but not illegal. The first cop car pulled off and the Lincoln disappeared right after him.

"Aw, leaving so soon." Gidion laughed and petted Page's chest. She was proud of herself, having scared away the "big bad" outside their house. He gave her a couple of dog treats for that.

The remaining cop car sat out there a little longer, probably to make sure the guy they'd run off didn't come back. If he did return, Gidion was definitely going to call the cops again. Cops didn't like dealing with problems twice in the same night. Do that, and after enough return trips, they'd find a reason to arrest somebody.

Gidion went upstairs and hooked up the camera to his computer. With any luck, he'd gotten his first look at one of the local coven's members. Now, he just needed to figure out how to use this to his advantage.

# CHAPTER NINETEEN

Tracking someone's movements used to require a nondescript car, keen eyes and an expandable bladder as tough as Kevlar. These days, tracking someone only required Internet access.

Gidion started with Facebook. A quick name search led him to a list of almost one-hundred-fifty Charles Finleys, but when he refined the search to Richmond, that took the list to just one guy. He had a nose the size and shape of Rhode Island, and his hair style screamed "going-bald-but-in-denial."

His Facebook page exposed an unhealthy addiction for Farmville and other pointless games. Fortunately, the info section included a link to Charlie's Twitter feed, and he updated his Twitter status with where and what he was doing as if the world's survival hinged on his nightlife. Didn't take Gidion long to figure out the guy went downtown almost every night. His favorite haunts were the Tobacco Company and Siné.

Wednesday, Charlie was hanging out at the Tobacco Company and thinking about getting his "waitress as a carryout order." Given the guy's looks, Gidion didn't think Charlie would be bringing her home anytime soon. That gave him plenty of time to snoop around the guy's place.

Charlie owned a ranch style house dressed in vinyl siding the shade of chain-smoker yellow. The yard, front and back, was flat, treeless and fenceless. There was no breaking into that house without being noticed. Fortunately, what Gidion wanted most wasn't inside.

He passed the house one time to scope out the terrain just before sunset. As soon as the sun went down, he zipped his car into the driveway, got out and went straight for the back. He walked, despite the urge to run. Strangers running through people's yards set off "nosey neighbor radar." He found the trash can, blue and boxy, next to the back door. He flipped it open, pulled out the top two bags, flipped it shut and took both bags straight to the back of his car.

The smell was hideous. He hoped it wouldn't rain tonight, because he was gonna have to leave his windows down all night if there was any chance of getting rid of the stench. His nose fought to identify the rotted odors, but he refused to let his mind make the connections. Charlie lived in the far East End, so the drive home required almost a half hour of nose denial.

Gidion didn't waste any time getting the trash out of his car. He'd hoped he could take them inside, but that wasn't happening. All the air freshener in Virginia wouldn't mask Charlie's refuse from Dad. He took both bags to the back porch and threw down a large plastic sheet. Next came his trusty box cutter and a liberal cut to one of the bags. Fast food bags, leftover chicken fried rice and a lot of things Gidion didn't want to recognize spilled onto the plastic. He covered his mouth and nose with one hand while he picked at the pile of nastiness with a tree limb he'd picked up from his backyard.

A small bottle rolled free of the pile. "Iron supplements." That was promising. Grandpa Murphy said some feeders went through iron supplements like candy, thinking it would somehow help them last longer, kind of like Viagra for blood donors.

He also spotted the leftover stems from beets and two empty containers of orange juice, more of the other helpful suggestions for blood donors you could find online. Feeders didn't want to face the fact that it didn't matter what they ate or drank, they'd eventually run out of blood and die. He wondered what Pete's trash looked like these days.

Gidion went through the second bag of trash. He didn't find any other obvious sources of iron or vitamin C. After digging with his stick, Gidion did find a matchbook with the "Old World" logo on the cover. He'd hoped there might be some address or phone number written inside the matchbook, but no such luck.

What was missing was any obvious sign of Band-Aid or bandage use. Vampires had a way of sealing their bite marks, something in their saliva, but after a lot of bites and repeated blood loss, feeders ended up with some pretty thin and weak skin.

Perhaps Charlie was in the early stages of donating his type O to the local vampire coven. Then again, he might just have an iron deficiency and a similar taste in night spots. Either way, Charlie's trash didn't offer any hints on where the vampires went to sleep at sunrise.

That's when he found the rope. Nothing about the type of rope stood out, just that it was the half-inch thick variety. As he studied it closer, he realized a small spot little bigger than a thumbprint was soaked red. Blood? No way to be sure, but as he considered the length of the rope, he felt certain there was more than enough length to bind a person's wrists. For all he knew, a ketchup packet in one of the fast food bags had burst and stained the rope. What he wouldn't give for a CSI lab tech. The real question was what use Charlie had for the rope.

He'd have to ask Ms. Aldgate, but the question would have to wait until tomorrow. She hadn't given him a phone number to reach her with yet. In hindsight, maybe knocking her phone into the James hadn't been his brightest move.

A flash of headlights to his right caught his attention. His house sat on a corner, and the rays of bluish light crawled down the side street. The body of the car resembled a Lincoln Town Car, and while the sky had darkened considerably, he felt certain the car was silver. Had his visitor from the previous night returned? Gidion opted for discretion and folded the plastic tarp to gather up the trash. He dragged the borrowed trash to the green trash can on the far side of the house.

Just as he was about to walk back inside the house, headlights stroked the asphalt again. Unless silver, late model Lincoln Town Cars had gained in popularity, his visitor was taking a new approach to surveillance. His fanged peeping Tom wasn't going to park across the street waiting for the cops to pay him a visit. This time, he planned to keep his car moving, probably circling the block. Gidion wouldn't be calling Chesterfield Police to run off his pest tonight. He couldn't move without the vampires knowing it. At least the bastard would burn through a lot of gas and money in the process.

Well, Grandpa Murphy had said he wanted Gidion to rest tonight. Looked like he was going to get his wish. That was all right. Gidion could put the time to good use. He already had plans that didn't require him to leave the house.

# CHAPTER TWENTY

Sprouting fangs only changed a person's dietary habits. According to Grandpa Murphy, Gidion's dad believed becoming a vampire didn't truly change a person. Certain habits were locked in place for the remainder of the bloodsucker's existence. Learn what they were like in life, and a good hunter could exploit mortal weaknesses to send an immortal to their final grave.

"Yeah, Dad was like one of those FBI, Quantico, serial killer profiler guys, Page." He scratched behind his dog's ear, and she curled up next to him in his bed. "Except, just for vampires."

He loaded the pictures of his new shadow onto his laptop and started looking for useful details. Most of the pictures had produced fuzzy crap, but he'd taken close to four dozen snapshots of his new friend. That was the number one rule of photography: shoot far more pictures of a subject than you could ever need. He only needed one good image. He was rewarded with five for his efforts.

He'd gotten a good picture of the guy's face. At least, Gidion wouldn't have any trouble recognizing him. The real question was whether he was dealing with a member of the local coven or one of those nomadic bastards, maybe hired in another text blast to take out Gidion.

"Hair doesn't look all oily and greasy." Gidion had noticed the nomadic vampires he'd dealt with didn't tend to look all that clean. He supposed a good shower was hard to come by for those guys. Turning into a member of the undead didn't automatically make a vampire smell better or worse. True they didn't sweat as much as a mortal might, but they still got dirty. After a few days without a bath, those hard to reach places stopped smelling nice.

One of the pictures hadn't offered a good picture of his target, but he got a good look at the interior of the car. It looked too clean to be one of those vampire "mobile homes" like the Crown Vic he'd found near the Canal Walk. The other Crown Vic he'd borrowed from the guy at the safe house had leather seats which were all tore up. That guy had piled on the mileage. The seats in his shadow's Lincoln were in much better shape.

This guy was definitely a local, and that meant he was part of the Richmond Coven.

"That might be useful." Gidion rubbed Page's back, and her throat rumbled with content.

After months of hunting, he'd finally found a direct line to the coven. He just needed a way to take advantage of it.

He glanced at his cell phone to check the time, just a quarter to nine. Most businesses would be closing, but there would still be enough left open for what he wanted to try.

"Hold down the fort, furball." Gidion hopped off of his bed and "suited up." He wasn't planning to go one-on-one with this freak—not tonight, but if the guy came after him, he needed to be ready.

Gidion took his time locking the front door to his house and getting into his car. Sure he could have timed his exit to slip away without his shadow seeing him, really put him to the test, but best not to play that hand yet. He just wanted to get a feel for how close this guy would follow. If he just wanted to kill Gidion, then he wouldn't be making himself so obvious. He'd go all stealth mode and go in for the kill.

He saw the Lincoln's headlights coming up his street as he pulled out of the driveway. Within the neighborhood, the Lincoln didn't have any cars separating it from Gidion. Only once Gidion turned onto Reams Road did the traffic increase. Courthouse offered a six-lane road and slightly thicker traffic, even at this time of night. The Lincoln never allowed more than one car to come between them, and he mirrored every lane change Gidion made, which was a bit obvious given he didn't have to go very far along this road.

Gidion drove straight to Chesterfield Towne Center, one of the larger malls in the metro area. The clock on his dash showed it was just after nine o'clock, so the mall itself would be closed. Plenty of the surrounding restaurants were still open, though, as well as the Barnes & Noble.

He didn't normally worry about getting the closest parking space when he went to the mall, but under the circumstances, he wanted as short a distance between his car and the front of the bookstore. He found a space within sight of the café and parked. As Gidion got out and walked to the entrance, he noticed his shadow parked one row over. That meant his shadow could watch Gidion's car and the front entrance from the comfort of his driver's seat.

Gidion didn't go too far into the store, just down near the information desk. He picked up a book named *Shiver* by some writer whose name he wasn't sure how to pronounce and opened it. From here, Gidion couldn't see the Lincoln or his car, so it was a safe bet his shadow couldn't see him either. He still had a clear view of the entrance, though. His shadow didn't appear interested in keeping an eye on him while he was inside the store.

He carried the book with him over to the café. He couldn't see the Lincoln from where he was standing in the line, but he saw his car. He'd locked it in case his shadow tried to search it.

Gidion bought a café mocha—a big one. He didn't buy the book but took it with him over to one of the two-seater tables. This spot gave him a perfect view of both cars. He opened the book as if to read it.

Then something curious happened. His shadow got out of the Lincoln. Not looking directly at him proved harder than Gidion had expected. What was fang boy doing?

The guy didn't head for the front door of the store, though. He strolled over to Gidion's car and resorted to the old, "Oh, gee, I suddenly have this overwhelming need to tie my shoelaces" routine. A pity Gidion wasn't in his car. He could have thrown the stupid thing in reverse and flattened the bastard. If the guy was any closer to his car, he could have given the tailpipe a blow job.

Then his shadow looked up at Gidion. The jerk looked straight into Gidion's eyes and flashed this big toothy grin, the kind a vampire never displays in public. What the hell happened to discretion? Was the guy testing him for his reaction or had he already seen something in the back of Gidion's car that had outed him for a hunter?

Whatever it was, the vampire stood and walked back to his car, got in and drove off.

"Shit."

What just happened? He abandoned his drink and the book and ran out to his car. He needed to know where this guy was going. He'd taken too long, though. By the time he cranked up the Little Hearse, the silver Lincoln was gone. Gidion sped onto Midlothian Turnpike, hoping to spot the Lincoln before it might get onto the Powhite and head downtown, assuming that was where he was headed, but he didn't see it. Gidion plowed through three red lights trying to make up the lost ground, but it was useless. He was lucky he hadn't gotten pulled over as it was. Better not to press his luck.

Gidion cursed as he drove home. What the hell was that about? Had he done something wrong? He couldn't begin to guess what that might be. What was it about the back of his car that could possibly have given him up? He circled the block to see if his shadow's Lincoln had come back here, but there was no sign of it, just the usual cars.

Pulling into his driveway, he got out and looked at the back of his car. None of his vampire hunter gear was visible. His sports gear camouflage was all in place. He kicked the back of the car and cursed. He'd missed something, but what was it?

Page was barking a blue streak of her own as he walked up to the front door. "Oh, shut up, Page!" He flipped through his keys for the one to the front door. "It's just me."

Then he realized that Page was flipping out the same way she had the other night when his shadow was across the street. That and a hint of the vampire's reflection in the screen door's glass gave him just enough warning. He ducked beneath a fist aimed for the back of his head. Bastard either meant to knock him out cold or take his head off.

Gidion dove into the vampire. They fell back onto the lawn. The vampire took the brunt of the impact with Gidion landing on top of him. He reacted much faster than Gidion had expected, though. The second they hit the grass, the vampire shoved Gidion off and scrambled to his feet. The guy moved faster than a cat dropped in water.

Before Gidion could get to his feet, the vampire was on him. Caught off-balance, Gidion was knocked into the shadows along the side of the house. A large, low hanging tree hid both of them from view. The vampire wanted privacy to make the kill.

The vampire raced at Gidion, fangs bared and going straight for the throat. No time to go for a sword or his box cutter, Gidion stabbed the vampire with the keys still in his hand. They might not be sharp, but those jagged edges delivered plenty of damage. Blood sprayed out of the vampire's eye. Momentum denied him a chance to retreat. Gidion grabbed the vampire by the shirt and pulled him down, shoving his face into the dirt. Keeping him down took all of Gidion's strength. Screams were muffled by the ground.

"Shut up!" Could he suffocate this stupid thing? That was one of those details Grandpa Murphy had never answered. All Gidion could do was keep that face pinned in the grass and dirt. He was forced to rely on his left arm. His right was still sore from getting swatted by the frying pan the last time he'd tangled with one of these things.

He couldn't keep this thing down, and it wasn't getting any weaker. Gidion stabbed the keys into the throat, but he had a bad angle of attack. The attempt put him off-balance. The vampire shoved him off. A punch to the gut winded Gidion and kept him from getting up.

The vampire's hands latched onto Gidion's shirt and flung him back against the side of the house. Gidion wasn't sure how he kept his head from cracking against the bricks. Damn good thing, because otherwise, he wouldn't have had enough sense left to defend himself. He threw up his legs to hold back the vampire. Those fangs were going straight for his throat. Two well-placed knees into the guy's chest were all that held him back. The vampire hissed, his glare all the more horrid with the left socket a bloody mess from Gidion's keys.

Gidion drew his box cutter and went for the throat. Wasn't a pretty strike, but he drew blood. His shadow released him as he jerked back from the slice. There wasn't time to catch his breath. Gidion grabbed the vampire by the collar of his aviator jacket. The fur, soaked in blood, nearly slipped free. He held him long enough to stab the tip of the box cutter into the vampire's remaining good eye.

He screeched and ran from Gidion, but he didn't get far. The blinded beast tripped on a protruding root and then slammed his head on a low-hanging branch. Gidion grabbed the vampire by the back of his jacket and flung him facedown on the ground.

The wakizashi delivered the next injury, driving the blade straight through the back into the heart and into the ground. He buried the sword to the hilt. A kick to the head knocked the vampire out.

"Dammit." Gidion gasped as he stumbled back. He needed to keep moving. The vampire wasn't dead, and if he was going to do what he intended, he needed to move fast. "Move it, Gid," he told himself.

He ran for his car and popped open the trunk. Grandpa had bought him stuff for just such an occasion. He just never thought he'd get to use it. He threw the bats and other crap into the backseat until he reached the blue backpack.

Just as he was about to run back to the vampire, a woman's voice startled him.

"What was all that racket?"

Gidion screamed, and much to his ego's bruising, very much like a little girl.

"Sorry, young man, didn't mean to scare you." This time, Gidion realized the voice was coming from the front door of his neighbor's house. He'd seen the old lady in passing, but he couldn't remember her name. She was leaning out, dressed in an orange, floral nightgown that made her look like some kind of withered hipster. "I just heard the most dreadful noises."

"Yeah, I heard it, too, ma'am." He held the backpack so that it would hide the bloodstains on his hoodie. His car hid his soaked pants. "Feral cats, I think. Found them fighting on the other side of my house. One of them got mauled pretty good."

"Oh, dear. Is the poor thing still alive? That just sounded dreadful."

"No, afraid it's dead. I was just getting something out of my trunk to wrap it up and throw away."

"We should probably call the police about those cats."

Gidion fought down the urge to roll his eyes. She didn't think to call the cops while he was getting his ass kicked? It's a sad world when even nosey neighbors can't be relied on to call 911 in a timely fashion.

"I'll call them as soon as I toss this cat, ma'am. I can let them know what the other cats looked like."

She nodded in that old lady way that made it look like she might fall over if she wasn't still gripping the knob to her front door.

"That poor thing. Are you sure it's dead?"

"Yes, ma'am. I better take care of it before it attracts any other animals." He waved to her. "You have a good night."

"Oh, yes, good night."

She disappeared back into her house, and Gidion ran back to the vampire's body. He was still there and unconscious.

First thing he did was kick the vampire in the head a few more times. Blood trickled from his ears. If this guy had been human, Gidion would've worried he'd gone a little too crazy on him. In this case, probably meant he'd done enough damage to safely do what he needed to next.

The best gag in the world isn't going to completely silence someone, but the most effective kind requires shoving something in the mouth which isn't the safest proposition with a vampire. Gidion turned the guy's head to the side and planted his foot down on the side to limit his ability to move it. A really large wad of insulation foam came next. After that, he applied a liberal amount of duct tape. "Yeah, that's me, your friendly neighborhood redneck vampire hunter." The duct tape also bound the wrists behind his back. The last touch was a slice to the tendon in the back of the ankle. For a vampire, the injury would heal fairly quickly, but not before Gidion could get him in the car.

Gidion ran to the front door. He struggled to keep Page from running out when he cracked the door open and reached inside to turn off the porch light. The best "drunk-friend-carry" in the world couldn't conceal all that duct tape wrapped around his prisoner's head. Even without any light, he needed to do this fast enough to keep anyone from getting a good look at them. There's no graceful way to throw a guy into your car, especially when the guy was as tall as this one. That he wasn't conscious to struggle certainly helped, though. Gidion buried him in sports gear.

Gidion gathered his sword and box cutter, tossed them in the passenger seat and drove off. With any luck, the guy wouldn't wake up on the way, but he couldn't risk speeding lest he get pulled over. Even if the guy didn't scream or move around with an officer at the car's window, the bloody mess of his pants and shirt were sure to invite an officer's curiosity.

He wondered what the chances were of Grandpa being at the funeral home. He always called him before going out to hunt, so Grandpa could drive there ahead of time and fire up the cremator once he'd caught a vampire.

"Lord, don't be drunk." He called Grandpa's cell first and got the voice mail. "Shit."

He tried the landline to Grandpa's house next. That went to the generic greeting that the answering machine came with (Grandpa didn't have the patience to figure out how to tape his voice to it). The beep seemed to take forever. "Grandpa! Pick up the phone! GRANDPA!" The machine cut him off.

He called back both numbers. He didn't bother with the cell's voice mail. Grandpa didn't know how to access it anyway. He saved his message for when he got the answering machine at the house the second time. "Grandpa, it's a little before ten on Wednesday. I've got a package, a live one. If you get this in the next few hours, I need you to meet me ASAP."

This was not good. Sure he'd watched Grandpa operate the cremation equipment lots of times, but he'd never really shown Gidion how to do it. The only time Gidion had asked Grandpa to teach him, the reply had been, 'It's a one-step process, boy. You call me.'

"Yeah, that's working just great, Grandpa," Gidion said to himself, after getting the answering machine for what was probably the tenth time since he left the house. "One-step process, my ass."

By this point, he was already getting off the interstate and onto Staples Mill Road. At least it wasn't after eleven o'clock. No danger of getting pulled over for that curfew nonsense. As long as he didn't speed, he should reach the funeral home without any problems in less than five minutes.

Then he heard a groan from the back of the car. That's when it occurred to him that in his haste to get the hell out of Dodge, he'd never bothered to duct tape the legs together. His prisoner might not be able to climb out of the back of the car, but that didn't mean he couldn't kick out a window. Body parts sticking out of shattered car windows tended to guarantee calls to 911.

Gidion kept silent. With any luck, his "friend" was too out of it to even realize where he was. Hearing a strange voice would probably guarantee a freak out sooner than later. At least, that sounded good to Gidion. Then he heard a thud.

The hell with the speed limit. He was two blocks from the funeral home. He'd risk it. There were enough speeders on the road anyway. He was just part of the pack.

He contained a cheer as he saw Milligan's on the left. Cars were coming from the other direction, but he felt safe in saying there was enough of a gap to make the left turn into the parking lot without stopping in the median. A muffled shout from the back protested the sudden lurch as the car zipped into its turn. A car horn from one of the oncoming cars joined his passenger's protest.

The Little Hearse felt like it went airborne as it reached the curb. That received another muffled screech from the back. A grunt followed as all of the sports gear shifted, probably smacking the vampire in the face and other places. Another thud came from the back as he reached the rear parking lot and hit the garage door opener. Thank God he hadn't borrowed this guy's car like the last one.

He didn't worry about backing in this time. He just zipped inside and threw the car into park. Gidion nearly tripped over his own feet as he scrambled out of the car and threw open the car's rear door. A baseball glove flew at Gidion as the vampire kicked into the open air.

Gidion grabbed the ankle, jerked the leg taut and slammed his elbow down on the knee.

"Goddammit!" His shout was louder than the gagged scream from his captive. He'd forgotten how sore his right arm was. "Just shut up!" Gidion shouted at the vampire. "Shut up!" He grabbed the bat and smashed it down where the head was buried under the black, plastic tarp. That did the trick. No more grunts or struggles.

With a weak laugh, Gidion sat on the ground against the bumper. "For what it's worth, my grandpa is probably gonna have a hangover worse than yours in the morning," he said to his unconscious companion. "You better give me something useful after all the crap it's taken to get you here in one piece."

He'd been expecting to have Grandpa here to take the lead for what came next. This was his first chance to interrogate a vampire, and to hear Grandpa tell it, this wasn't going to be pleasant.

# CHAPTER TWENTY-ONE

The vampire prisoner resembled some kind of West Virginia mountain mummy by the time Gidion finished wrapping his legs together with duct tape. He placed the vampire on the conveyer in the cremator room. The most movement the vampire might manage would be to roll off the conveyer and onto the floor. If he could make his getaway trussed up like that, the jerk deserved to escape.

Gidion made one last try to reach Grandpa by phone, but the call went to the machine again. He'd have to do this on his own. Of course, if this vampire didn't wake up soon, he'd probably have to just take his head off and leave him for Grandpa to cremate in the morning or whenever he decided to show up. That was assuming Grandpa even showed. What if he was dead? Gidion thought about that arsenal of swords and other weapons planted around Grandpa's house. Could an old enemy have come calling? Dammit, what if the Richmond Coven had taken him out to send Gidion some kind of message? He knew that last thought was stupid. If the coven wanted to deal with him, they'd go directly for him, not waste time on Grandpa, but being unable to reach him was making Gidion panic.

While he was waiting, he searched this vampire's pockets. No weapons. He just found his keys and a cell phone. "This is a really nice cell phone," he said to its unconscious owner. "I guess membership in the coven has its privileges, huh?" This baby was all tripped out with a touchscreen and lots of apps. "Angry Birds? Really?" His respect for this guy hit a new low. He wondered if this moron had been playing games on his phone the entire time he'd been staking out his home.

A search of the previous calls made and received provided a bit of good news. He hadn't spoken with anyone since following him to the bookstore. Still, it wasn't like his coven wouldn't know the person he'd been tracking. The question was how soon they'd miss him and what Gidion could do to leave them uncertain who was to blame for him being MIA. He could deal with that later. The question that bothered him the most was what to do if Grandpa didn't show.

Before Gidion could search through the phone more, a groan from his prisoner announced it was time to start the interrogation. He powered down the cell phone and set it aside.

He wondered if his guest's eyes would have healed. They opened, but one look told him all he needed to know. This guy needed a seeing eye dog to go anywhere, and since vampires freaked the hell out of dogs, that left this guy shit outta luck.

"Sucks being blind, doesn't it?" Gidion plucked a follicle of hair from his head.

The vampire screamed in surprise. "Fuck you!"

"Whatever." Gidion poured as much indifference into his voice as he could manage. "Bet you wish you'd stuck with driving circles around my house."

"Think you're clever, don't you?" The vampire laughed. "You'd be a lot more impressive if I couldn't hear your heart beating like a baby squirrel pissing in his nest."

Heightened senses. He hadn't considered that in planning his approach to this. Of course, he wasn't all that sure how good those senses worked. Maybe it depended on the vampire.

"That's what gave me away back at the bookstore, wasn't it?" Gidion laughed. "You smelled my previous kills."

"Vampire blood is distinct."

Gidion clapped in a slow fashion that was full of contempt. "I'd almost think you were smart, but the fact there were several passengers' blood in there, you were pretty arrogant coming after me by yourself."

"You're just a scared little boy."

"And you're a blind vampire on the conveyer belt of a cremator. If you want to roll into those flames with your lungs still turning oxygen into carbon dioxide, just keep being an uncooperative asshole. Won't bother me a bit."

His prisoner snarled at him. The sound of it echoed in the small room and made Gidion jump back a step.

"Oh, that is scary." Gidion laughed. "Probably would be a lot scarier if you weren't all wrapped up in duct tape and blind...but scary." He playfully punched the vampire on the shoulder as one might when picking on a close friend.

He picked up his baseball bat and gave it a quick swing, the whistle of air inches from the vampire's ear. "You'd also be a lot scarier if you didn't feel pain." He brought the bat down with all his strength on the vampire's legs, just above the ankles. The aluminum bat delivered a satisfying crunch. Gidion winced and was glad the vampire couldn't see that. He needed to be brutal and unforgiving. He hadn't expected that to be difficult. This thing wasn't human, not even truly alive, but he looked it. He doubted the vampire could sense that hesitation through the pain of those broken bones.

"Yeah, I'd be a lot of more worried if I couldn't hurt you, but clearly, that's not an issue, is it?"

The vampire said nothing to that.

"Let's discuss your options here." Gidion plucked another hair. "Option one: I ask questions and you answer them truthfully. I like that option, because it's productive. Then there's option two where I smash the ever loving crap out of you with my bat. Oh, I should point out that I kind of like that option, too, because I enjoy the irony of beating up a vampire with a bat."

He tapped the tip of the bat against the edge of the conveyer next to the vampire's ear.

"My, you are the funny one, aren't you?" The vampire sighed. "Ask your questions, Gallagher."

Who was Gallagher? Gidion decided not to bother asking. Was probably one of those generation gap things. "Why don't we start with who the leader of your coven is? Who is it?"

"That would be Satan." He smirked.

Gidion brought the bat down on the legs again. The swing was rewarded with a loud scream from his captive.

"Here's a tip. Leave the jokes to me. You stick with the honest answers." He tapped the bat on the conveyer again as a reminder. "Let's try that question again. Who's the leader of your coven?"

A growl rumbled within his throat, but the vampire finally spoke. "His name is Alistair."

Gidion had started his swing when he heard the word "His." Thanks to Pete, he already knew who the coven leader was. This just gave him a way to know when his prisoner was being honest with him. This swing struck just below the knees.

"Now, that's just not nice. I'm starting to think you like option two." He wiped the sweat from his brow.

The vampire choked as he tried to respond. "Why don't you suck my—"

Gidion placed the tip of the bat on the appendage he was sure the vampire was about to refer to and just let it sit there, the weight of it. "I'm betting those heightened senses aren't limited to hearing and smelling, are they? I gotta think your sense of touch is pretty phenomenal. Just how much do you think it's going to hurt when my swings work their way up to here?"

"I think you are a monstrous child."

"I think you better start answering my questions!" Gidion shouted, his lips inches from the vampire's ear. This time, it was the vampire who flinched. "Who leads your coven!"

Still no answer. "Who is it!"

Gidion raised the bat and smashed it down on both kneecaps. The sound of cracking bones was joined by a disgusting pop. Tears flowed from the vampire's eyes.

"I'm getting really tired of option one."

The response wasn't what Gidion expected. The vampire laughed, a sound that resonated with the pain he'd inflicted, but he laughed at him. "No, hunter. I think you're getting tired of option two."

This wasn't working. He couldn't even get the information he already knew out of this guy. What would Grandpa do? He'd probably tell Gidion to use his fool head for a change.

Gidion pulled out his box cutter and delivered a small cut to the vampire's arm. Blood dripped from the wound but then healed.

"You don't care about your bones, do you?" Gidion thumped a finger against the injuries to the legs. They were already trying to heal, he suspected. "Only thing you give a damn about is blood, right?"

He made another small cut, this one to the cheek.

A panicked hiss answered.

"You're right. I am tired of option two." Gidion shrugged. "Too much work, but I can cut you all night. It's just a few drops at a time, mind you, but at some point, I'll bleed you dry. You can heal your flesh, restore your bones, but you can't replace that blood, not without feeding...and you aren't getting any more blood."

The next cut was to the vampire's throat.

"Elizabeth!" The answer startled Gidion. He hadn't really expected it work. "Her name is Elizabeth."

Gidion placed the edge of his box cutter's blade against the throat again. "And why should I believe you now? You've been lying to me up to this point."

"Her name is Elizabeth." He growled, an angry but desperate sound.

"And where do I find her?"

Something in the vampire's spirit sank when Gidion asked that question. He suspected that reaction meant one thing, and the possibility seemed ridiculous.

Gidion cut the vampire's throat again.

"Dammit!" The frustration in his captive's voice only made Gidion more certain his fears were true. "I don't know where she is."

"Right." Gidion cut his arm.

"I don't know! I swear!"

Gidion stabbed his box cutter in the center of the vampire's chest. "No! You have to know a way to reach her."

"Her feeder! Her damn feeder is how we communicate."

A feeder, and Gidion had a hunch who that might be. "The feeder's name, what is it?"

"I only know her first name." He banged the back of his head against the conveyer. "Stephanie."

Gidion kicked the base of the conveyer. He knew more than his prisoner. Everything kept going back to his schoolmate Stephanie Drake.

Gidion pulled out the vampire's cell phone. "You were ordered to watch my house. Where did that order come from? Did she call you? Text you?"

"Email." The vampire bit out the word as if to chew it in half. He was getting his spirit back.

"Don't," Gidion cut his shoulder, a long deep gash, "get snippy with me." He looked at the touch screen to the cell phone and saw what looked like an email icon near the top of the apps displayed. A tap of the icon opened straight to the inbox, no password required. How nice of him.

The vampire lunged at him. The movement caught Gidion completely off guard. He didn't think the guy could manage to bend his body like that as bound in duct tape as he was. The attack knocked down Gidion and sent the vampire tumbling to the floor beside him. Fangs snapped after him. Gidion scrambled away. Any slower and Gidion would have lost a chunk of forearm. He snatched up his sword and slammed it down through his prisoner's neck. The head rolled away from its body.

Gidion's hands shook as he stared at the now vacant eyes. He balled his hands into fists. His fingernails nearly drew blood as he forced himself to steady. He'd expected this to be simpler than hunting down a vampire and killing it in the field. He thought he knew the nature of the thing he hunted. He'd been wrong.

What finally calmed his nerves were thoughts of Grandpa. Gidion needed to make sure he was all right, but he couldn't go anywhere until after he'd cleaned up this mess.

# CHAPTER TWENTY-TWO

Grandpa Murphy didn't live in the worst part of Richmond by any stretch, but his neighborhood had seen better days and far better nights. Dad had never flat-out forbidden Gidion from coming down here after dark, but his curfew on the nights he visited Grandpa changed with daylight saving time.

The outside resembled the inside in the sense that Keep hands were to blame for its current condition. Grandpa considered the peeling paint a part of its charm and the warp of the front steps the equivalent of snarled lips to discourage unwanted guests...which included anybody with two legs. Gidion suspected one-legged and no-legged folks would do well to avoid the place, too.

The light to the front porch didn't work, the bulb long since burned out. Grandpa had insisted he'd get around to replacing it and refused any offer from Gidion or Dad to do it for him.

Gidion's headlights flashed across the front porch as he turned into the driveway. At least the front door didn't look disturbed. His car's lights glared back at him as they pulled within inches of the dented bumper to Grandpa's pickup. The Ford had a paint job to match the house.

He turned off his car. After his eyes adjusted to the dark, he unlocked the doors and got out. The temperature had taken a winter-steep dive since sunset. He zipped up his hoodie and gripped his box cutter in the front pocket.

From the front, everything looked fine, but one of Grandpa's rules of vampire hunting warned never to enter any potentially-compromised building by the front until you've checked the back.

Walking down the driveway, he placed a hand on the pickup's

hood. Grandpa hadn't been anywhere, and if he had, he certainly hadn't driven there.

Gidion continued his three sixty. He knew all of the best hiding places this property had to offer. The tree in the backyard had thick branches ideal for climbing, but most of the leaves had fallen by now so it didn't provide any cover. A bush near the back neighbor's fence was a good place to hide. Nobody was there.

The house was dark and all of the curtains closed. He couldn't see anything moving. At least the back screen porch was closed. Nothing looked out of place or damaged, at least not from anything other than simple neglect.

The air unit, sticking out of a side window, rumbled to life just as Gidion passed. He drew his box cutter and turned in a full circle looking for the attack that wasn't there. He cursed and headed for the front. This time, he didn't bother putting his box cutter back in his pocket.

He climbed the front steps and cringed to a halt as the third and final one creaked, the house laughing at how easily it had caught him. Letting the silence reassert itself, he stood there while he inspected the front door more closely to confirm all was as it should be. If anything was wrong, he couldn't see it. He lifted his foot from the step, and the house laughed at him again. Between the steps and the air unit making him squeal, Gidion figured anyone who was here would know he was.

Just as he was about to knock, the front door flung open. He jumped back and ducked to the right as twin barrels shoved their way out of the shadows to glare at him.

"Get the fuck off my property!" Grandpa shouted, although the words slurred their way out of his mouth. Probably didn't have his dentures, but Gidion suspected the stench of stale beer had more to do with the poor enunciation.

"Grandpa, it's me!"

Grandpa didn't lower the rifle in his hands. His body swayed left to right. Eyes squinted until they found Gidion at the bottom of the steps.

"Gidion? What the hell you doing here?"

He moved to the left to get out of the rifle's line of fire, but when Grandpa tried to follow him with his eyes, the gun moved with him.

"Jesus, Grandpa! Put the gun down!"

Odds favored the only way he'd successfully shoot something at this point would require doing so at point blank range, but the way Gidion's night had gone thus far, he wasn't going to risk it.

"Boy!" Grandpa's face pinched as he continued to sway in place. The task of forming a sentence from raw thought looked as if it required all his mental power. "What are you doing here?" At least, that was what Gidion assumed he was trying to ask, because what he said might as well have been in Korean.

"You weren't answering your phone." Gidion kept his words slow and precise. Even doing that, Grandpa didn't look as if he'd understood anything he'd said. At least that placed them on an equal playing field, because whatever Grandpa said next, there was no deciphering it.

Taking slow steps at first, Gidion climbed to Grandpa and took the rifle from him. "Are you all right?"

Grandpa swayed a bit and then grabbed him in this big hug that forced Gidion to support all of his weight. For a man who didn't look that big, he about knocked Gidion to the ground.

"Let's get you back to bed."

To his surprise, Grandpa didn't resist. Gidion used the same arm-over-the-shoulder carry to get Grandpa to bed that he'd used to drag more than one vampire's corpse to his car, a detail he tried not to dwell on as they dodged an empty bottle of Killian's on the way to the bedroom.

Grandpa rambled in his drunk "Kor-english" the entire way which meant Gidion understood none of it. He did his best to make the drop into bed as gentle as possible, but the fall resembled a belly flop. Grandpa didn't seem to mind and snored within seconds of landing.

The front door was still open. The rifle was leaning against the front porch railing where Gidion had left it. He brought that back inside. He was about to put it back in its rack beside the bedroom door then thought better of it. Being threatened with bullets once in a night was enough. He shoved it under the sofa where he knew he'd be sleeping tonight.

Running back out to his car, Gidion pulled out the blue backpack. He'd shoved some of the vampire's belongings into it before rushing out of the funeral home. He tossed the backpack onto the couch. Grandpa's snoring vibrated through the walls from the bedroom, so Gidion hunted for something to drown him out. Grandpa didn't own a TV or a computer, but he had an old CD player. His music collection was pretty damned pitiful, mostly people like Ella Fitzgerald and Rosemary Clooney, whoever the hell they were. Gidion found the one CD he'd enjoyed as a kid during his overnight visits, a collection of songs by Louis Armstrong.

*Ain't Misbehavin'* turned Grandpa's snoring into a memory as Gidion unzipped his backpack. His shadow had carried the usual items: a wallet and cell phone. He'd already seen the driver's license which had named his shadow as Milton Robbins. That had to be legit, because what self-respecting vampire would use "Milton" for an alias?

The cell phone offered the most promise. He clicked on the touchscreen and went straight for the email icon. The inbox didn't offer a lot. What he wouldn't give for a vampire who had a packrat mentality towards email and text messages. At least there were a few emails: mostly Facebook and Twitter notifications. Interesting. This guy must have been a young vampire.

An email from "RichmondCoven@gmail.com" caught Gidion's attention. The message was a reply to a "status update" his shadow had emailed Stephanie yesterday morning. The nimrod had started circling his place less than an hour after the cops had run him off. On the bright side, the jerk had confirmed that Gidion hadn't gone anywhere last night. Stephanie had just told him to keep watch, or rather that Elizabeth wanted him to stay on Gidion until she was satisfied Gidion really just thought they were dealing drugs and ignorant that they were vampires. She also wanted him to email them updates each morning.

Gidion sifted through the sent emails. The last email sent was the status report Stephanie had replied to. That was a good sign. A closer inspection of the phone revealed no outgoing phone calls or text messages between the trip to the mall and the ambush outside Gidion's house.

"He lives somewhere different," Gidion said to himself. If he didn't, then he wouldn't need to email those reports. He could do them in person. On the downside, that meant he couldn't track down this guy's home to find the rest of the coven, but that also meant the coven wouldn't know right away that Milton was dead. Gidion just needed to email Stephanie status reports with this phone to keep them off his scent. If he could hunt down and kill a vampire tomorrow night, then Gidion could email an update telling them he'd never left his house. They'd be convinced Gidion wasn't a hunter, at least long enough for him to find the rest of the coven and finish them.

Nothing else immediately useful popped out at Gidion. He wanted a better look at this guy's Facebook page and Twitter feed, but it was close to one in the morning and his laptop was at home.

He set his alarm to go off about 5:30 in the morning and groaned. He still needed to get Grandpa to the funeral home to torch that vampire's corpse. If he had any hope of getting some sleep, he needed to sleep here. This wasn't the first time he'd used the sofa in Grandpa's den for a bed, but the last time he'd done that, he must have been about nine years old when it was rare for Dad to work overnight and he still needed someone to look after him.

With the den lights turned off and Milton's belongings put away, Gidion's mind returned to Grandpa Murphy. He'd never seen his grandfather like this, drunk and out of control. Had Grandpa really changed that much, or had Gidion finally gotten old enough to see what was always there? That thought and the thin pillow he borrowed from Grandpa's bed kept him awake for another hour. Just as he fell to sleep, another thought struck him. How would he hunt if he didn't have Grandpa there anymore?

# CHAPTER TWENTY-THREE

The *James Bond* theme blared from Gidion's cell phone at the appointed time. He hit the snooze, but Grandpa stumbling out of his bedroom rendered that moot.

"Gidion? What the hell you doing here, boy?"

He sat up and rubbed his face, as if to force feed himself alertness from his palms. "You don't remember?" No, of course, he didn't.

"Don't get wise with me." The way he snapped his fingers suggested he was well-rested without a bit of the hangover he deserved. "What's going on here?"

"What's going on is there's a vampire's corpse at the funeral home. I need you to get there ASAP and cremate it."

Grandpa's left eye twitched. "You lose your marbles? You know damn well that you don't hunt without calling me first."

"I wasn't hunting. The jerk ambushed me outside of my house, and I did call you. How many beers did you drink last night? Is that why I'm supposed to call first, so you know when it's safe to get plastered?"

"Listen here, boy. I don't take that guff from your daddy, and I sure as hell ain't gonna take it from you."

Holy crap. No wonder Grandpa drove Dad insane.

"Grandpa, you nearly shot me with a rifle last night!"

"Bullshit." He hobbled to the kitchen. "I'm gonna make myself a cup of coffee before we go. That's assuming it fits into your busy schedule."

"And yes, I'm fine," Gidion called after him. "Thanks for asking."

"Don't need to ask, when I can see it with my damn eyes."

Grandpa banged around a lot for someone who was just making a pot of coffee. "You wouldn't be getting ambushed at all if you did like you were fucking told. This is what you get for bringing home stragglers and trying to protect a damn feeder."

"Whatever." Gidion stumbled his way to the bathroom. Damn, he was a sight: bed head, bags beneath his eyes and a royal nasty case of morning mouth.

He splashed water on his face, not that it did much. Was his brain swelling, because it felt like it was trying to push his eyeballs out of his head? This was when his dad sleeping during the day just sucked. It wasn't like Gidion could play hooky and sleep in without getting caught.

"What did you do with the body?" Grandpa shouted from the kitchen.

Gidion swished some water around his mouth and spit it out to mitigate his morning mouth. "Beheaded it. Put it in one of the plain, pine boxes. I trust the cremator can handle duct tape?"

Grandpa didn't answer. Instead, Gidion heard his own voice coming from the kitchen. Grandpa was playing the answering machine.

*Crap*, Gidion thought, *here it comes.*

"Are you out of your Goddamned mind!"

Gidion didn't answer. He kicked the bathroom door closed and splashed water onto the top of his head. He mangled his fingers through his hair, trying to rub out the anime-character-worthy waves. A look in the mirror told him he wasn't having much success. The bathroom door muffled Grandpa enough to make him unintelligible, so he decided to give his hair a few more tries instead of facing that nonsense.

Having fixed his appearance to something resembling school-acceptable, he abandoned his hiding place. "You ready, Grandpa?"

Grandpa was slurping coffee from a plain, white mug. "Waiting on you." He'd put on his work clothes while Gidion had hidden in the bathroom. The black suit and tie made him look more like a mobster than a funeral home director.

"I'll follow you." Gidion dreaded how slow Grandpa would

probably drive, but that was preferable to the lecture he'd get for speeding and picking a non-Grandpa approved route.

They didn't say much once they got to the funeral home. They'd made it there by a quarter after six. The sky was still dark with a hint of pink in the east.

Grandpa didn't say much. He'd returned to the grunting method of communication from the other night. Gidion kept his mouth shut. Doing his best not to be obvious about it, he watched everything Grandpa did to operate the cremator. For every button pushed and sensor checked, Gidion sent himself a text message noting what the step in the process had been. That way he'd not only be able to study the order of the steps later, but he'd know how long it had taken Grandpa to get to that step. He decided he'd need to do this several times before he felt certain he could do it himself.

Between texting himself, Gidion had Milton the vampire's cell phone out, and sent Stephanie his status report. Just to keep things real, Gidion included the trip to Barnes & Noble minus all the "fun" that had followed.

The *James Bond* theme sounded from his cell phone about a quarter to seven, the usual time he set it to go off in the morning. "Gotta get to school," he said.

Grandpa didn't look at him, just grunted as he checked the temperature on the panel.

"I'm going hunting tonight."

Another grunt.

Dammit. Gidion didn't need this crap. Dad gave him enough grief as it was. Last thing he needed was for Grandpa to start. Gidion got in trouble for stuff as simple as getting his pants dirty, but Grandpa gets drunk and nearly shoots him with a freaking rifle and gets a free pass. Total BS!

What he wouldn't give to stay home today. He needed the sleep, and he wasn't sure he'd finished all of his math homework. Maybe he could get a nap after school. He needed to rest sometime, because hunting with his head in a fog guaranteed getting himself killed.

# CHAPTER TWENTY-FOUR

The rest of the day didn't go well. The Little Hearse roared into the driveway with barely a minute to spare thanks to a stupid gray hair in a silver land yacht. The lady hadn't recognized the difference between the Smart Tag lane and the Exact Change lane at the Midlothian tolls until she was sitting in it with Gidion right behind her and six more cars behind him. A chorus of horns attacked her for being the moron she was. She was so flustered that she'd nearly backed into Gidion's car.

From her early morning perch on the den sofa, Page watched Gidion sprint into the house. "Dad'll have to get you when he comes home," he said, careful not to use the word "out." She didn't look worried, not that he had time to study the look on her face. He darted into his room and tripped over a box of Kleenex he'd left on the floor. The edge of the bed saved him from a total wipeout. He threw his school books into his backpack and tossed in his laptop.

Flinging on his backpack threw Gidion off-balance, but he kept upright. He ran through the den for the front door with an indifferent yawn from Page.

The drive to school was blessedly free of any more idiot drivers. Good thing, too, because he still had to sprint from his car to his first class. The bell sounded just as he ran through the door to the classroom. His teacher gave him an evil eye that suggested she'd still like to mark him tardy, but decided against it. She exacted her revenge when she went around checking everyone's homework. Gidion hadn't finished the last two problems.

Mrs. Brown marked up his paper with her infamous red pen. She drew an "X" followed by a long line at the bottom of the page.

"Finish those problems and get your father to sign this."

Ugh! Uptight bitch! Why couldn't the vampires have gone after her instead of Ms. Aldgate? Killing her would be a service to every student in the world. Of course, for Mrs. Brown to get killed by a vampire, she'd need to get a real life first.

Dad was gonna go off on him when he saw this. He really needed to learn how to forge Dad's signature. Maybe he could ambush him on the way out the door for work tonight, limit the time he'd have to endure the "Wrath of Dad."

The rest of the school day went downhill from there. His English class had provided a pop quiz on the first act of Shakespeare's boring-as-hell play *Hamlet*, which Gidion hadn't read yet. At least Dad wouldn't have to sign that.

He'd never been so glad for lunch. In his dash from the funeral home to school, food hadn't really been an option. His usual PB Twix and Mountain Dew weren't going to cut it, so he drove off-campus for lunch.

He went for Café Caturra since his lunch period was early enough to get there before the midday crowd. Even then, that would be cutting it close. At least it would give him Wi-Fi access.

Gidion cracked open his laptop and went straight for Facebook for a look at Milton the vampire's page. Turned out he was a local guy. In fact, Milton graduated from Gidion's high school just ten years ago—West Chester High. That didn't feel like coincidence, not that he could pin down why. He didn't know anyone with the last name Robbins from school or his neighborhood, but the more he dug into the Richmond Coven, everything kept hitting close to home.

Milton's employer was listed as "Old World." That could be a problem. He'd need to check Milton's phone for a work schedule, if he even had one listed in it. For that matter, he needed to look for Milton's car. He must have parked somewhere within walking distance to his house. Maybe he could find something useful in it.

Any hope of finding something helpful in Milton's friends list was abandoned. The guy was a total Facebook whore with close to two thousand friends. He must have friended anyone in his life who ever sneezed in his direction.

He went to Milton's Twitter feed next. The number of people he followed was even worse than his Facebook friends list.

Gidion remembered there was a Twitter app on Milton's cell phone. He pulled it out to get a look at what the people Milton followed had to tweet. The feed was moving fast. Following close to three thousand people will do that. Fortunately, it wasn't so fast that Gidion missed a tweet from a guy: "Enjoying an ale with my lunch. The waitress is a definite NINE out of TEN. Hellooo, Nurse!"

The tweet was from Ms. Aldgate's ex-husband.

# CHAPTER TWENTY-FIVE

Gidion made it back to class with just a minute to spare. Ms. Aldgate gave him an odd look halfway through class, and he suspected it was probably because of how anxious he was.

"Gidion, would you please quit tapping your pencil on your desk."

Jeez, he hadn't even realized he'd been doing it. "Sorry." He just wanted this class to end.

Trying to focus on class didn't help make the time move more quickly. He noticed Andrea kept smirking back at him in that way girls seem to do when they know something about you. What was her deal? Seth had probably told her about one of his more embarrassing moments—lousy traitor.

With just ten minutes left, Principal "Vermin" interrupted class for a conversation in the hallway with Ms. Aldgate.

"This might take a few minutes," Ms. Aldgate said. "Use the time to read over page sixty-eight. I will be just outside the door, so no talking."

She left the door open just a crack, but he couldn't make out anything they were saying. He tried to read his textbook, but all he could think about was what he'd learned during lunch. Would this class never end?

"Psst! Gidion!" The guy sitting in front of Gidion whispered as he planted a folded slip of paper on his desk.

He opened the note. 'I hear someone has a secret, you sneaky stud.'

What the hell? He looked up and realized the note must have been from Andrea. If her smile widened any more, her face would split in half.

Everything in his gut twisted. Andrea might be perky as a jackrabbit after five espressos, but she wasn't stupid. Not many freshmen made it into honors world history, proof enough she had brains in there somewhere. Could she be tied into all of this somehow? She was one of Ms. Aldgate's students, after all.

He wrote a reply and stuck with print, because his cursive resembled bad line art on crack. 'I don't know what you're talking about.'

She muffled a laugh as she read his reply. Her pen danced across the shrinking space of the paper. This time, she leaned back and handed it directly to him. Lord, he hoped Ms. Aldgate didn't catch them passing notes. Bad enough everyone in the classroom could see it.

'Everyone's talking about it! You're dating a senior! Is it true???'

Holy crap! Was "everyone" really talking about it? At first, he enjoyed the ego boost of that thought, but then he broke down the implications. How would anyone even know that? Could this be a clever way for the coven to figure out if he was connected to Tamara, waiting to see if he'd confirm it? Even if it wasn't, the rumor was already circulating. If Stephanie hadn't started it as a test, then it wouldn't be long before she heard it, if she hadn't already.

Rumors were tricky things, and given the low rung on the social ladder he usually hung to, he didn't know squat about how to stop or mitigate these things. Confirming it just felt like a bad idea, and denying it would suck. No matter which way he went, he was adding more information to feed the rumor's fire.

Ms. Aldgate returned before he could write a reply.

"All right, everyone. We're almost out of time, so let's quickly go over what will be on tomorrow's quiz."

Thank God! How bad off was he when he was glad to have a teacher talk about a quiz? At least this would leave Andrea guessing, and it wouldn't seem like he'd intentionally kept quiet. If he didn't respond one way or the other, maybe the rumor would die before it could reach Stephanie or anyone else in the coven.

That last thought stilled his pencil. Had Pete heard about this? If he was at school today, Andrea would have been sure to mention it at lunch.

Grandpa's warning about not being able to trust Pete gained newfound credibility. Dammit, he didn't know what to do. All of his options sucked. He needed to confront Pete, find out what the coven knew, what they were saying. That was assuming he could trust a word out of his friend's mouth.

Chairs creaked as everyone stood and shoved their books into their bags. Had the bell rung? He looked at his watch. Sure enough, he'd missed it.

Andrea winked at him as he stood. "You sly devil."

Funny, he didn't feel all that clever. He kept to his silent look of confusion. Under the circumstances, wasn't difficult to maintain the appropriate expression. He took his time packing his bag, waiting until after everyone else had left the room.

"Gidion?" Ms. Aldgate looked towards the door and then back to him.

He walked over to the door and closed it. "You know anyone named Milton Robbins?"

She shook her head. "Who is he?"

"He was a vampire in the Richmond Coven until I killed him last night." Had it really been less than twenty-four hours since that happened? Too much had gone down between then and now for that to feel possible. "He's listed as a friend of your ex-husband on Facebook and Twitter. I'm not sure how closely connected they might be, but it's a direct link to the coven."

She sat behind her desk and didn't meet his eyes. "Gidion, I have a hard time believing Charles—I mean...Dammit!" She stood and planted her fists on her desk. "Gidion, I cannot sit and wait like this. I'm scared to go home. I haven't even slept in my bed in almost a week!" He'd been so focused on his own problems in all this that he hadn't even picked up on the wear and tear on his teacher. Her shirt and pants were wrinkled, and her clothes usually looked ironed sharp enough to pass a military inspection. He sat a few rows back, so he hadn't noticed the bags under her eyes. Up close, her makeup couldn't conceal just how tired she was. That he looked little better probably added to her doubts in him.

"Ms. Aldgate, I'm close to finishing this. You've gotta believe me."

She held up a hand for him to shut up. "I'm not even sure I believe any of this anymore. That I want to. For God's sake, Gidion, you're just a boy."

"I'm not a boy!" Holy crap. He'd just shouted at one of his teachers and at school, no less. He took a deep breath. "I know I'm only sixteen, but I'm right about this. All of it."

"That might be, but if my ex-husband has anything to do with this, then how are you going to prove it? Did you find any messages between him and this vampire? What was his name? Milton?"

"No, I haven't found any communications between the two of them, not yet."

She crossed her arms, but the way she did it looked as though she was hugging herself. "Charles is many things. He's a philanderer and a chauvinist, but I've also seen him go out of his way to help many people over the years. He can be very generous, and frankly, I don't see any reason he would want to kill me. It's not as if I'm really a part of his life anymore. He's moved on."

"Then why were you crying the other night? He definitely wasn't feeling all 'generous' towards you then." He had to find some way to turn her back around on this. She was going to get herself killed.

"He was drunk. I was there with a friend, and he came over to make a pass at her. He didn't even know I was there, not until after she didn't answer and he realized she was staring at him and me. I'd pointed him out to her just before he walked over, so she knew who he was." Her voice shook as she said the next part. "Then he saw me; tried to apologize, tried to hug me and I slapped him." She wiped a tear from her eye, trying to catch it before it could smear her makeup. "Truth is, Gidion, as embarrassed and humiliated as I felt, I think he felt worse."

Damn. He didn't know what to say to that. Before she'd said

all that, he'd meant to ask something. He needed a moment to remember what the question was, and the words scratched their way out. "He's taking iron and eating a lot of beets."

"What?"

"They're common traits among feeders—I mean, vampire servants."

"How would you even know—?" She shook her head and raised a hand to stop that line of thought, a gesture she often used to stop students who had rambled too far off topic in class. "He's anemic. Always has been. Can't tell you how many ways I found to prepare beets to make them somewhat edible when we were married." That last part drew a smile out of her even as she caught another escaping tear on her fingertip.

"He's anemic." Crap. Grandpa said vampires could smell when someone was anemic. Most of them wouldn't even bother with a person who had blood like that, especially not to keep one as a feeder. Too much effort for too little reward.

He was about to ask her why she hadn't mentioned that beforehand, but how would she have known it mattered? It wasn't like he'd thought to ask about it.

"If it's not your ex-husband, then someone else must want you dead. Can you think of anyone who might?"

"I'm sure there are more than a few students I've taught over the years." She crossed her arms. "Fortunately, the kind of student who does poorly in school typically doesn't have the industriousness to follow through on something like that."

He supposed she had a point there, and even as much as he despised Mrs. Brown, he didn't think he'd give her much thought after he was done with this school year. "That doesn't change that these vampires want you dead. You saw the text message for yourself."

She leaned forward, her chin resting on her intertwined fingers. "Gidion, the threat might be real, but I can't hide forever. There comes a point when running from something is the same as choosing not to live."

Even though she was talking about herself, Gidion couldn't

help but think of Dad and his mom's portrait. As far as he knew, Dad had never gone on a date since Mom died. A vampire took her from them. Even if Dad and Grandpa would never say it, he knew that's what happened. As far as Dad knew, Gidion was completely ignorant about vampires, but their entire lives were organized around their existence and always had been.

He nodded. Doing that made him feel beaten, as if he'd just taken one of Dad's scoldings. "I'm not going to stop," he said. "I'm close to finding the rest of the coven. I'll let you know if I learn anything else."

She picked up a pad and wrote him a hall pass. "Suppose you'll need this."

"Uh, yeah, there's something else I need, if you don't mind."

"Oh, God, yes." She ripped off the note and wrote something else on the next sheet. "I've got my new cell phone. This is the number. I had it changed just to be safe."

"Thanks, that'll help, but I was wondering if you could repeat the stuff you said we were going to have on tomorrow's quiz? I was a little distracted when you said it the first time." He shrugged. "Sorry."

She laughed. "I'm finding it difficult to think of you as a student. For what it's worth Gidion, while you're still a boy to me, you're more like some kind of Van Helsing than someone I teach."

"Thanks." He'd never had a teacher say anything like that to him. After the way Grandpa had acted this morning, it was nice to be treated in a way that ranked him a step above others his age.

"Just make certain you do well in my class, Gidion Keep, or that will change very quickly."

Well, that was short-lived. "Understood, Ms. Aldgate." He picked up his notebook and wiggled his pencil to indicate he was ready to write the topics for tomorrow's quiz.

# CHAPtER tWENtY-SIX

Even running late for P.E. class, Gidion managed to get changed into his shorts and in the attendance line on time. That was fine with him. Meant he didn't need to use his hall pass which drew less attention to him having stayed back to talk to Ms. Aldgate.

This was the one class Gidion shared with both Seth and Pete. At the start of the school year, he'd looked forward to this class. This week, he'd come to dread it.

Given Pete's last name was Addams, he was usually first in line, so it was obvious he wasn't there. As tall as he'd gotten, it wouldn't have mattered what his last name was. You'd have to be a dwarf or blind not to notice he wasn't there.

"Seth," Gidion whispered down to him, "where's Pete?"

"Haven't seen him all day." He tossed in an exaggerated shrug in case Gidion hadn't been able to hear him. "Wasn't even sure you were here."

The coach started talking then and divided them into four groups for volleyball. Gidion and Seth ended up on different teams at different nets, so they didn't get to talk again until after class in the locker room.

"You heard from Pete at all today?" Gidion asked. He was eager to get to his car and turn his cell back on so he could send Pete a text.

"Nah. He must have called out sick. Dude looked pretty awful yesterday."

Gidion stole a page from Grandpa and Dad's books and answered with a grunt instead of the, "You should have seen what he looked like the day before," he was thinking. He just slid his jeans back on and decided that changing shirts wasn't all that important.

Seth didn't press the matter, though. His mind was focused on matters that related to between his legs. "All right, I promised my girlfriend I'd ask, so…"

"Oh, Jesus." Gidion slammed his fist on the door of his locker. "Tell that stupid twit you call a 'girlfriend' that my personal life isn't any of her damn business." He grabbed his backpack and marched out of the locker room. The look of shock on Seth's face and the collective "Ooooo" and laughter from the other guys within earshot brought him up short as he stormed out of the locker room.

"Classy, Gidion," he whispered. "Way to make a total jackass out of yourself." He knew he should go back in there and apologize, but he just couldn't bring himself to do it. He needed to get to Pete's and find out what he knew, make sure he was all right. All true, but it was also total bull. He was just too embarrassed.

# CHAPTER TWENTY-SEVEN

Gidion pulled up to Pete's house about fifteen minutes later. Death was parked in its usual place in the driveway, so he decided it was a safe bet Pete would be inside.

He hesitated when he saw the front door. He ran his finger over a large dent in the middle of it. The frame was splintered where the lock was. Had someone kicked it open? Normally, Gidion would have placed his money on Pete's dad as the culprit, but in light of Pete's current crowd, that wasn't a sure thing.

His knock was all it took to open the door. "Um, Pete?"

A head peeked around the corner of the hallway, but it wasn't Pete's.

"Hey, Gidion." He hadn't seen Pete's little sister in a long time. Sendy (poor kid's parents really didn't do her any favors spelling her name like that) must have been eleven now. She'd started middle school this year. She had short, curly blond hair that looked about as haphazard as the house.

"Where's Pete?"

She shrugged. "Haven't seen him."

"Since this morning?"

She shook her head. "Not since yesterday. Mom and Dad and I went to dinner. Pete stayed home, and when we got back he was gone."

"But his car is here."

She didn't sound concerned, and given how the Addams house was, a kid running off wasn't exactly a first. He'd be surprised if Pete's folks had even bothered to report him missing to the police. Only thing was, Gidion didn't think Pete would've left without his car. Maybe it wasn't working, but he wasn't getting that vibe.

"Yeah, Dad was really mad, too. He said he's gonna beat Pete a new one for what he did to the door."

There was no way Pete could've done that to the door, not with the condition he was in. Not unless, he'd gotten a vampire transfusion last night. "Did your Dad see Pete kick open the door?"

She shook her head. "Found it that way when we got home. That's when Dad said he was gonna beat him a new one."

"Mind if I come in for a minute?" Gidion looked past her. Didn't look like anything was stolen, not that he could see. The Addams owned a big flatscreen TV, and that was still leaning against the far wall on the floor of the family room. Pete's Dad had never gotten around to hanging it, so they just left it there. Gidion suspected Pete's Dad just didn't have a clue how to hang it and didn't want to prove it by having it fall.

"I don't mind." Sendy waved him in and then followed close behind as he went to Pete's room.

"Daddy was really mad when he saw it."

"I'll bet." The room looked even worse than it had the day Gidion had last visited. Whereas the place had just resembled a pigsty the other day, the room now resembled a murder scene, minus the blood and the body.

He wasn't sure what he was looking for, and he was damn sure he didn't want to be here when Pete's parents got home. Just before he was going to walk out of the room he noticed a picture on top of the dresser's pile of crap. The picture was old. It was of Pete and his two brothers. Pete must have been about five. His brother who was now in the military was decked out prophetically in a camouflage t-shirt. The oldest brother Roddy was in the middle, gripping his siblings in headlocks. Only where Roddy's head should have been, the photograph had been vandalized with a ballpoint pen. What looked like the shape of a "W" was worn all the way through the paper. Roddy's torso was circled with an arrow pointing at him from the word "Shithead." Was it possible Pete had run off? His brothers had done the same, although, they'd at least waited until they were adults to do it. He knew Pete had always envied them for getting out, but he'd never realized he might also hate them for leaving him behind.

Gidion looked at Sendy, standing in the hallway, too scared to come into the room.

"You see Pete, promise me you'll tell him to call me right away," he said. "All right?"

She nodded and followed him to the front door.

"Um, Gidion, can I ask you a question?"

"Sure."

"What did my daddy mean when he said he was gonna beat Pete a new one? A new what?"

"Um," he cleared his throat as he figured what might be best to say, "probably just meant he was gonna give him a bruise."

She appeared crestfallen by his answer. "Oh, I thought he meant a new asshole."

"Oh, uh, could be," he said. "Just make sure you tell Pete to call me when he comes home."

She didn't say anything else, allowing him to walk to his car and leave. He was glad, because what he'd said wasn't what he'd been thinking. When he'd told her "when he comes home," he'd intended to say "if."

# CHAPtER tWENtY-EIGHt

Every call Gidion made to Pete's cell just went straight to voicemail. A text message warning his friend that he'd better not have "fallen off the wagon" went unanswered. Everything in his gut said the shit was hitting the fan, and worst of all, he couldn't do anything about it.

Dad wasn't working any overtime tonight. At least he was going into work at ten, but that left Gidion trapped at home. He holed up in his room under the premise of studying for tomorrow's quiz. Dad was preparing dinner, all excited about an early evening of "quality time," oblivious that the world was hitching a basket ride to the lowest pits of Hell.

Gidion was rereading page eighty-nine of his world history book for the tenth time when something chimed in his room.

"What the hell?"

The chime had come from his blue backpack. He'd stuffed it on the backside of his bed where he tossed most anything that didn't have a home in his room or he'd been too impatient to bother with putting away. He pulled out Milton the vampire's cell from the bag.

"Who's sending you a text message?" He pressed the buttons to find the text.

The message was to the point: *Where the fuck R U?*

"Nice."

The contact info identified the sender as "R.A."

"Hey, son!" Dad's voice had that tone that could only be followed by, "Dinner's ready!"

"Be there in just a minute, Dad!"

He stared at the message and considered his options. A glance out the window confirmed it was already dark, just a little before seven. If Milton hadn't been beheaded and cremated this morning, then he probably would've been circling the block by now.

Gidion decided to answer the text with, *'Watching after the brat like I'm supposed to.'*

"Gidion!"

Crap. He didn't wait for a reply, just set the phone to vibrate and put it in his nightstand so Dad wouldn't hear the phone if "R.A." answered.

"What were you doing up there?" Dad asked as Gidion jumped down the stairs and skidded into the kitchen.

"Homework." Gidion hoped Dad wouldn't ask for specifics. Those kinds of details only got him trouble.

"What kind of homework?"

Crap. At least Dad didn't see him shake his head. Dad was too busy pulling a pan of teriyaki chicken from the oven.

"Um, world history."

"That's Ms. Aldgate's class, right?" He glanced at Gidion as he closed the oven with a hip bump. "Finish setting the table, would you?"

"Sure." Gidion didn't have to do much, just pull out the silverware.

"So, that's Ms. Aldgate's class?" Dad asked again.

"Yeah, that's the one." Gidion tried to contain a smirk, but failed miserably.

"What's so funny?"

"It's just you never remember most of my teacher's names," Gidion said, "except for the pretty ones."

"Excuse you?" Dad's face hardened. Most of Gidion's life, that look intimidated the hell out of him, but tonight, it just made him laugh.

"Well, it's true." He sat in his usual spot that placed Mom's portrait to his right.

Dad set a plate of chicken and sautéed peppers in front of him. "That is not true."

"Uh huh." Gidion knew he should probably back down from this one, but he couldn't resist. "Who's my algebra teacher?"

Dad's lips twisted as if to squeeze the answer free. Yeah, fat chance.

"My science teacher?"

The only answer Dad mustered was a grunt to clear his throat.

"Mrs. Brown and Mrs. Eckert," Gidion said. "Both ugly, old hags."

"Mind your manners," Dad switched to the raised eyebrow look of intimidation. Sooooo not working by this point. "And that doesn't prove anything."

"Really? What was the name of my seventh grade English teacher?"

Yeah, Dad's eyes widened and retreated to his dinner. Oh, he remembered Mrs. Reynolds, all right. She was one of those right-out-of-college teachers who dressed every day like it was Friday night—lots of short skirts and high heels.

Dad glanced back up as he cut off a piece of chicken. "Still doesn't prove anything."

Gidion laughed as Dad shook his head with an amused sigh of defeat. Ah, sweet victory.

Then a thought struck him. "You know, I bet Ms. Aldgate would like you."

The amusement vanished from Dad's face. "That really wouldn't be appropriate."

"Why not?" Gidion knew it was kind of silly, but he could totally dig Ms. Aldgate as a stepmom. Wasn't like Dad had done wrong by him or anything, but there were times when Gidion wished he still had a mom. May had always sucked in elementary school when the teachers would get all the kids to do Mother's Day art projects. Gidion ended up giving most of them to Dad, but one year, he'd given it to his teacher. She was another cute one whose name Dad could probably still remember.

"She's your teacher. It's a conflict of interest."

"What if I promise to do well in her class?"

"You better do well anyway." Dad tapped the edge of Gidion's plate with his fork. "Eat."

This was just stupid. "Look, it's not like you're still married. I mean, it's been more than a decade—"

"Enough!" Dad glared at him, and this time, he scored enough intimidation to force Gidion's eyes back to his plate.

Gidion cut his chicken into several pieces. He noticed Dad wasn't holding his fork or knife anymore. Several times, he'd caught Dad looking up at Mom as if he felt guilty about discussing this in front of her.

"Mom was pretty special, wasn't she?"

A delayed nod answered him. When Dad looked back at him, he managed a smile. "We were like a perfect picture God split into two pieces when we were born and put back together when we met. I never felt like anyone else ever understood me the way she did."

"Do you think she'd be upset if you dated?" Gidion didn't need to look at Dad to sense the defensive wall go back up. "I'm just asking."

Dad looked at her portrait. "Yes, I think she'd mind. Your mom would probably never admit it, but she could be a mighty jealous thing. One girl from our high school who had a crush on me was scared of her even years after we graduated. Your mom was proud of that, too."

"Wow. Mom was bad ass, huh?"

"Once she decided she wanted something, she was tenacious."

Gidion tried to remember that about her, but he couldn't remember much of anything. She was a blurred memory wrapped in fog. One part of him envied Dad's clarity of Mom, but he also pitied him. It was like Dad wanted to die with her, and the only reason he was still here was because of Gidion.

"I met a girl this week," Gidion said.

Dad got this big smirk on his face. "Oh really? And just who is this girl?"

"Her name's Tamara. She's a senior."

"A senior?" The way Dad said "senior" made it sound like

Gidion had lost his marbles or that he'd heard him wrong.

"Yes, they have those in high school."

If Dad were a computer, he'd have worn a big, grey error message on his screen, because he looked totally baffled. "You're dating a senior?"

"Well, we haven't really been on a date yet, but I'm meeting her at the football game tomorrow night."

"But you're a sophomore?"

Jeez, thanks for the vote of confidence, Dad. "I know what grade I'm in."

"And are you sure she likes you?"

"Well, she did kiss me."

Dad smiled all proud and stuff, but then he sat up and waved his hands in front of him as if something was blocking his view of Gidion. "Wait, I mean—" He stopped and shook his head before talking again. "You said you haven't been on a date yet, but this girl kissed you. How did you meet her?"

That's when Gidion felt a big stamp on his forehead that could have only said "World's Biggest Idiot." After giving Tamara that big lecture about getting their cover story straight for her parents, he realized he'd never put one together for his dad.

"We, uh, well, I mean—I met her at the bookstore." He gave himself a mental pat on the back for that one. He'd even gone to the bookstore this week.

"When was this?"

Drat! Which way to go? He'd gone to the bookstore last night which his checking account would prove, but he'd met her Monday. "I ran into her in the café at the Barnes & Noble last night. She goes to Midlothian Springs."

A big, dopey grin appeared on his dad's face. "Let me get this straight. You're telling me you met some girl who goes to a different school than you at the Barnes & Noble, and managed to kiss her even though you weren't on a date."

"Well, yeah."

"How did you even get on this girl's radar?"

Gidion couldn't decide if Dad was mocking him or interrogating him. Having a cop for a dad, even a former one, sucked sometimes.

"I don't know what it was, but it worked." Gidion tossed in a shrug for good measure.

"Well, son, I am impressed."

*And apparently in total denial given the way you keep shaking your head,* Gidion thought.

"So you two are going out tomorrow night?"

Gidion nodded without meeting his dad's eyes. Instead, he focused on his food. He made a mental note to let Tamara know about the cover story for his dad. He also realized it would be a good idea to keep Dad and Tamara's parents from meeting anytime soon. Knowing Dad, he'd realize the origin stories didn't match up and then it was "game over."

Dad's questions didn't let up, but they at least moved into safer territory, mainly what she looked like. About the only thing he didn't ask was what her breast size was, not that Gidion would've known.

After shoving his food into his stomach as fast as he could, Gidion popped out of his chair, tossed his dishes into the dishwasher and ran up the stairs. "Gotta finish my homework."

Dad's voice chased him. "I'm going to want to meet this girl." The jerk was getting a big laugh out of this for some reason. You'd think he'd be proud. Hello! He was dating a senior!

As he hopped onto the bed, it dawned on him that saying he was "dating" Tamara might be a bit premature. Technically, they hadn't been on a date yet, after all. Crap! What if she'd only kissed him as some kind of reward for saving her and that was it? That would be hideous. Then he thought about the rumor floating around school about him and Tamara.

He pulled out his cell phone to text her, but then wondered what to say. 'Hey, are we dating?' That imaginary "World's Biggest Idiot" stamp on his forehead itched. Could he sound more desperate?

The thought of text messages reminded him of the one on Milton's phone. He pulled it out of his nightstand's drawer. Sure enough "R.A." had responded.

*'We're done playing with the kid. If he leaves the house, text me and we'll grab him.'*

"Crap."

Gidion didn't bother answering the message. He didn't get the feeling it needed one. He wondered if R.A. was a man or a woman and if it even mattered. More than anything else, he needed a way to end this mess fast.

It was only 7:30, but that gave him time to do some research. Time to see what other goodies Milton's cell phone and wallet might contain.

# CHAPtER tWENtY-NINE

Dad left about a quarter after nine o'clock, but Gidion forced himself to play it safe and not leave until it was almost ten. He didn't want to risk Dad running back home because he'd forgotten something like his ID card. He'd done it more than once.

Gidion put a fresh blade in his box cutter and drove to where he assumed Milton had lived. He would have expected somewhere downtown, but instead, the address took Gidion further west to Carytown.

The area consisted mostly of locally owned shops, some classier than others. Gidion came to Carytown mainly to see movies at the Byrd Theater, because the tickets only cost two bucks. Movies didn't show there until after they'd left the more expensive theaters, though.

All those businesses were located on Cary Street. Gidion's destination was one block over on Ellwood Avenue. The quality of the homes changed block to block, transitioning from upscale to piece of shit and back again, all within walking distance. He wasn't surprised that Milton's address fell into the POS area. At least the neighborhood wasn't so bad that Gidion felt like he might get mugged at any minute.

He circled the block and even drove through the back alley before finding a place to park on Ellwood. The closest place he managed was a block past it.

No lights were on in Milton's rental. The exterior was brick like most of the other homes. Someone had gotten industrious at some point in the distant past and painted the brick a bright orange, but time had worn it down so that more of the natural red of the brick was visible than not.

The door was in about the same condition, only painted red. Whoever the poor bastard was must have used the cheapest paint he could find. Gidion stepped onto the front porch without any creaks from the wood. The door wasn't unlocked as with the safe house. Fortunately, Gidion had Milton's keys.

Once inside, he put on a pair of tight-fitting, leather gloves. No guarantee anyone would be fingerprinting this place for any reason, but he preferred not to risk it. He'd also been careful not to use his fingertips on the door knob.

Milton had the typical bachelor's den: big screen TV, Playstation and stereo system. Beanbags were the only furniture and a ceiling fan offered the only lights that Gidion could see. This morning's newspaper was left on the kitchen counter. There was a refrigerator with only beer and wine in it. He assumed that was more for show than anything else, probably used to keep prospective meals too inebriated to realize they were about to die.

He went upstairs. There were two bedrooms with the doors closed and a bathroom.

Gidion opened the door to the front bedroom first. That's when he got his first big surprise. Sitting in the middle of the room and bathed in a wide beam of moonlight from the window sat a coffin.

"Oh, this boy was hard core."

Grandpa had said some vampires really went for the coffin thing. Wasn't like in *Dracula* where they needed their native soil or any nonsense like that. It was just one of those practical matters of avoiding sunlight. Especially in a rattrap like this, there was only so much a guy could do to block out the sunlight. Of course, some of the young ones liked to play up the whole gothic thing, too.

Milton had gone cheap, though. In a bit of irony, this was a plain pine box just like the one Gidion had tossed him into at the funeral home.

The furniture was pretty sparse in here, too. About the only effort made was a bookshelf. Gidion wasn't sure what he'd hoped to find that would lead him to Elizabeth's home, but he wasn't optimistic as he sifted through the pile of newspapers and porn magazines. Jerk didn't even have a computer in here. He wondered if that might be in the other bedroom. He'd get to it after he finished going through everything here. Sitting at the bottom of the pile was Milton's senior yearbook from West Chester High. He decided to take it with him. Maybe he'd find something useful in it. Wasn't like he'd found anything else useful yet.

Giving up on this room, he went for the next. Not as much natural light was coming in through the window here, but it was enough for him to see yet another coffin in the middle of the room.

"Oh, crap."

A second coffin. Milton had a roommate. The earlier text from "R.A." suddenly made sense. No wonder he'd asked where Milton was. That's when he realized he'd already missed the obvious sign. The newspaper in the kitchen was today's paper.

He needed to get out of here. Just as he ran for the stairs, he heard a sound from below, a key sliding into the front door's lock. If he weren't in panic mode, he might not have noticed it, but fear had him hyperalert. What really turned his heart into a full rock 'n roll drum set was that the person at the door was going to every effort to keep quiet. Whoever it was knew Gidion was here.

Even as Gidion tried to think of a way out, the details clicked into place. The text to Milton's phone had been to test if Gidion was in possession of it, not if Milton was alive. They knew Milton's driver's license would lead him here. They'd set a trap, and he'd walked right into it. There'd be more than one out there, too.

He didn't know the odds, and that meant he needed backup. He pulled out Milton's cell phone and dialed.

A woman's voice answered. "Richmond 911."

"I'm at 2858 Ellwood Avenue," he whispered to conceal the call as best he could from the vampire outside. "Someone just broke in my front door, and I think he has a knife. Please send help. Oh my God!" He hung up.

Time to move. If the forced entry didn't get the cops going lights and sirens, then the promise of a weapon would for sure.

He ran for the front bedroom as he heard the door open

downstairs. The vampires were still going for stealth, hoping to catch him by surprise. At least, that's what he hoped, because that gave him a few more seconds.

He grabbed the window, trying to lift it open. Damn thing wouldn't budge, painted shut. No time for subtle. He dropped the yearbook and grabbed the lid of the coffin. Just before he lifted it, he saw the cover of the annual. Gold letters were engraved on the front, but the name wasn't Milton. No time to think about it. He flung the coffin lid through the window. Glass exploded as the lid shot out like a ball from a cannon. The plank of wood thudded and banged about as it slid off the roof of the front porch and to the ground.

Footsteps pounded up the inside stairs. Gidion climbed out the window. His sleeve snagged and tore on a jagged piece of glass still attached to the frame. He looked over his shoulder to see the outline of a man rushing towards him. He jerked free of the window, cutting his arm.

"Come back here, you little shit!"

Gidion jumped. Grandpa had warned him about stunts like this. A jump from this height wouldn't get him killed, not likely, but if he broke a leg, the vampires would finish him well before the cops got here. The key was to start positioning himself as soon as he jumped, land on the balls of his feet with his knees bent and roll to distribute the force of the landing. Most of all, he had to protect his head.

Grandpa would've been proud. He managed it without breaking anything.

"Get him!" the guy inside the house shouted from the window.

Sirens whined in the distance, Gidion's backup was getting close. Sadly, the two vampires waiting in front of the house were a whole lot closer. One man and one woman rushed him. He got to his feet, drew his box cutter and ran at the smaller of the two, the woman. A slice, aimed for her throat, slit across her face instead. Not even close to a killing blow, but good enough to make her flinch and let him past her.

Nothing else to do now but run as fast as possible. This was where being a long-distance runner versus a sprinter really didn't work in his favor.

A low growl warned Gidion he was losing ground. He wouldn't reach the corner before the male vampire caught up to him.

He stopped and dropped into a crouch, balling up his body. The vampire tripped over Gidion, screaming as he skidded to a stop on the sidewalk.

The female vampire caught up just as Gidion got back to his feet. She threw a punch that caught him on the cheek. He rolled with it enough to keep from getting knocked silly. He grabbed her by the shirt. Fangs snapped in vain at him as he slashed across her throat with his box cutter.

The sirens got louder, just a block or two away.

"What the fuck?" the male vampire was on all fours and looking down the street at the approaching blue and red lights.

Gidion ran past him and turned the corner, going as fast as he could for Cary Street. He didn't slow down. The vampires weren't far behind. He needed someplace public and busy that wouldn't throw out a kid this close to eleven o'clock.

He got his bearings as he rounded the corner onto Cary Street. He recognized the red exterior of the game shop, One Eyed Jacques. Sadly, the place was closed, but just across the street, he spotted the neon sign for the Galaxy Diner. He just ran into the road, banking that any drivers coming down Cary would be going slow enough to stop in time if they were about to hit him.

He darted inside as soon as the sliding glass door was open enough to admit him. He heard a winded "Shit!" from the male vampire who'd managed to get pretty close. It was too late to grab Gidion, though, not unless he wanted to make a scene sure to prompt calls for the police.

Gidion climbed into a booth near the front. He could see the two vampires who'd chased him still outside and arguing with each other about what to do. The logo on the guy's black t-shirt distracted Gidion for a moment. It was the picture of a cat in the style of an old western mug shot with the words "Wanted Dead

& Alive: Schrödinger's Cat" around it. A vampire with a sense of humor Fabulous.

"What can I get you?" The waitress eyed him a bit suspiciously. He hadn't caught his breath yet. He was sweating buckets and his arm was bleeding.

"Iced tea, unsweetened." He offered his best smile as she handed him a menu.

As soon as she walked away to get his drink, he pulled out his phone to call his real backup.

"Grandpa?"

"You okay, boy?"

He laughed. "No, but I'll live. I need a pickup. Got chased by two vampires into the Galaxy Diner in Carytown. No chance of getting to my car from here, not on foot."

"Sit tight. What do these fang freaks look like?"

Gidion leaned out of his booth for a better look. The female vampire glared at him as he smiled at her and waved. "One white female with short, blond hair, wearing a dark green jacket. One black male with cornrows and wearing a black t-shirt with an off-white logo on the front and black jeans. There was a third male, a white guy, at the house I went into on Ellwood. I called the cops to the address, so not sure if they'll have him stuck there. Didn't get a good look at him, but I'm pretty sure he's tall and has shaggy brown hair."

"If you didn't get a good look, then how do you know that?"

Gidion laughed as his mind's eye drifted back to the name on the cover of the yearbook.

"Just hurry. Not sure how long they'll wait before they try something." He hung up the phone just as the server returned. He ordered two hamburgers to go. No reason not to make this detour practical, and he knew Grandpa wouldn't mind a bite to eat.

The side walls were covered with mirrors, creating the illusion this narrow place was twice its size. That didn't stop the grip of claustrophobia Gidion felt as Milton's roommate stepped through the door. The vampire walked over to Gidion's table and sat across from him.

"I always thought you were a little prissy bitch, Gidion. Not surprised you ran."

Sure enough, he had the brown hair that was all scruffy. The jerk hadn't changed much since Gidion had last seen him about seven years ago. He even recognized the leather jacket from the picture he'd seen earlier today in Pete's bedroom.

"R.A." Gidion didn't bother with false bravado. Given his lessons from interrogating Milton, he knew there was no hiding his fear. "Roddy Addams. So who dragged who into the 'Fangs 'R' Us' club? I'm betting it was Milton who recruited you. Little doubt you sucked your brother Pete into this mess."

"It's not like he was ever going to amount to anything anyway." Pete's oldest brother laughed. "Besides, a guy's gotta pay his bills. Delivering a willing feeder to the Queen Bee earns a lot of cred."

Gidion leaned forward despite every urge that said he should keep as much space as possible between him and this monster. "Suppose it shouldn't surprise me that you'd sell out Pete."

"Shouldn't really surprise you that Pete sold you out, too." He smiled, not bothering to hide his fangs. "The whole 'my friend is into drugs' thing had us going there for a bit. That was very clever. The little scene with the bat outside my old house was a nice touch, too."

"Is he still alive?"

Roddy shrugged and there was nothing feigned in his indifference. "Not my call. The Queen Bee is really pissed at him."

Gidion wondered if "Queen Bee" was the required code reference to Elizabeth. Using her name seemed borderline forbidden outside of the coven. He didn't say anything to stop Roddy from running his mouth. He'd had to cut up Milton just to get what little information he'd already known. Milton had brains. Roddy was just a jerk with a mouth, and Gidion hoped that might give him something useful, maybe even a lead for finding Pete or Elizabeth's daytime lair.

"My little sister should be ready for it in a few years, lot sooner than he was. The Queen Bee likes the girls young." Roddy all but vibrated with giddiness. "Oh, don't give me that look. You and I both know I'll be doing her a favor."

"By turning her into a whore who's worth little more than a blood bag?"

"At least she'll get something out of it. Queen Bee treats her girls better than her own kind. You wouldn't believe what she's willing to do for them."

Something in the way Roddy said that reminded Gidion of Pete. Back when he'd caught Pete pretending to breastfeed that baby doll, his friend had lashed out like some cornered animal defending his turf. His jealousy for Sendy had bordered on hatred.

"We both know that's better for her than what'll happen if she stays with my old man," Roddy said. "Minute she starts growing tits, he'll probably be trying to fuck her more than Mom."

The server came back to the table. "We'll have your order ready in just a moment," she said to Gidion and then turned her attention to Roddy. "What can I get you?" The way she asked made it sound more like she was warning them not to start any crap in her diner.

"Nothing." If they were all talking in hidden meanings, then that must have translated into "fuck off," because the waitress got the message and went back to the bar.

"Wow, I suddenly realized why Pete hates you so much," Gidion said. "You might not look like him, but you act just like your dad."

Roddy went so still, he didn't even breath.

"Was that a little too personal?" Gidion offered his biggest smirk.

"Not at all." Roddy checked his watch, which he wore with the face positioned on the bottom of his wrist. "Oh, look at the time. What do you know? It's on my side. Place only stays open until two, Gidion. We can wait."

He stood and knocked over the iced tea, sending an orange waterfall from the tabletop onto Gidion's lap.

"Oops." Roddy laughed as Gidion jumped out of his seat, too late to avoid his jeans getting drenched.

"Hey, Roddy!" Gidion's shout stopped the departing asshole just short of the door.

"What?"

"Tell Elizabeth I'm really looking forward to meeting her."

Using the "Queen Bee's" name smacked the cockiness from Roddy's face. He didn't say anything else, just walked out.

The server came over with a small towel to wipe up the spill and offered him one for his pants. He made a token effort at drying them off. At least he still had a change of clothes in his car, assuming he could get to it.

"You want another glass of tea?" she asked.

"No, thanks. I've had enough."

He sat and divided his attention between checking the time and watching what the vampires were doing. For the moment, they appeared content to wait him out. With any luck, that would last long enough for Grandpa to get here. Even in public, he'd need to move fast to make his getaway.

His cell vibrated in his hand, startling him as it displayed a phone number he didn't recognize. A glance at the vampires confirmed it wasn't one of them. He decided to answer it, wondering who it might be. Perhaps, the "Queen Bee?"

"Hello?"

"Gid, hey, it's Andrea."

His mind was stuck in vampire hunter mode, so much so that it took him a moment to realize it was Seth's girlfriend.

"Andrea?" How did she even know his number? Puzzling together that answer didn't take much effort: Seth. "What do you want?"

"Look, Seth told me about what you'd said to him in gym class today. I just wanted to apologize."

Apologize? Like he really cared? Truth was, he did, but not with three vampires outside waiting for a chance to de-limb him and bleed him dry.

"Andrea, this really isn't a good time."

"I know it's late and all." Truth be told, she really did sound sorry, enough so that he regretted the tone he'd had in his voice. "It's just that I know what good friends you and Seth are. I'm not wanting to mess that up or anything. I mean, I know I can be nosey and all, but I was just all excited when I heard about you and Tamara Gardner."

Just great. The rumor running around had him and Tamara connected by name. He was about to hang up on Andrea, but the next words out of her mouth froze him.

"I can't wait to hear what Stephanie Drake says when she finds out. I'll bet she'll be hot. She's always so moody. I think it's all that black she wears. I read somewhere that wearing dark colors is really bad for your inner chi. You know, you should probably dress in lighter colors, too. I bet you'd look good in aquamarine or maybe persimmon."

"Wait." Holy crap. Had he heard her right? "Why would Stephanie Drake care about me dating Tamara?" Sure he knew the vampires wanted Tamara dead, but Andrea wouldn't know jack about that.

"Oh, so you really are dating her? That's so cool, Gid! I hear she's a really nice girl."

Jesus. "Andrea, just answer the question. What do Tamara and Stephanie have to do with each other?"

"Oh!" She sounded excited that he'd finally shown an interest in the gossip he usually tuned out during their lunch break. "Well, this past summer, the bands from our school and Midlothian Springs and a bunch of other Chesterfield high schools went to camp together. You see, Stephanie was dating this guy from Midlothian Springs. He was a rising senior and from what I hear, he's really hot but a total slut."

Oh, dear God. Would she get to the point already? Gidion glanced outside. The female vampire caught him looking and glared at him. Jeez, whoever the guy was who wrote girls were made of "sugar and spice and everything nice" never got caught in that Medusa's gaze.

"Anyway, this guy dumped Stephanie after less than three days at camp and hooked up with Tamara. Three days! Can you believe that? Such a creep."

She rambled on, but Gidion stopped listening closely as the dots connected in his mind. Roddy had just said Elizabeth would do almost anything for her girls, treated them better than her vampires. Good God! Could it really be that simple?

"Andrea!" He had to cut her off. Lord, he hoped she was as deep into the school's gossip as she sounded. "What's the deal with Stephanie and Ms. Aldgate?"

"You don't know about that?" The way she said that made him wonder if he was the only person in school who didn't know. Knowing his luck, she'd probably even mentioned this at lunch when he was trying NOT to listen to her.

"Just answer the question, Andrea," he said and quickly added, "please."

"Well, remember when Principal Vermin came by our class earlier today?"

"Yeah, what about it?" Ugh! Like he wanted to think about the Vermin flirting with his teacher. Dad would be so much better for her.

"Well, I hear Ms. Aldgate caught her plagiarizing on a term paper last year. Stephanie took AP World History as a freshman, just like me. Word has it she bought the paper from some guy who graduated from our school almost a decade ago, some Mallard or Milburn guy or something like that."

Sweet Jesus. "Milton Robbins. She got the paper from Milton Robbins, didn't she?"

"That might have been the guy's name. Anyway, I'm not sure how Ms. Aldgate caught Stephanie cheating like that, but it actually ruined her streak of all-A's since sixth grade. Oh, how horrible, right? From what I hear, her parents have been harassing the Vermin for weeks now trying to get Ms. Aldgate to let it slide and change her grade for the last nine weeks of the previous school year from a C to an A."

Gidion laughed. All his vampire hunting, digging for a connection, and the answer had been staring him in the face all along.

Stephanie Drake.

What was it Roddy had just said? Elizabeth would do almost anything for her little girls. Was it that big of a stretch that "almost anything" would include hits on two people Stephanie hated?

"Andrea, I gotta go, but I owe you one. Thanks. I promise I'll talk to Seth later so I can apologize to him." After he hung up, he realized he probably owed Andrea an apology, too. He'd blamed her for all the distance between him and his friends, but in hindsight, they'd done all the damage themselves.

Fixing things with Seth and Andrea would have to wait, though. Finding Pete came first.

He tried to craft a plan while he waited for Grandpa. His order was already prepared and paid for by the time Grandpa stopped in front of the Galaxy Diner in his white and rust pickup.

Gidion was already running out the front door before the truck stopped. He had his cell phone in hand, in case he needed to dial 911 again. The vampires didn't chase after him right away. They'd probably been expecting to grab him as he made a run for his Kia.

"You okay, boy?" Grandpa didn't really look at Gidion, his eyes assessing the trio of vampires.

"Yeah, take the next left and floor it. I'm gonna need my car."

The vampires chased after them, but Grandpa did as he'd been told. That would give Gidion about a minute to hop in his car and roll. He readied for the pickup to stop as it made the turn onto Ellwood.

"I'm three cars down on the left." He glanced right to see the cop cars were still in front of Roddy's house. They were probably still trying to find a key holder. "I'll meet you back at the funeral home."

The Little Hearse came into view. He jumped out of the pickup and ran for the driver's seat. Just as he pressed the button on his keychain to automatically unlock the doors, he realized the car was leaning too far on its side.

"Son of a bitch!" The vampires had slashed both of the driver side tires.

He threw open the trunk and grabbed the blue backpack and black bag with his change of clothes.

"Hurry up, boy!"

Gidion slammed the trunk shut. He glanced over his shoulder

to see the vampires rounding the corner at a sprint. He tossed his bags into the back of the pickup and scrambled into the passenger seat. Grandpa hit the accelerator before he could close the door.

The Little Hearse honked and flashed its lights as he used his keychain to lock it. The headlights gave him a brief look at Roddy's face, good and pissed.

"I'm gonna need to borrow the truck, Grandpa."

Grandpa laughed in that smoker, phlegmy way. "Getting run down like a rabbit by three vampires isn't enough for one night?"

"No, because I plan to end this tonight."

# CHAPTER THIRTY

Grandpa Murphy spent the entire drive bitching about Gidion's plan.

"Not that I haven't had my share of school teacher fantasies, boy, but keeping this bitch in my house is a bad idea."

"It's either your place or the funeral home, and as to that first part—EWWW! Don't feel like you've got to share every thought that goes through your brain." Gidion looked up from the map book. "Take the next left."

Grandpa chuckled, clearly enjoying messing with him. This had to be punishment for last night and the plan for tonight.

"There it is." Gidion pointed to the street sign at the next corner. "Crater Street. Turn right and look for 8912."

They pulled into the driveway just three houses down. The rancher reminded him of the one Ms. Aldgate's ex lived in. Only, this version looked much better. Even in the glow of only the front porch light, he could tell the yard was trimmed and landscaped. He wondered if she did it herself or paid someone.

"We'll follow you in her car." Gidion got out of the pickup. "Try not to treat it like a Sunday afternoon." He shut the door before Grandpa could get off a smart remark, or what he would assume passed for one.

A small elephant statue was standing guard next to the front door. Gidion knocked. There was the sound of shuffling from inside but no voice. He gripped his box cutter as he saw the light coming through the peephole go dark, suggesting someone was looking at him.

Only Ms. Aldgate came out when the door opened. He'd called ahead, but part of him worried the vampires might go after her before he got here. She wasn't looking as put together as she usually did for class, wearing a t-shirt and jeans. She'd pulled her hair back into a ponytail and was wearing glasses. She looked more like a librarian. A random thought as to whether Grandpa had any fantasies about women in that occupation made him queasy.

"Are you certain about this?" She had a large bag slung over her shoulder along with a purse as she locked her door behind her.

"Not one doubt. We need you somewhere safe if this doesn't go well."

She scowled at him. Given how the conversation had gone over the phone, he was surprised she hadn't changed her mind and refused to leave.

"What about the girl from Midlothian Springs?"

"Already warned her. Called her after I got off the phone with you," he said. "She lives with her parents. I don't think they're as likely to go after her."

He waved to Grandpa to roll out as they climbed into her dark green Honda Accord. "Nice car."

"Thank you." She pulled out and kept a close tail on Grandpa's truck. A heavy sigh slipped out and she directed a scowl towards him. "I was looking forward to sleeping in my bed again for the first time in almost a week."

"With any luck, you're just delaying that by one more night." Dear God, could Grandpa drive any slower? It was a miracle Gidion wasn't still waiting in the Galaxy Diner the way he drove.

His cell phone lit up and vibrated. Crap, who was calling now?

"Shit, it's Tamara." Considering he'd practically just talked to her, he didn't think this could be good. "What's up? You all right?"

"Remember you told me to keep track of any cars outside my house? Well, one just pulled up a few minutes after you called. No one's gotten out of it yet either."

"Tam, hold on a moment." He covered the mouthpiece to his phone as he saw an oncoming car. "Ms. Aldgate, you might want to sit lower." He did the same. As the car neared, he saw it was a blue, four-door Toyota. He didn't recognize the car, but he definitely recognized the two in it. It was Roddy's pals, Schrödinger and Medusa. "Crap."

"What?" Ms. Aldgate looked over her shoulder. Gidion didn't need to. He heard the other car's tires squeal as they turned around to follow. Didn't matter how low they'd been sitting. There was no way those two wouldn't recognize Grandpa's beat up truck.

"Don't panic." Gidion looked back to see the Toyota rushing to catch up, but slowing as it got closer. "They're just going to follow until we stop." At least, he assumed they would. A car wreck invited police and potentially left them without a car to drive their catch to a more convenient killing place.

"Gidion, what's happening?" Tamara sounded pretty freaked.

"We've got two vampires following us. We're okay for the moment. What about your guy?" He was willing to bet it was Roddy and wondered if he had any other friends with him.

"Still hasn't gotten out of the car." Her voice was rising, even as she struggled to whisper.

"I want you to call 911. Tell them you've got a suspicious vehicle outside your house. Don't embellish. Just give them what you can see. And if they ask if you want to be seen by the officer, tell them 'no'."

"Why not?" Ouch! She did not sound happy about that.

"Because they're going to wonder why you're so jumpy about it, and what are you going to tell them?"

"Okay, okay…" She wasn't happy about it, not that he could blame her. "Sorry, I just wish you were you here."

"Me, too. I'll call you back as soon as I've dealt with the two following me, so keep your phone on vibrate."

"Got it."

He hung up and called Grandpa, hoping he was paying attention.

"Listen sharp, boy," Grandpa answered without giving Gidion a chance to speak. "If you're calling to say anything like, 'I told you so,' just remember who signs your paychecks."

"I want to set up an ambush. Let's go for the elementary school on Reams Road. We're coming up on Midlothian Turnpike. You go right. We'll go left, take the long way."

Gidion could hear Grandpa grumble. "All right, boy. I'll head to Pullbrooke Drive. You better give me enough time or you'll be on your own."

"You got it, Grandpa," he said. "By the way, I told you so."

He hung up and looked over to Ms. Aldgate. She was giving him that look she usually reserved for students who didn't show up with their homework. Somehow, her librarian look for tonight made it a little more intimidating.

"Mind telling me what we're doing?"

He smiled and laughed nervously. "Just turn left onto Midlothian when we get there and head down to 288. If our friends get out of the car at any of our stops and try to approach, just run the light. Stay in the left lane unless you're certain you can pass any car in front of you. Leave extra room between you and any car stopped in front of you. We don't want to get boxed in."

A quick check confirmed the doors were already locked.

"You know how to get to Reams Road Elementary?"

"Yes, I've been there a few times. But heading towards 288 is in the opposite direction."

"Just trust me. I want to take our time on this. No matter how aggressive they get, don't speed if you can help it."

When they reached the intersection with Midlothian Turnpike, the vampires followed Ms. Aldgate's car. Gidion had been pretty sure they would, but he'd had a brief moment of fear they might prove unpredictable and go after Grandpa. The pickup disappeared from sight. From this point forward, they were operating on faith.

"Why are we going to the elementary school?" Ms. Aldgate had her eyes on the rear view mirror more than the road ahead.

"Home field advantage. My little league football team used to practice there every evening in the fall. Perfect place for some privacy so I can finish off these jerks."

He was sitting so that he faced the rear of the car, keeping an eye on the vampires. "You make it sound like this is a good thing. Couldn't we just try to lose them?"

"Gotta kill them sometime, Ms. Aldgate. I'd rather face them two-to-one than take on the entire coven at once. I'm good, but I'm not exactly Jason Bourne. Killing them now also improves my odds later when it's time to finish off the coven."

"Assuming you don't get killed."

He decided against finding a pithy comeback to that.

The next fifteen minutes crawled by as they played out their slow-paced cat-and-mouse chase. Route 288 helped keep things simple. The road was nothing but trees, grass and asphalt, basically the same as an interstate.

"Still behind us?" she asked.

"Oh, yeah." Gidion smiled, even though he could tell it was irritating her. "Stay at the speed limit. I want to go over a few things before we get to the school. When we get off of 288 onto Courthouse, I want you to get some distance between us. Just make sure we don't lose them."

"Oh, of course. How difficult could that be?" He'd say this for Ms. Aldgate, she wielded sarcasm like a bat.

"There's a gate that leads onto the basketball court, which is right next to the football and baseball fields. I need you to park there. The bad news is that your car will be blocked in. The good news is they won't be able to drive their car onto the football field and try to run us over. We're going to run for the treeline. Make sure you turn off the car and kill the lights. We don't want to be noticed by any cops driving down Reams Road."

"I don't see why not."

Good grief, did these people not get it? "We need these vampires dead. Police don't help with that. All they do is delay the confrontation. We have an opportunity to fight these two on our terms. That's better than having them surprise us later when we might not be ready for them."

"Sorry, Gidion," she said, "but somehow the idea of having grown men with guns trained for this sort of thing is more appealing."

"You're missing the point. They haven't been trained to deal with vampires. I have." He cut her off before she might say anything else. "That's the exit we need."

She jerked the car to the right and onto the off-ramp. That nearly flung him on top of her.

"Sorry."

"All good," he said. "Be ready to turn early, because we've had them following us for a while, and there's not much out here. If there's any place they might try to grab us, it's at this light."

They crawled to a stop without any other cars in front of them. The Toyota stopped close enough that Gidion could feel the rumble of its engine vibrating the Honda. He could see the two vampires arguing. Neither was on a cell phone. That was a good sign. He'd worried about them trying to set up an ambush of their own. The glow of the traffic lights changed from red to green and their slow-speed pursuit continued.

He slipped out of his hoodie so he'd be able to get to his sword more easily when it was time. "I'm going to check on Tamara."

He sent a text to her this time. *What's happening there? You all right?*

That she didn't answer right away had him worried.

"Your plan doesn't give us a way out." Ms. Aldgate looked nervously in her rearview mirror as they neared another stoplight where they'd have to stop.

"If they take me down, you run into the woods. They aren't too deep, and there are houses behind there. Go for the nearest one with lights on and bang on the door until someone answers."

He glanced at her bags in the backseat. It suddenly occurred to him that Grandpa had all of his gear from the Little Hearse. At least he had his sword and box cutter. "I don't suppose you ever got a box cutter like I'd suggested?"

"Dammit, no!" She slammed her fists on the steering wheel. He needed to get her calmer and focused.

"That's all right. Better to leave the fighting to me anyway." He smiled at her. "Just know that you're getting an 'incomplete' for failing to do your homework."

She did a double-take at that. "Funny," she said with a swing of her sarcasm bat. "Very funny."

"Well, I figure if I don't make it as a vampire hunter, I can always fall back on comedy." He pointed as they neared the turn for Reams Road, but she was already swerving into the turn lane. She'd sped up, making their hunters work for it a bit more. They didn't have quite as much distance as he'd have liked, but it would have to do.

"When we stop, remember to turn it off, kill the lights and run like hell. Just stay with me. I need to be between you and the vampires at all times. When I stop running, stay at least a meter behind me. You stray too far, I can't protect you. You get too close, and I won't have room to fight."

Grandpa had discussed this kind of fighting. He called it "Secret Service Style," because it involved protecting someone.

"There it is!" she said, about to turn into the first parking lot.

"No!" He slammed the palm of his hand on the dashboard. "Not here! The next lot!"

Her correction nearly sent them into the ditch, but she managed to get back onto the road. He grabbed the handle just above the door and hung on for dear life.

The road curved in snakelike fashion as they approached the right turn. "Here?" she asked.

"Yes!" He decided he better throw one last joke out there in hopes of getting her to calm the hell down. The way she was driving might kill them sooner than the damn vampires. "Next week we'll cover defensive driving techniques."

"Not funny!"

He looked back and saw the Toyota turn into the lot behind them. They'd have maybe a five second head start. He hoped like hell it would be enough.

She went straight for the gate he'd told her about. The car screeched to a halt. Jeez, could they make more noise? They'd be lucky if all this crap didn't prompt someone to call the cops.

"Go!"

They jumped out. To her credit, she did everything he'd said with great efficiency. Car off, lights out, dash! Perfect.

The only pity was that she didn't run quicker. Even in sneakers, she wasn't a track star hopeful by any stretch. He heard her gasping for breath, and they weren't even halfway to the tree line. They needed to get close to those trees, or they were screwed.

Twenty meters from the trees was as far as they could get before the vampires were on them. Having to go slow enough to stay with his teacher meant he wasn't out of breath and had plenty of fight left in him.

He turned, drawing his sword, wishing for once it was a longer one. The swing fell just short of Medusa's stomach. Her body tipped forward even as she struggled to bend back and stay out of the sword's path.

Schrödinger was coming up behind his partner, but more to the right.

"Back up!" he shouted at Ms. Aldgate. He needed the trees behind them to act like a wall. He just hoped she wouldn't panic and run into the woods. Not only would the vampires be able to see far better in the dark, but Grandpa said some vampires could navigate the treetops like gold-medal gymnasts. Speaking of Grandpa, where was he?

The guy hissed at him. The lady crouched and looked close to going to all fours. Bad sign. Grandpa said the older ones moved less like humans and more like animals. That made them twice as dangerous.

The pair closed in on him, moving in slow steps. That was good. They were trying to drive them into the trees.

"Here, kitty, kitty." Gidion flicked the sword in a taunt. The guy bit first, lunging forward. The move was only a feint to give Medusa an opening.

She leaped at Gidion. He tried to dodge and swing at her as she passed but she was too fast. She tackled Ms. Aldgate.

The guy came after Gidion from behind. Gidion heard him coming and spun around. This swing didn't miss. He got knocked down but not before his sword buried into the guy's back. The vampire tried to scramble away, but Gidion recovered faster and got him right on the throat. Neck said bye-bye to its head with a satisfying sucking sound.

"Enough!" Medusa hissed. She had a firm grip on Ms. Aldgate: one arm wrapped around her waist and the other hand holding to the ponytail.

"One step closer, and I'll rip her throat open."

Ms. Aldgate wasn't making it easy on her, though. Even with the vice she was being held within, the vampire couldn't keep her still. Getting that bite into her throat wouldn't be a simple strike.

"Ms. Aldgate, be still. Just stop struggling." Her eyes widened and demanded if he'd lost his ever-loving mind. He didn't blame her, but he needed her to quit moving around. "Trust me. Please, stop moving."

The vampire grinned at him. "Wise choice, hunter."

"I know."

She laughed. "Now, drop the sword."

"No, I don't think so."

A soft whistle was swiftly followed by a loud thunk. The arrogance disappeared from Medusa's face and her grip on his teacher released. Ms. Aldgate dropped to the ground and scrambled away from the vampire, who was now too busy trying to remove the arrow Grandpa had just buried into the back of her head.

Medusa screamed as she spun around. Gidion's sword silenced her, sending her head bouncing across the field like the footballs he and his teammates had passed back in his elementary school days. The vampire's body collapsed next to it.

"You certainly took your sweet time," Gidion said.

Grandpa's laugh came from the woods. "Well, if you'd been thirty yards over, I might have taken out both of those fuckers for you."

Gidion took Ms. Aldgate by the hand and helped her to her feet.

"Why didn't you tell me he was going to be in there?"

"Was worried you'd be looking for him and give away that he was there." Gidion shrugged. "Sorry, but figured it was best."

Grandpa limped out of the trees' shadows and onto the field. "Thanks for staying still, ma'am. I'm a good shot with this crossbow when I got a target that ain't moving, but I ain't no Robin Hood."

"Glad to know that after the fact and not before you took the shot with my head next to hers."

"You all right, Grandpa?" He always had trouble walking, but his limp was more pronounced.

"Tripped on a damn root coming in here from the other side."

Fabulous. They didn't have time for injuries.

"Ms. Aldgate." He pulled out the bag he kept folded up in his back pocket and handed it to her. "Collect the heads. I'm going to drag their bodies into the woods. I can come back for them later," he told Grandpa before he tried to protest. "We can't waste anymore time here. If someone called the cops, they won't take much longer to get here."

"Fine, but you're giving me a ride back to my car."

"Whatever. Let's just move." He grabbed Schrödinger's body first since he looked heavier. Getting him the twenty feet to the trees and well out of sight about threw his back out. Lady vamp went a lot more easily after that. He threw leaves and dirt on them like a dog digging a hole.

Gidion and Grandpa got in the vampires' car. Ms. Aldgate followed in hers.

"You sure you can drive, Grandpa?"

He grunted. "Pickup's an automatic. I think I can handle that."

Getting around to where Grandpa parked on Pullbrooke Drive took about five minutes. From there, they formed a three-car caravan with Grandpa in front and Gidion in the rear, driving the vampires' Corolla. It was a nice car, too, complete with an iPod mount. Sadly, the vampires' taste in music was dreadful.

"Seriously?" he muttered as if the vampires were still there to hear him. "You were in a car chase while listening to Buddy Holly? God, how pathetic."

He realized as they were about to turn onto Reams Road that he hadn't seen if Tamara had ever texted him back. When he pulled out his phone, he was relieved to see he had an unread message from her and with a picture attached. His relief stopped as soon as he flipped open his phone. He saw Tamara's face with tears streaming from her eyes and a hand wrapped around her throat, keeping her still for the picture.

The message with it read, *'Come get her, lover boy. –R.A.'*

# CHAPTER THIRTY-ONE

Gidion was getting tired of seeing blue and red lights tonight. Police cars were parked all along the block where Tamara lived. He didn't bother trying to turn onto the street. He wouldn't get near their house, and it was a safe bet nobody around here would really know any definite details.

If he had to guess, he'd wager Tamara's parents were dead. What had him puzzled was that she'd been taken alive. That could mean a lot of things and none of the options were good.

For all he'd done, he still didn't know where Elizabeth's lair was. For that matter, there was no guarantee Tamara or Pete would be there.

As he was leaving the neighborhood and police cars behind him, his phone rang. The call was from Tamara's phone.

"You're a goddamned psycho, Roddy."

A low purr answered, followed by an equally unexpected voice: a woman's.

"Gidion Keep, you have been most taxing."

"I take it you would be Elizabeth." He hadn't expected this, and now that he had her on the phone, he didn't have a clue what to do with her. Of course, that was probably why she was the one making the call, to throw him off-balance. It was working. He transferred a quick kiss from his lips to the red bat on his shirt, hoping for a little extra good luck.

"Tell me, Mister Keep, what do you hope to accomplish? Kill me? Destroy my coven? Save your friends? Tsk tsk…So naïve."

"Why not meet me face-to-face? We'll see how naïve you think I am then."

She laughed, and the tone was disturbing. She sounded like some grandmother but with the voice of a woman who hadn't yet developed the rattle of old age. How old was she?

"You are a delightful child. It's so rare to find a challenge in this world, and even less likely to see such a talented killer who is so young."

Gidion pulled his borrowed car over near the entrance to Tamara's neighborhood. They'd called almost as soon as he'd gotten here. That couldn't be coincidence.

"What can I say? I have a lot of natural talent." He looked around, trying to see if anyone was watching. She must have had a set of eyes near the neighborhood, but there was no guessing where. That's when a thought struck him. Why was she calling him at all?

"So why the call, Elizabeth? I thought you were the shy type."

He kept focused on his surroundings, worried they might try to attack him where he was. Driving required him to divide his attention from the conversation, but the fear he was about to get attacked at any second wasn't any better.

"Inquisitive and deductive," she whispered. Was she simply taking his measure? Trying to flatter him?

"What do you want?" he said as he pulled back onto the road.

"Actually, Mister Keep, the question is 'What do you want?'"

"Fair enough. I want my friends back."

There was silence. "I don't believe you have any friends in my care."

His chest went cold as he realized they might be dead. Was that what she meant? She might be calling just to let him know just how thoroughly screwed he was.

"Where are Pete and Tamara?"

She didn't answer right away. Taking a deep breath, she said, "I believe they are being looked after."

"Well, those are the ones I consider my friends."

She made that strange purr that wasn't exactly a purr again. "I believe we define friendship differently."

"Are they alive?" Jesus, what was this, a really bad game of

"Twenty Questions: the Vampire Edition?"

"How would you define 'alive,' Mister Keep? I suspect my definition is a tad more liberal than yours."

Cute.

"Lady, are you just messing with me? If so, I've got better things to do. If you want to negotiate, let's negotiate. Until then, why don't you go do something creative for a change and rob a blood bank?"

He hung up on her. The act felt bold and clever at the time he did it, but in the silence that followed, he just felt foolish.

While sitting at an intersection, waiting for the light to change, he realized she was testing him. There was more to it than that, though. She was putting him in his place. She hadn't killed Pete or Tamara—not yet. Unfortunately, that gave her leverage over him.

He needed to change that.

# CHAPTER THIRTY-TWO

When it comes to war, the more someone knows about their enemy can make all the difference. Gidion knew only a few facts about Elizabeth. None of them let him know where to find his friends or Elizabeth's lair. Thanks to Pete's brother, though, he knew there was at least one way to get to the "Queen Bee."

Gidion drove to the safe house where he first met Tamara. He was glad to see Stephanie's car wasn't in the driveway of her house. That gave him the time he needed.

The best traps are the ones that an enemy can't avoid, even if they know it's a trap.

Gidion kept watch from the den window of the safe house. From there, he could see down to the corner. About two o'clock he saw a car make the turn onto Tolliver Court. By the time Stephanie turned into her driveway, he was blasting the stereo in the house and cranked it as loud as it would go. He'd made sure to choose a rap song with lots of bass and plenty of vulgar language, the kind of music guaranteed to make the white-bread suburbanites on this street call the cops. "No loud music" was rule number five on the nice pamphlets kept in the foyer.

For good measure, Gidion left the front door sitting open a few inches. He'd kept almost all of the lights, including the one on the front porch, turned off. No one would be able to see the front door was cracked open, unless they walked up to it.

Stephanie was guaranteed to do that.

The last thing she wanted was for the police to come here and find the door sitting open. For all of the handy rule pamphlets and Stephanie's daily cleanings, which he assumed she did after school, the basement still had its share of suspicious bloodstains. The walls were lined with benches and shackles which he assumed would keep a tasty snack confined if a vampire wanted to save it for later.

Cops searched insecure properties, and the one light he'd left on inside this house was the one in the basement. He'd also left the back door sitting wide open. The tall hedges in the backyard wouldn't let neighbors see that door very easily, but the cops would do a three-sixty of the property and find it. He was willing to bet that Stephanie would, too, assuming she didn't go right inside to turn off the music.

Of course, the police weren't going to come. The music had only just started blasting. Stephanie wouldn't know that, though. For all she knew, the music could have been going on for hours and the cops were already on the way.

He'd frustrated her for sure. She ran towards the house, but hesitated several times. She pulled out her cell phone, probably calling for vampire or feeder backup. Odds favored they wouldn't get here that quickly. Stephanie would have to get things under control before that point lest irritated neighbors call the police.

Gidion had borrowed the portable stereo from Grandpa's house for this. The stereo was a Christmas gift from him and Dad. Good thing they didn't go cheap.

The stereo was sitting on the floor in the center of the room. Just as she walked up to it, Gidion attacked. Even through the blasting rap music, he heard her scream, not that anyone else would. She fell back to the floor, all without Gidion landing a single punch or a kick.

Gidion stood from behind the chair where he'd been hiding. Stephanie's body convulsed. He quickly shoved a rag into her mouth and covered it with duct tape. Then he turned off the music. She still screamed, but at least it was muffled. He closed and locked the front door. That was him being a jerk, because he was willing to bet the only person with the keys would be Stephanie.

"You enjoying the Taser, Steph? Found that in the trunk of your vampire friends' car."

Her body shook, and she grunted just before he rolled her onto her stomach. Unfortunately, stun guns and Tasers don't automatically render a person unconscious like in the movies. Sometimes the blow to the head from the fall might do that, but he hadn't gotten that lucky. For the moment, Stephanie was at least knocked pretty senseless.

"The first shot's the worst, I'm told. Those little jolts you're feeling just keep you too incapacitated to rip out the nodes I shot at your back." He slapped a pair of handcuffs on her wrists. "Look on the bright side; it's a lot kinder than what my box cutter would do to you."

Another pair of handcuffs went around her ankles. Then he carried her to the Toyota he'd parked in the garage, threw her on the floorboard of the backseat and covered her with a tarp the vampires had kept in the trunk along with their handcuffs and the Taser.

He wished the Taser would have kept shocking her, but that only lasted for about thirty seconds. She started to recover from the shocks about the time he was turning back onto Midlothian Turnpike.

Stephanie kicked the back of his seat. She screamed through her gag. He glanced back to make sure she wasn't getting up. Not likely with the way he had her cuffed up.

"Just be patient, Stephanie. I won't leave you back there for long."

And she sure as hell wasn't going to like things any better once he got her out of the car.

# CHAPTER THIRTY-THREE

Binding Stephanie to a tree turned out a lot trickier than he'd expected. Fortunately, he discovered he could use the Taser gun even without the little nodes shooting out the front of it. Knowing his luck, she'd gain superpowers from all of these repeated shocks and start zapping him with lightning bolts from her hands.

After making her a bit more compliant, he bound her with a set of bungee cords he also kept in his blue backpack.

She screamed as loud as she could, and did pretty well considering she was still gagged.

"What's that?" he asked with a taunting smile.

She glared at him and screamed.

"Oh, you're calling for help? Allow me." He stepped back and shouted as loudly as he could. "HELP!" He laughed at her and then turned his back to her as he dug through his backpack. He wasn't getting anything else out of the bag. He just needed a moment to get his game face reset. The minute Roddy had let slip how important Elizabeth's "little girls" were, he'd known he'd have to do this. Interrogating that vampire at the funeral home wasn't nearly as daunting as tying up and threatening a girl, even one all gothed out like Stephanie.

"These woods," he said without looking back at her, "are a little ways off of I-64. You might enjoy the irony; it was Pete who found it. We came out here a few times with our toy lightsabers and beat the snot out of each other. Not a soul bothered us, and nobody's going to hear you screaming either. Even if it wasn't the middle of nowhere, the traffic on the interstate would drown out your screams. The car's too far off the road for anyone to see it either."

He stood and walked back over to her and waved the cell phone he took from Milton in her face. "Now you stay nice and still. I want a good picture of you to send to your vampire mommy."

How he didn't flinch when he snapped the shot of her, he wasn't sure. Now that he was this close, he could see her eyes were blue. There was no missing them, bulging from their sockets in desperation.

"That'll work."

He petted her on the head like he would his dog Page. "Good girl." He grinned at her. "Is that what she does after she bleeds you? Or does she give you a little tummy rub and throw a ball in the house for you to fetch? You're just a pet, after all."

Desperation was replaced with the rage he'd grown accustomed to seeing from Steph. The guttural cry must have hurt her throat.

"You know, my parents had a cat when I was born." He typed his text to go along with the picture he'd just taken. "My mom loved that little furball, had owned it for years, but then it tried to suffocate me in my crib. Guess which one of us got sent to the pound after that?"

He held up the cell phone for her to see her picture and read the text. "I'm willing to bet Elizabeth is going to have a similar reaction when she sees this."

The text read, *Elizabeth, call me. It's time to negotiate.*

"Of course, she might just decide you really are worth saving and trade you for Pete and Tamara." He shrugged. "See, this is what I like to call a win-win scenario. Even if your owner doesn't make the trade, I get the satisfaction of knowing you're gonna die out here, and probably long before Tamara, too."

He pressed the send button on the phone and watched as the picture uploaded. A pretty little graphic with the words "Message Sent" appeared. He held it up for Stephanie to see it.

"Let's discuss options here, Stephanie, because I'm guessing Roddy isn't going to want to show that to the 'Queen Bee' right away." He walked back to the car and sat on the hood. "Now, I suspect you're still too pissed to have really considered your situation.

I'm assuming you got your vampire blood fix tonight, but I'm also guessing you made a donation. You don't feel how weak you really are, because you're still riding your high. You get daily doses of that crap? Yeah, I'll bet you do, so you're gonna feel the withdrawals by tomorrow night, if not sooner."

He narrowed his eyes, looking hard into her stare. "And I bet they're gonna hurt real bad."

He drank some water from a bottle he also kept in his backpack. "Now, since I'll wager your vampire friends aren't bothering with giving Pete or Tamara any food or water, I plan to give you the same treatment. Bet you're plenty thirsty, too, after all that screaming."

Did she have any clue how difficult it was for him to meet her glare and keep a smile on his face? He doubted it. Unlike his interrogation with Milton, Stephanie wasn't working with heightened senses. She couldn't hear how fast his heart was working or see the shake of his hands. If her senses were telling her anything, it was probably how tight those bungee cords were, how uncomfortable the tree's bark was against her back and how chilly the night air was.

He glanced at the phone to give his poker face a small break. "Hmmm...still no reply. Not looking good for you. Right now, I'd guess Elizabeth is trying to decide if you're worth the trouble of saving. After all, your little vendettas with Ms. Aldgate and Tamara are the whole reason her coven has been exposed.

"Why'd she let you do it? Some kind of gift she offered you for being a good little blood whore?" He took a sip of his water and put the bottle away. This wasn't all about payback for him, treating Stephanie like this. He needed her to realize how desperate her situation really was, because he didn't expect Elizabeth to make the trade. If he was right, and there was no deal to be had, then he'd need to get what information he wanted out of Stephanie. She wasn't going to talk if she thought for one minute she had any other way out.

The phone in his hand vibrated. "Ah, look who's calling." He hopped off the hood of the car, walking to Stephanie and waggling the phone in her face. He hit the button for the speaker phone mode. "Hello, thank you for calling Feeders 'R' Us."

"Mister Keep, I'd be more impressed if you were holding a hand more impressive than mine."

He grinned at Stephanie and mouthed the words, 'Told you so,' before he responded to Elizabeth's comment.

"Well, I won't lie," Gidion said, "I think Tamara is a far better catch than your little goth princess."

"How fortunate you should feel that way, because I assume you're calling to offer a trade, are you not?"

He had her amused. He wasn't sure if that was a good or bad sign.

"Glad to see you're not as dumb as your followers, Beth. If you want your little girl back, then I want Pete and Tamara returned unharmed."

"No, Mister Keep." She laughed as if they were trading jokes over tea. "You misunderstand me. I realize you hope to trade Stephanie for your friends, but I am only interested in an even exchange. If you return Stephanie to me, I will free Peter: a feeder for a feeder."

"That's a bullshit trade, and you know it." Sure she'd free Pete first. He was just as likely to crawl back to them on his own for a hit of blood. He'd hoped for an outright refusal from Elizabeth. The token offer for a trade might work against his attempt to manipulate Stephanie, give her false hope.

"Are you suggesting such a trade is unfair?"

He laughed. "I'm suggesting you're an idiot if you think I'll settle for anything less than both Pete and Tamara's safe return."

"It seems we have reached an impasse."

Gidion looked up at Stephanie and saw her glare. Worst of all, he saw his strategy wasn't working at all. He had to turn this around somehow.

"Let me ask you this, Elizabeth, if I were to offer an exchange of Stephanie for Tamara, what would you say?" He just hoped Pete wasn't listening in the same way he had Stephanie unwillingly doing so. It wouldn't be hard for Elizabeth to turn Pete against him with the same strategy.

"How chivalrous, saving the damsel in favor of your friend."

Shit. She was doing exactly that.

"Never said I was giving up on saving him, lady," he snapped. "Now just answer the question. Will you make the trade?"

The line went silent. He glanced down to verify the line was still open, which it was. She hadn't expected this. Score one for him maybe.

"If you have any hope of ever seeing Stephanie in one piece again, I'd recommend agreeing to this."

"No, Mister Keep, I don't—"

He hung up before she could finish whatever she was about to say. Odds favored it would mitigate the damage of her refusal, and he didn't want that.

"Seems your ex-boyfriend isn't the only one who prefers Tamara's company to you."

He shut off the phone and slid it into his pocket. Better not to give Elizabeth a chance to call back while he played this hand with Stephanie.

"Just to show I'm not completely heartless…" He ripped the duct tape from her mouth. She shrieked. Her skin was red and raw from where the tape had been. She spit out the rag and coughed.

He flicked two fingers at her from his forehead in a parting salute. "At least you can maybe drink a few raindrops," he said, "if it rains at all." He turned and headed back to the car.

"Where are you going!" The words sounded full of pain. "Gidion! She said she'd trade for me! She said she would!"

*Don't let your face slip now,* he told himself. This was where this either worked or failed. "That's right, Stephanie. What did she say? 'A feeder for a feeder'?" He laughed. "That's exactly how much she values you."

"She loves me!" Regaining her voice filled her with a new determination to get free. She struggled against the bungee cords, but he had them too tight for her to move anywhere. The handcuffs to her wrists and ankles didn't help.

"Loves you? 'A feeder for a feeder,' Stephanie. How much does she really value you? I remember your opinion of Pete. You called him a decoration and a gargoyle." He opened his car door, but didn't climb in right away.

"No! I'm her favorite! I'm—"

"What you are to her is replaceable!" He stormed back towards her. "How much do you want to bet she's already debating on how difficult it might be to convert Tamara into a feeder? She likes them pretty, and we both know how much more beautiful Tamara is than you. Your ex obviously agreed."

"You're a fucking pig!"

He got right in her face. Tears ran down her face, the memory of their paths marked by her dark eyeliner. "What I am is your wake-up call. Elizabeth is using you as a maid and a whore. If she loved you so much, there wouldn't be any question about trading you for Pete and Tamara. All she cares about now is killing me. Leaving you here to die is a kindness compared to making that trade."

Stephanie pulled back. "A kindness? Leaving me here to die? You're insane."

"Oh, really. What happened to the head feeder before Elizabeth gave you the honor?" He poured every ounce of sarcasm he could into that last word.

She didn't answer him. She didn't need to. Her blue eyes glistened from droplets of fear and desperation. They told the story of the little girl who'd come before her, and it wasn't a tale that ended happily. He didn't need to know what the mistake was. They both knew the details didn't matter.

"You can die here, or you can die by Elizabeth's loving hands. Just by being captured, you've failed her. By putting the hits on Tamara and Ms. Aldgate, you've endangered her and gotten three of her followers killed. That's twice you've failed her." He pitied her. He reached up and wiped one of those tear trails from her face. "I'm sorry, Stephanie. I wish we could have been friends, but it's too late for that."

She sobbed. His mind insisted he stay cold, but he remembered the Stephanie who'd been in his elementary school homeroom. That girl had been shy, sweet and pretty.

"I don't want to die." The words coughed out between her sobs.

"There's only one path left that lets you live."

She looked up at him. "You really believe you can kill her? She's more than three hundred years old."

"You know where she's holding Pete and Tamara, all of her habits, even where she sleeps." He nodded. "If you tell me all that, then yes, I can kill her…and you get to live to see another day."

The tears flowed again, reflecting the moonlight as they dripped to the ground. The answers spilled from her just as quickly.

# CHAPTER THIRTY-FOUR

Stephanie's screams and sobs had called after him as he left her in the clearing. He promised her he'd come back and free her, if what she'd told him was the truth. He didn't bother voicing that it depended on whether he managed to avoid getting himself killed.

Being on I-64 turned out to be fortunate, because Elizabeth's house was in the far East End. The interstate got him where he needed to go more quickly.

The drive reminded him how long it had been since he'd last slept. Grandpa Murphy would probably warn him against going after Elizabeth or any vampire in his condition, but he didn't see a choice.

The reason he'd captured Stephanie was by moving faster than Elizabeth had expected. He realized Stephanie added one more life to the list of those now riding on his success. Tamara's parents were already dead. He just hoped Tamara wouldn't blame him for that, because he'd underestimated how desperate he'd made the Richmond Coven, how far they'd be willing to go to stop him.

All he could do now was follow through with his plan to finish off Elizabeth and her coven. The supplies he needed required a stop by his Kia, but he knew that would be safe now. Elizabeth had called him with Roddy's phone earlier, so that meant he was with her. Thanks to Stephanie, he now knew the full roster to Elizabeth's coven. She only had Roddy and one other vampire left. That didn't leave her vampires to spare to watch his car in Carytown. Pity it still had two flat tires.

He retrieved two spray bottles from the trunk of the Little Hearse and a two-pack of lighters, the kind with the trigger and long, black wand. Despite how certain he was it was safe to be here, he moved quickly and kept an eye out for any possible feeders. There were still four of those creeps out there, according to Stephanie, but he suspected if they were staking out anywhere, then it was likely his house. They wouldn't be at Elizabeth's. Only the head feeder was ever allowed there.

By the time he reached the neighborhood where Elizabeth's house was hidden, the clock on the dashboard display on his borrowed Toyota was getting close to four. He legally parked his car on the road, positioned so that it wasn't directly in front of any single house. He wiped down the interior to make sure he wouldn't leave any fingerprints. There was a good chance he might not make it back to the car before any cops arrived, and he didn't want anything leading to him left here. He also needed to limit anything that would prompt a call to the police. The only thing he had in his favor was that Elizabeth wouldn't want police showing up at her house either.

This was where things would get risky for him, though. He would be putting his trust in Stephanie's intel. If what she told him about the house was true, then it explained exactly why Elizabeth had chosen 9718 Callums Hill Road as her home. From the outside, the two-story house with its white vinyl siding hid what made it unique. The entire subdivision had belonged to a wealthy family up until the 1970s when the family business had gone bust. The plot where Elizabeth's house was built happened to fall exactly where the original home had been, right on top of a fallout shelter that had been added to the property back in the sixties. According to Stephanie, the Cuban Missile Crisis had created a plethora of homes with underground shelters perfect for vampires. The designer for this house had cleverly altered the cookie-cutter design to include a set of stairs leading from the kitchen to the hidden bunker.

The house itself offered plenty of subtle warnings for people to stay the fuck off the property. The backyard was surrounded by a nine-foot tall, wooden privacy fence. The front yard was bordered by neatly trimmed bushes that, while not nearly tall enough to hide the house, created a subconscious deterrent to coming onto the property. The most obvious touch was a black sign on the front mailbox that stated "No Trespassing" in big orange letters.

Gidion approached the house from the side by cutting through the neighbor's yard and hopping the hedges. The house design didn't include any windows on this side of the house, because of the garage. From this point forward, it was all about moving too fast for anyone to see him and avoid arousing the neighbors' suspicions. Cutting through the neighbor's yard was about as great a risk as he could take.

From there he pulled out one of the spray bottles he'd hooked to the back of his belt. He sprayed the side of the house like an over-enthusiastic exterminator laying down a layer of insecticide. The vampires inside wouldn't likely miss the scent of gasoline outside the house, not with their heightened sense of smell. He was banking on that.

He hopped the privacy fence. Signs on the fence warned to "Beware of Dog," but according to Stephanie, there weren't any. Given how dogs reacted to vampires, he wasn't surprised. There weren't any lights on the outside of the house that reached over here, so that left him enough shadows to go unnoticed by any neighbors who might just happen to look out their windows, not that many were likely to at four in the morning.

He managed to spray most of the back of the house with gasoline before the door to the kitchen opened. The only thing missing was Bela Lugosi saying, "Enter freely and of your own will." He didn't drop the spray bottle in his hand to draw his box cutter. Instead, he waited, ready to draw his weapon if Roddy or his remaining partner attacked. Stephanie had said that one was a woman Elizabeth had turned a few years ago. The woman hadn't been a feeder, which had led to the deadly friction between Elizabeth and Steph's predecessor.

The vampires never came out, though. They wanted him inside. That was just as well. He'd been debating on how he was going to manage that without making a lot of noise, breaking a window and the sort.

He sprayed more of the back with the gasoline, emptying the sixteen ounce spray bottle. The vampires must have been pretty confident he wouldn't torch the house with Tamara and Pete in there. They were right. Despite his bravado with Grandpa, he couldn't just burn this place down. According to Stephanie, Tamara and Pete were being held in the underground bomb shelter. They'd probably be safe down there, but that didn't guarantee the vampires wouldn't kill them out of spite or simply hole up in the shelter with them.

Part of him had hoped the gas would draw Roddy or the other vampire outside. No such luck. They were being patient, forcing him into the dark and where the walls would muffle any screams.

No point in keeping them waiting. He remembered Roddy saying, "Time is on my side," in that sing-song voice back at the diner in Carytown. Had that really been this same night? It felt like a week ago.

The memory of Grandpa Murphy's wisdom chided him, 'Move fast, be smart and know when to run like Satan's close enough to lick your ass.' Running wasn't an option tonight. He walked onto the back porch to the open door. This was going to be close quarters combat. That meant he'd go in with the box cutter drawn instead of the sword.

The kitchen looked immaculate, likely by virtue of having never been used in the decade since Elizabeth acquired the place. Even though it didn't have a table, it did contain an island. The counter had a block of knives. He didn't want to think about what they did with those.

A flash of red light offered him his only warning, but it was enough. He darted to the right as the prongs shot out of a Taser. If he'd been a second slower, this would've been all over. The female vampire must have had the Taser, because Roddy immediately lunged at him from the shadows of the den.

Just before Gidion could swing at him with his box cutter, he realized Roddy had a switchblade in his hand. He dodged Roddy's swings and raced for the island, placing it between them. Roddy laughed. Gidion assumed Roddy was keeping him busy to let his partner reload her Taser.

Gidion decided to go for the unexpected and placed his box cutter down on the island.

"Dumb move, kid."

Gidion pulled the extra bottle from his belt with his left and sprayed Roddy's face with it as the vampire came after him. With his right, Gidion drew the multipurpose lighter and set the vampire on fire.

Roddy howled, dropping his knife as he drew back scrambling for the sink. Gidion sprayed him a second time, sending up a fireball in the kitchen. The bright light exposed the female vampire in the den. The flames distracted her in the middle of reloading her taser. Gidion decided there was enough room in the den for the sword and ran right at her.

She gave up on reloading and tried to get him with the Taser, using it like a stun gun. The sword won. The blade sliced off a finger as he went for her arms. The Taser fell. The vampire shrieked and fled from his attack, but it was already too late. He ran her through the heart with the sword and added a twist to increase the damage as he pulled it free for a slice at her head. She ducked, but not enough to avoid a cut to her forehead. They went back and forth, her trying to flee and him countering with a swing. The longer they took, the more fearful he became that Roddy would recover, despite the endless screams he heard from the kitchen.

Gidion achieved his checkmate. The final swing buried his sword's blade deep into her throat. He didn't take her head, but blood sprayed from the wound and dropped her to the floor with a pathetic mewl. He had to plant his foot on her chest to jerk the weapon free.

The fire that was Roddy was still blazing in the kitchen, sprawled across the island. Flames licked up the thick, black curtains over the sink. The only movement from him was the flames. Gidion scanned the house before drawing closer to him. The stench of burned hair and flesh had Gidion close to puking.

He decided it best to be certain and raised his sword to behead him. He slammed the sword down. Just before he struck, Roddy jerked back. The sword stabbed into the island's surface and stuck.

Roddy hissed at him. His face was reduced to a melted mass with a mouth. The fiery monster ran at him, forcing Gidion to retreat without a weapon in hand. The idea of getting burned in a bear hug made him panic. He ran into the den, Roddy screaming in his pursuit. Just before Gidion was out of room to retreat, he regained his nerve. He stood his ground and kicked Roddy as hard as he could in the chest. For all of Roddy's rage, the fire had weakened him to a charred husk. Even if he hadn't heard the crunch of bone, Gidion felt the ribcage cave beneath his foot. The kick sent Roddy over the back of the sofa. He fell to the floor and went silent after a long sigh as if to exhale his last bit of life. Bits of burning vampire clung to the bottom of Gidion's shoe. He stomped it on the floor to put it out.

Flames slid up the back of the sofa as Gidion waited to be sure Roddy was finished. The burning body didn't twitch. Satisfied that task was done, he looked up at the stairs, expecting to see Elizabeth, but no one was there. He didn't have time to search the house, not with the flames spreading. What mattered was getting Tamara and Pete out of here. He was willing to bet that if Elizabeth was here, then she had probably fled to the safety of the bomb shelter where she had her prisoners.

He wondered if he'd even be able to get in there. Did she want to confront him? The flames had reached the ceiling in the kitchen. Now that he didn't have to worry about a burning vampire coming after him, he worked his sword free. His box cutter had dropped to the floor, and he retrieved that, too.

The door down to the bomb shelter was positioned next to the refrigerator and cracked open. Halfway down the stairs, he crouched for a better look. The bottom wasn't an actual room, but a short hallway with two doors to the right. A small set of keys were placed on a hook on the wall between the doors. The hall appeared empty, so he hurried down with his sword drawn. With any luck, he could use the narrow space to his advantage, charge Elizabeth and run her through.

The first door was open, but the room within was unoccupied. The inside reminded him of the basement in the safe house with a single bench that doubled for a bed. Two chains were linked to the wall and connected to a pair of shackles which were open and lying on the floor. A drain was set in the center of the room.

The second door in the hallway was open with more light coming from it. He crept towards it, but stopped when he heard Elizabeth's voice.

"Gidion Keep, if your goal is to sneak up on me, you would do better to learn to float. You are quite loud."

He leaned forward to glance in the room. Tamara and Pete were in there...with Elizabeth. The Queen Bee smiled at him.

"If he steps through the door, please break her neck, dear Peter."

Gidion had expected some kind of winsome waif; Elizabeth was anything but. She was tall and built like a rock. If she'd been green, she could have passed for She-Hulk's twin sister. She was a black woman, but her skin had lost much of its hue, resembling a grayish-brown that was still strangely attractive.

She stood just behind Pete and stroked his hair with propriety.

"Hey, Gidion." Pete laughed. His smile was nervous and his glassy eyes refused to stay focused on one thing. As unfocused as he appeared, his grip on the chain wrapped around Tamara's neck was taut. The chain was bolted to the far wall and attached to the shackle on Pete's right wrist.

Tamara was pushed to her knees. Her fingers clawed at the chain choking her. He recognized it was a token effort, though. Thin lines of blood spilled down her throat to her light purple night shirt. She'd been fed on to weaken her. Pete appeared to have received the same treatment, only he'd been given a taste of vampire blood. Given how jittery Pete sounded, Elizabeth had probably fed him from herself. Odds favored he wasn't used to that kind of quality product and certainly not as weak as he'd been, like going from Advil to cocaine.

"Pete, let her go."

Elizabeth's hand gripped Pete's head. "If Mister Keep fails to do what I say, you will pull that chain tight until she dies." She spoke softly into his ear. "Do that, and I'll let you drink from me."

The way Pete's hand shook, he was half-choking Tamara already.

"Pete, she's just going to kill you."

"No." Her voice managed to cut at him and soothe Pete at the same time. "I take the pain away. Don't I, Peter?"

Pete nodded like he was fighting off a seizure. He was terrified. "Yes, ma'am." That's when Gidion finally understood just how far gone his friend really was. The threat of not having that blood was equal to a gun barrel pressed against his temple.

Elizabeth lazily pointed at Gidion's sword. "Mister Keep, place your weapon on the floor and slide it over here."

Gidion considered sliding it to Tamara, but the way Pete was holding her, she'd never be able to reach down for it. On the upside, she wasn't chained to the wall like Pete. They must have been holding her in the first room and brought her in here for Elizabeth's little show of power with Pete.

Did Elizabeth realize he had the box cutter in his hoodie's pocket? If not, that might work in his favor. He just needed to get close enough. She wouldn't go down easily, though. She'd just fed, and she resembled some kind of wrestler. He'd kind of hoped for one of those Victorian gals in some ridiculous outfit that made fighting impractical, but Elizabeth wore a bright green sports tank and black workout pants.

"So what's your play here, Elizabeth? You think that chain around Tamara's throat will keep me from stopping you from walking out of here?"

She didn't answer right away. Her head canted as if that improved her view of him. "I'd be tempted to try and turn you. You have such a talent for killing that it seems a pity to waste it, but I've seen other elders try to turn their enemies." She chuckled. "Such efforts always end in disaster. No, Mister Keep, I mean to kill you. Here. Now."

He took his time kneeling to set the sword on the floor. "Just to satisfy my curiosity, what have you got planned for Tamara?"

"Killing you seems waste enough." She reached around Pete to caress Tamara's bare shoulder. "I might try to keep this one. Killing her parents seems to have taken the fight out of her. I suspect you dying next will finish the job." She smirked at him. "Stall any longer and any option for Tamara's continued life will vanish with an unpleasant snap of her neck. Slide the sword over."

"Surprised you aren't willing to do it yourself." Gidion kicked the sword towards her. "You like fucking up the little girls, just not killing them. Why is that?"

Despite the fire above, the room dropped a few degrees from the chill in her eyes. He wondered what the chances were anyone had noticed the fire yet. Given the privacy fence and that it was about 4:30 in the morning, probably not likely if the flames hadn't moved outside yet. "Oh, I'm willing to get my hands dirty, Mister Keep. I simply need my hands free to get your blood on them first."

Pete's eyes continued to dance around the room, but now Gidion understood why. They were avoiding looking at Gidion out of guilt.

"I'm going to play with your friend, Peter," Elizabeth whispered to him. "Keep the chain tight."

Elizabeth stepped around Pete and hissed at Gidion. Damn she was tall. This crazy bitch looked like she wanted to beat him to death with her bare hands. The bad news was that she looked more than capable of it.

Only she wasn't going to settle for that. She stopped to pick up his sword.

"What's good for the goose, Mister Keep."

Was it too much to hope she didn't have any skill with a sword? The way she rushed at him answered that fast enough. Her swings were swift and controlled. Her third swing slit through the front of his shirt, and if he hadn't jumped back when he did, his stomach would have split open instead of sporting a light cut.

Gidion retreated back into the bunker's hallway.

"No, don't run away, Mister Keep."

He didn't answer. Instead, he pulled out his box cutter. The sight of the small blade received a loud laugh from Elizabeth.

A feint drew her into a swing at him, but she was too skilled to give him an opening. They went back and forth. The lack of sleep and the mass of bruises his body had suffered the past week were taking their toll. She moved with a lizard's speed and ease. That she hadn't run him through yet was a miracle or perhaps a sign she was just toying with him.

Desperate to gain the advantage, Gidion rushed at her. She slashed at his leg, sending him to the floor. Pain blinded him, the fall only adding to the pain. She'd driven the blade deep with that cut.

"Disappointing," she said.

He rolled forward as she swung the sword down at him. With one hand, he grabbed her wrist, stopping the attack short of his torso. He sliced her forearm with his box cutter. Blood rained onto his head, getting in his hair and his face.

Elizabeth's scream echoed off the bare, metal walls. Before he could deliver another cut, she flung him down the corridor at the stairs. He slid across the smooth surface, the top of his back cracking against the edge of the bottom step, sending lightning bolts of agony through his body.

He recovered just in time to see Elizabeth run at him, sword raised and ready to strike. She slammed the sword down, every bit of her strength behind the attack. He rolled to the right and felt the breeze from the swing. The blade struck the concrete with a chime and snapped.

Gidion planted his foot into her stomach. The break in his sword had caught her by surprise, put her off-balance. He wasn't sure how much the kick had hurt her, but it sent her falling backwards. She lost the sword trying to break her fall with her hands and it landed several feet behind her, just beyond his reach.

He took the opening he had and jumped on her. He slammed the butt of his box cutter at her face. The impact hurt his hand, but he heard something crunch. She'd heal from whatever injury it was quickly enough, but he'd hurt her and made her scream. He punched with his left at her throat. Her eyes widened as the blow cut off her air for a split second, her scream cut in half.

The next strike was with the box cutter, the blade intended for her jugular. Elizabeth grabbed his forearm, stopping him short of his target. Before he could counter, her other hand wrapped around his throat and lifted him off her. He gasped, unable to catch a breath. He tried to pry off her fingers as the lack of air made him panic. He needed to get free. His heart was pounding wildly, and he swore he could hear it like a drum in his ears. He forced down his fear, realizing he couldn't peel off her fingers, that getting free would require something thought out, if he had enough air to feed his brain for the task.

He reached at her face, hoping to stab her eyes with his fingers. She held her arm straight, and her reach was longer than his. No chance of that attack. Goddammit, think! Act! He scratched at her arm. His fingernails drew blood, but not enough to make her release him.

"Oh, don't worry. I won't choke you to death, just enough to put you down and drink every last bloody drop from you." A line of blood dripped from above her right eye and down into her mouth. Red shined at the edges of her fanged teeth, and he knew his blood would be there soon if he didn't do something in the next few seconds.

The sides of his head ached as if his skull might explode. His vision blurred, and his body felt as if it was falling in a wicked spin even though he wasn't moving.

Elizabeth stood, lifting him off his feet. Crap, he was going to pass out. He tried to kick at her, but he wasn't sure his legs were answering his commands.

He realized he was going to die with Elizabeth's fanged smile for his last vision. The thought angered him, but all the fury in the world wasn't going to put air back in his lungs.

Then the smile on Elizabeth's face vanished. Her jaw dropped open with a gasp. Her eyes which had been boring into his looked down. Gidion fell to the floor. He tried to land on his feet, a vain hope. He was too close to the brink to jump back like that. The best he managed was to keep on his knees and his body somewhat upright. Blood flowed down the front of Elizabeth's body. The shattered end of his sword jutted out from between her breasts.

She turned with a hiss. Gidion looked past her to see Tamara. Her body shook, probably from the exhaustion of being fed on and getting free of Pete, however she'd managed it.

Gidion needed his box cutter. He'd dropped it and saw it on the floor between him and Elizabeth.

The vampire rushed at Tamara, who collapsed to the floor. Tamara's shrill scream threatened to shatter his eardrums, but it pushed him into action. He scrambled to his feet and snatched up his box cutter.

Elizabeth grabbed Tamara by her face and shoulder. She was pulling her close to bite her throat open.

Gidion snagged hold of Elizabeth's long hair and yanked hard. In the same move, he slit open her throat and shoved her head forward, her chin pressed against the top of her chest, much as he had with the vampire on the Canal Walk a week ago. The hilt of his sword, sticking out of her back, made holding her that way difficult.

She tried to shake him loose. He refused to release his hold. She thrashed about, but the narrow corridor helped pin her. He slammed the top of her head against the wall, the crack audible above her growls. His hands shook as he struggled to maintain his hold. Blood splattered from her wounds onto the white walls like a red Rorschach. Her attempts to break free devolved into stumbles. She ran into the walls until she dropped to her knees and crawled.

Gidion shoved her face to the floor. He ripped the bottom half of his sword free from her back. It didn't have much length left, but it would be enough.

The narrow space combined with his shortened weapon made her beheading a gruesome act that required several attempts. Each swing cut deeper until her head came free. He wouldn't settle for anything less than a certain death for Elizabeth. For good measure he tossed her head into the shelter's empty room.

Pathetic sobs and screams drew his attention back to the far end of the corridor. Tamara stared at him. Blood covered her face. She'd probably been covered when Gidion slit open Elizabeth's throat. The weak cries weren't from her, but rather from Pete, still chained in his cell. She was on the edge, though. That she wasn't a bubbling mess surprised him, but he needed to focus her.

He snatched the keys off the hook on the wall and went to Tamara. "The house is on fire." He kept his voice calm and soothing. "Don't talk, just run. I'll be right behind you, as soon as I free Pete." She reached out for his hand, and he pulled her to her feet.

Her grip on his hand tightened. "I'm not walking out of here without you."

He didn't argue with her. "Wait here."

She let him go as he went back into the small room with Pete. He was still sobbing in the room as Gidion went to him. His body was sprawled across the floor.

"Pete, we have to go." He wasn't as gentle with Pete as he'd been with Tamara. He jerked him up and slammed him back against the bench.

"I'm sorry." Tears and snot ran down his face, and he didn't seem to care enough to wipe off either.

Gidion unlocked his shackles and jerked him to his feet.

"Just shut up and move! I'm not going to die in a fire, because you're fucking sorry." He shoved him into the corridor. "Move!"

Gidion had to hold him by the back of his shirt and push him forward to keep him moving. Tamara kept a step ahead of them, stepping around Elizabeth's headless corpse, trying without success to not step in the puddle of her blood. Pete stared at the blood and groaned. He only turned his head forward when they reached the top of the steps.

The heat crushed against them. The kitchen and living room were consumed in fire.

"Keep low!" Gidion nodded to Tamara, and she ran out first. He went right behind her, pushing Pete out of the shelter's safety. If no one had called 911 yet, it would be a damn miracle. Flames were licking out through the windows and the open door. By the time they went out the back, Pete no longer needed Gidion's prompts. They raced into the backyard.

Tamara was sitting on the ground on her knees. He was shocked to see her smile. "I didn't think we'd make it out of there."

He hugged her. "I'm sorry." She clung to him, and her body felt good. His own exhaustion nearly bested him then, but they couldn't stop yet. The flames were rushing around the house where he'd sprayed the gasoline. "We have to go before the fire department gets here."

They ran out the gate. The sky was still black but the stars were lost with dawn drawing near. He led them to the vampires' Corolla. They piled into the car, cranked it up and sped away. As they turned out of the subdivision onto the main road, a yellow fire engine screamed past them, its sirens strong enough to shake the car.

Gidion pulled into the parking lot of a convenience store that was still closed and not far from the subdivision. He parked as close to the edge of the road as he could get. Some stores like this set up cameras on the parking lot, and he didn't want to risk being caught on camera.

Another yellow fire unit, this one a large truck, raced past them. Its red lights washed over them for a few seconds before disappearing down the road.

Tamara and Pete both looked confused but neither mustered up the obvious question as to why they'd stopped here. Pete was still crying, his sobs more muted than within the shelter. Tamara was in better control of herself. She'd probably already cried more than once for her parents.

"We aren't done. We need to be smart about this, or all of this could blow up in our faces." He looked Tamara in the eyes, trying to decide if she was really up for this. "Tamara, what comes next is up to you."

He hoped she'd forgive him for what he was about to ask of her.

# CHAPTER THIRTY-FIVE

A pair of police cars rolled into the parking lot of the convenience store. The headlights revealed Tamara sitting on the ground beside the payphone, near the corner of the building. Gidion wondered what it was she said as the officers got out and approached her. He didn't wait to find out.

Gidion had parked across the street in the back lot of a car mechanic shop. The lot opened onto an intersecting street. Now that he knew Tamara was safe with the police, he pulled out onto the connecting road and drove away. If she did what they'd discussed, Tamara would claim to have been abducted by Elizabeth and her cohorts, saying they were a bunch of freaks who "thought" they were vampires. She wouldn't know why they came after her. She still didn't know. There hadn't been time for Gidion to tell her about Stephanie's vendetta with her and his teacher. Her story would still include a rescuer, but she wouldn't tell them it was Gidion, rather that it had been a stranger. They'd agree that she would describe her ex-boyfriend, just to make sure she'd be able to give a consistent description. There was no hiding her abduction. The best thing was to keep it as close to the truth as possible. Only in this scenario, she'd run until she'd gotten out of the neighborhood and to the nearest payphone. Grandpa Murphy said the best lies were always easier to cover with lots of truth.

Gidion had saved her, and now, he needed her to do the same for him. Police didn't believe in vampires, and there was no hiding the bodies in that house. Not even a fire that big could hide the corpses or that they'd all died before the house was torched. If she didn't convince the police and fire investigators with a consistent story, then he could end up in jail for murder.

Pete sat next to him. They didn't say anything. Gidion remembered how tense things had been between them after Pete had broken that window all those years ago. Pete had never thanked him for taking the fall, and Gidion had resented that. He'd never admitted that, not even to himself, not until now when he had something worse to hold against him.

The silence lasted all the way to Pete's house. Gidion parked across the street, same as he had the day he'd confronted him about being a feeder.

Pete stared at the floorboard. The tears had stopped, but their memories had trailed through the smoke stains on his face to make him look like some kind of goth clown. "I didn't want to hurt her." Gidion realized Pete was talking about Tamara. "I couldn't bring myself to let her go, though."

Gidion nodded. He already knew that. Part of him had hoped Tamara had gotten free, because Pete had found the willpower to let her go. Tamara had told Gidion how she'd managed enough strength to smack the bottom of Pete's chin with the top of her head. Doing that had taken most of her strength, but it had been enough to get free of him and into the corridor where she'd found the sword to drive through Elizabeth's heart.

"Pete, the point is that it's over. They're dead, and they can't hurt you anymore."

"Yeah." He didn't sound convinced.

"You're safe." Gidion put a hand on his friend's shoulder and felt Pete flinch at the contact. "We can get back to our lives, the way they were before all of this. Who knows, maybe you can even get your job back at the car shop?"

Pete nodded. He glanced at Gidion and then at his house. He licked his lips. "I'm tired."

"Me, too. I'm definitely not going to school today." He laughed, but his heart wasn't in it. "Look, get some rest. We can talk about all this later, if you want to."

"Yeah, good idea." Pete forced a smile, and it reminded Gidion of that day in the parking lot outside the comic book shop. He hadn't understood then what his friend had been trying to hide.

Pete climbed out before Gidion could say anything else. He stopped a few feet from the car. After a moment, he walked back and stopped in front of the driver side door.

Gidion rolled down his window. "Pete?"

He never looked up from the road. "You need to change the oil in your car next week." This noncommittal smile cracked his face. "Life blood of a car, you know."

Pete crossed the street and disappeared inside his house without giving Gidion a chance to respond. It was good to see something of the old Pete was still there.

Gidion didn't linger. There was more he needed to do. He drove towards 288. He needed to release Stephanie from where he'd left her on I-64. With any luck, she'd have enough sense to realize that if she ever opened her mouth, Gidion could implicate her in Tamara's abduction.

On the way, he called Grandpa, got him to call the school to report he'd be out sick. With Grandpa calling, he wouldn't have to worry about Dad finding out. Gidion needed to shower and sleep, and at this point, the order was optional.

As tired as he was, though, Gidion felt a renewed buzz of excitement. Against all the odds, he'd saved all of them: Tamara, Ms. Aldgate, and even Pete. The relief gave him the energy to keep going but faltered once he reached the place he'd left Stephanie.

She was gone.

All that was left to show she'd been there were the bungee cords he'd used to tie her to the tree. Someone had piled them neatly at the tree's base. He worried over that long into the weekend, but she never showed up at school again. Perhaps she'd freed herself and realized that no matter how Gidion's battle with Elizabeth ended, her safest option was self-exile from Richmond.

# CHAPTER THIRTY-SIX

Grandpa's theory that the previous Sunday was the last for cooking on the grill turned out wrong. He was back on the deck of their porch cooking steaks to help them stomach yet another Washington Redskins loss.

"Damn proud of you, boy," Grandpa said when Dad went back inside to cut up some vegetables to cook on the grill after the steaks were done.

"Yeah, but I think I've put myself out of a job."

Grandpa laughed as he reached down to check one of the steaks by pressing a knuckle into it, the way he always did. "Naw, plenty of strays to watch for, but best to let you lay low a while. After a kill that big, too risky to jump right back into the hunt."

Gidion sat on the back porch's railing. Grandpa had always seemed bigger than life when he'd been growing up. Somehow, the past few days had diminished his view of him. The old man was frailer than he'd realized.

"Grandpa, do you always drink like you did the other night?" He still remembered that shotgun's barrel pointing at him, how close he'd come to getting shot.

The question didn't get an immediate answer, but Gidion felt the sudden stillness in the air between them.

"Boy, I got a lot of mileage on me. I'll be fine."

"I might not." Gidion glanced towards the back window at Dad. "I need you here, if I'm going to keep doing this."

"I'm not going anywhere." He looked at him as if Gidion wasn't making any sense.

"Why do you drink like that?"

"What the hell kind of question is that?" Grandpa snapped.

"I've seen how you are, what Dad is like, and you were both hunters, too. Just kind of worried that—" He stopped when he realized what it was he was about to say, that he was scared of ending up like both of them—scared to live.

"I'm not in the habit of explaining the way I choose to live, Gidion." He grumped as he flipped one of the steaks. "We've got a good thing going here. Let's not mess it up by talking it into the crapper."

Gidion sighed. He wasn't going to get anywhere with this.

"Dad's going to figure it out eventually," Gidion said. "You do realize that, right?"

"Yep, and he'll be one pissed hombre." Grandpa smirked over at him. "And when he's done fumin' and bitchin', he'll be like me— damn proud of ya. He still believes in the hunt, just ain't up for it anymore."

He looked back through the window at Dad. Gidion felt like he understood him a little better than he used to.

"Any chance I could get an advance on my next paycheck?" he asked.

Grandpa laughed. "How much of an advance are you talking about? You've got a lot of vampire corpses on that check."

"A hundred would be nice. Dad's letting me take Tamara out tomorrow night."

"On a school night? He actually agreed to that?" Grandpa looked over his shoulder at Gidion's dad.

"It's the only time I'm probably going to get to take her anywhere. She's been staying with a friend's family, but her aunt and uncle are flying into town on Tuesday morning. They're going to have her move in with them in Arizona."

Grandpa grumbled. "Sorry, boy. Tough break."

"So does that mean I get the advance?"

Grandpa smiled at him. "Yeah, you'll get it. I'll even throw in an extra hundred so you can take her somewhere really nice. Make it count. You don't want regrets when it comes to women."

"Thanks, Grandpa. By the way, do I get a bonus for killing an elder vampire?"

Grandpa scowled at him. "Don't push it. You're lucky I popped for those two new tires on your car."

It was good to have his car back in drivable condition. Grandpa had gotten it towed and the tires replaced by the time Gidion had woken up at his house. He'd gotten two slightly used tires, too, to keep Dad from noticing they'd been replaced.

● ● ●

The anticipation of his date with Tamara had Gidion's spirits riding high even as he went back to school Monday morning. The excitement took a dive when he pulled the Little Hearse into the campus parking lot. There was almost always at least one cop on duty at the school, but today there were four. The cars were parked in the carpool drop-off in front of the main office.

Two police officers were standing on the front sidewalk. Gidion gripped the shoulder straps to his backpack to conceal the shake in his hands. The officers looked right at him, but as he walked past them, he realized they weren't looking for him. They were simply noting another arrival for the school day.

The mood on the campus just felt off. Students were gathered in all the usual places with their usual crowds, but everyone seemed quieter. What the hell was going on?

He got to the bench where his crowd hung out. Pete, Seth and Andrea had yet to arrive. During the past few days, he realized that it was time to cut Andrea some slack. She wasn't going anywhere, and the only reason he'd found her annoying was because he hadn't wanted her there. For better or worse, she was part of the group. In light of how she'd helped him the other night, it was time to accept those lemons. Besides, at this point, facing Pete on a daily basis was going to be more difficult than putting up with Andrea's motormouth.

"Gid!"

He turned and saw Seth running to him.

"Hey, Seth." Gidion smiled. For once, Andrea wasn't attached to Seth's hip. "What's up?"

Seth stopped short and winced. "Oh, shit."

"What?" There was something in the way Seth was looking at him. Gidion could tell whatever was on Seth's mind, it was bad.

"You haven't heard, have you?"

"Heard what?" Gidion gripped his shoulder straps again, as if that would somehow hide the sudden panic he was feeling.

"About Pete? You haven't heard?"

Gidion swallowed before he answered. "No, what is it?" But even as he asked, he remembered Grandpa's words about feeders. He knew what Seth was going to say.

"Pete's dead."

• • •

The rest of the day didn't feel real.

The way the teachers and other students were looking at him differently didn't have anything to do with that. They all knew he'd lost one of his best friends. A few tried to offer their sympathies. He thanked them, insisted he was fine and tried to get away.

The weather wasn't to blame either. The sun was shining bright like it had on hundreds of other Mondays in his life, but it was the first time he ever felt like the sun was mocking him.

The day didn't feel real, because he didn't want it to.

He walked through his personal fog with teachers blessedly leaving him alone. None of them asked him any questions in class. Maybe they had, and he just hadn't noticed. He wasn't sure, because he didn't notice much of anything even after the bell for lunch rang. He walked to their bench, the one they'd "owned" for more than a year now. After five minutes of sitting in silence, he realized he was the only one there.

Seth had sent a text to his phone right after the lunch bell. Andrea was taking him off-campus for lunch. Seth said he'd call him after school and asked if he was okay. Gidion started to type a reply, but only got as far as, 'I'm.'

He put the phone away and walked until he reached Ms. Aldgate's classroom. She was sitting at her desk with a salad in a plastic container on one side and a pile of papers she was grading in the middle.

"Gidion." She stood and walked around to him. "I heard about your friend when I got to school this morning. I'm so sorry."

Principal Vermil had mentioned Pete's "unfortunate and untimely death" in the morning announcements and how they would have counselors available to students who wanted to speak to one. He left out the part about it being a suicide, the part about how Pete had taken his dad's gun with him into the shower and stuck the barrel in his mouth and pulled the trigger.

Seth had given him the details before that. He hadn't wanted to. Gidion had grabbed him by the shirt and made him say it. He hadn't cried then. He didn't want to.

"Do you want to talk?" Ms. Aldgate asked.

He shook his head doing his best not to look at yet another sympathetic face. "Can I just stay here until class?"

"Of course."

Despite his best efforts, he saw her concerned smile as she nodded.

He went to his desk and sat. He pulled out his world history textbook, but he didn't open it. That mundane book sat there laughing at him like the sun.

There were no vampires to hunt and no more souls to save. He wanted to run, and there was nowhere to run to.

That was when he cried.

He didn't see Ms. Aldgate come over to him, but he felt her there when she hugged him. "I'm sorry, Gidion. I'm so sorry."

She didn't ask him any questions. She just held him until the tears slowed.

"Just stay," she said. "I'll be back in a moment."

She went to her desk and wrote something on a piece of paper before leaving the room. She closed the door behind her. He was glad to have the privacy. When the bell rang for the end of lunch, he suddenly realized nobody from his class had come into the room.

When Ms. Aldgate returned, she left the classroom door cracked open and sat in the chair of the desk next to his.

"Where's the class?" he asked.

"They're in the library," she said. "I'm making today a research day."

He put his book back into his bag. "Do I need to—?"

She touched his shoulder to keep him from standing and shook her head. "No, you're going home."

"I'll be fine."

"I know you will, but you're not fine right now. There's no reason to be ashamed of that."

"I couldn't save him." The admission had him close to crying again.

"You saved me. You saved that girl, too."

"Her parents were killed." Much as he was looking forward to seeing Tamara tonight, he knew this wasn't going to be much of a date. Her parents were going to be buried tomorrow afternoon. Grandpa had made the arrangements, insisting this one was going to be on the house, although he'd said it with more class to Tamara.

"Gidion, you didn't kill them, and I'm certain her parents, wherever they are, are grateful to you for saving their daughter."

He wasn't sure if he believed that, but it sounded good.

"I'm taking her on a date tonight," he said.

"Where to?"

He shook his head. "I don't know. My grandpa gave me about two hundred dollars to spend, but I've never been on a date. I was going to ask my dad for a suggestion, but I don't think he's been on a date in more than a decade."

"Do you mind if I offer a suggestion?"

"I was planning to ask you when I got to school, but then…" He couldn't say the rest. He didn't need to and sure as hell didn't want to.

She didn't answer right away. She rubbed the tip of her thumb against two of her fingers, a gesture he'd seen her use when considering difficult questions from his classmates. "There's a French bistro in Carytown called Can Can. On a Monday night, it probably won't be too crowded, but I'd still suggest making reservations."

"I'll do that." He wondered if he ever would have had a conversation like this with his mom, if she'd still been alive. Life would have been a lot different with her around.

There was a knock at the door. It was his dad.

"Hi, son." Going by the concerned look on his face, he already knew about Pete, but then again, why else would he be here?

"I called him when I stepped out." Ms. Aldgate stood and shook Dad's hand.

"Thank you," Dad said.

"I'll give you two a moment."

Dad waited until she walked out to say anything and sat in the chair where she had been. Gidion was scared he'd be upset, but Dad smiled at him. He must have been asleep when she called. He was just in a pair of jeans and a Henrico Police sweatshirt, and there were bags under his eyes.

"I'm sorry about Pete," Dad said, "and I'm sorry what I said about him the other day."

"No, you were right. Pete was an idiot."

"It's all right to cry."

"No, I don't want to." He shook his head to fight back the tears that were damn close to getting out again. "I couldn't save him."

"You knew he was having problems." Dad wasn't asking. Gidion had told him about as much the other day.

"I don't think 'having problems' really covers it."

"Yeah, I guess not." Dad got a distant look in his eyes before he continued. "One of the worst calls I ever took while working in the 911 center was from a man whose wife shot herself. She was bleeding out of her chest and her back. He was trying to put pressure on the wounds to stop the bleeding while I got help on the way. The police and the ambulance crew got on scene, but they couldn't get inside because the doors were locked. I had to make him let her go to open the door. They pronounced her dead at the hospital." He stopped to take a deep breath. "I still remember how desperate her husband sounded, begging to have the police just break in the door, and I was terrified I'd done the wrong thing in making him leave her side. I came home and cried."

Gidion could see just talking about it had Dad choked up, too, and it was kind of crazy to see that.

"You never told me about that call."

Dad laughed and wiped his nose. "Son, you were twelve or maybe younger than that—far too young for me to be unburdening my woes from work to."

"So why tell me now?"

"Because I didn't put the gun in that woman's hand anymore than you put the one in Pete's. If there's anything I've learned from my job, it's that you can't stop someone from hurting themselves once they've made the decision to do it. They'll always find a way."

Gidion considered that. "But you're still upset by that call, and you didn't even know that man or woman."

Dad smiled. "Yeah, I know. The head and heart don't always work with the same logic."

"Is that why you've never been on a date since Mom died, because you blame yourself?" He'd wanted to ask this ever since he'd realized her death was probably tied into his dad's vampire hunting days. Grandpa wouldn't talk about it, and even if Dad didn't realize he knew about the vampires, this was probably the best chance he'd ever get to force some kind of answer out of him.

Dad shifted in his seat, glancing towards the door. Gidion didn't think Ms. Aldgate was still there, but he thought it was interesting that Dad seemed worried about it.

"Son, what happened to your mom," he paused and the way he stared at Gidion almost seemed to question why he would even ask this, how he'd make that kind of connection without knowing about the vampires. Maybe it was just Gidion's guilty conscience at work, but that's what it felt like he wasn't asking. "It's more complicated than that. I'm not ready to date yet."

"It's been twelve years. That's longer than you were married to her."

Dad leaned back. "I don't think this is the time to discuss this."

"Yeah, and it never will be, will it?" Gidion saw Dad didn't want to answer that, and he knew that was answer enough, so he decided to go for broke. "I see Grandpa, and I don't think he even likes himself. I love him, but I don't want you to end up like that."

That got a laugh out of Dad. "I haven't had enough sleep for this conversation. Do you really think me dating will somehow magically improve my disposition?"

"Yes."

*That's right, Dad,* Gidion thought to himself, *sarcastic questions will not save you today.*

"I'll make you a deal," Gidion said. "If I make all A's in Ms. Aldgate's class, you agree to ask her on a date at the end of the school year."

That definitely made Dad check the door again.

"It's not like I'm asking you to date one of my old hag teachers. At least she's one of the pretty ones."

He held up his hands as if he was agreeing to be handcuffed and hauled off to jail. "Enough. I'll agree to that, but just remember she might turn me down."

"She might not."

"Yes, but if she does, you get to deal with my even worse disposition at having been shot down by a beautiful woman."

Gidion smiled. "I like my odds."

"I'd like to see the report cards first." They shook on it. "Ms. Aldgate told me you came in here at the beginning of lunch. Have you eaten at all today?"

He shook his head. "Wasn't really hungry."

"I am. Want to get some breakfast?"

"Yeah."

There was another knock on the door. Ms. Aldgate was back.

"Hope I'm not interrupting," she said. "I wanted to make

sure you were both all right, and I needed to get a few things from my desk."

"Not at all." Dad stood. "Thank you again for calling me."

"You have a unique son." She smiled at him, and Gidion smiled back. "You have every right to be proud of him. I can tell you are."

"Thank you." He looked back at Gidion as he slipped on his backpack. "Let's go eat."

Ms. Aldgate walked over to her desk, picked up a note pad and wrote something on it. "Mister Keep, before you go," she turned and held out the small sheet of paper to him, "if there's anything I can do to help you and your son, this is the number to my cell phone." Gidion saw a smile tug at her lips. "And you might need that in June."

Dad's face turned red. His lips worked for close to ten seconds before he managed to say anything.

"Thank you."

Gidion covered his mouth, not that it did much to hide he was laughing. Dad took him by the arm and almost dragged him out of the room.

"I think my odds just improved, Dad."

Dad tried to glare at him, but he was smiling too much to pull it off. "Just make sure you get all A's in her class."

# CHAPTER THIRTY-SEVEN

When Dad found out Gidion was making reservations at Can Can, he handed him an extra fifty bucks and made him get a new dress shirt and tie so he wouldn't walk into a nice restaurant "looking like a bum."

The shirt was royal blue and the tie black. He thought Dad was being a worrywart up until he saw the green dress Tamara was wearing. She looked nice, really nice.

Dad also came through by making him get some flowers, two purple roses. He said purple roses were Mom's favorite.

The restaurant was dimly lit and really cool. It reminded him of the inside of an old subway station with its white tiles.

"You look really handsome," Tamara said after they'd ordered dessert. She'd said it about three times, but it hadn't gotten old to hear her say it.

"Thanks," he said, thinking quickly for a different way to repay the compliment. "I needed to. I knew I was going to be with a beautiful girl."

"Nice." She smiled, something she'd done very little tonight. There was no getting past what happened to her parents. He hadn't intended to tell her about Pete, but the rumors of his suicide had traveled to her school. She hadn't been to school today, but the friend she was staying with had.

"I talked to my aunt before you picked me up." She sipped her sparkling water with lime, which was about the only "bubbly" the restaurant could legally let them drink, according to their server.

"What did she say?" He figured it couldn't be good, if she'd waited this long to mention it.

"Our flight to Phoenix leaves Wednesday morning."

"That sucks."

"A lot." She smiled again, but the expression was sadder than before.

"Well, if we can't have a second date, then I say to hell with our curfews."

They raised their glasses of non-alcoholic bubbly and toasted the idea.

After they ordered dessert, she reached into her purse and pulled out a small box, covered in silver paper and blue ribbon. He felt bad as soon as he saw, because he hadn't thought of a gift for her, nothing beyond the flowers.

"It's okay." She smiled at him as she placed it in his hands. "Open it."

He ripped off the paper, trying not to be too loud. The gift was nestled inside the box, resting on a layer of white tissue paper.

"A rabbit's foot!" That was too cool! The fur was grayish-brown and soft. "Where did you—?" He stopped when he realized the answer to his question.

"I saw it on my dad's desk this morning, and I thought of you." She stopped there, and he could tell she was about to cry.

"Thank you." He ran his thumb against one of the tiny toe nails. "I'll keep it with me every night."

"You better." Having fought back her tears, she smiled at him and reached across the table to hold his hand. "Don't you dare go hunting without it."

Dessert arrived. They'd gone all out with their order, getting three different desserts to split: all chocolate. Now that they knew they'd be staying up really late, they decided to get some coffee, too.

"You know," Tamara said between bites of chocolate crème brûlée, "it's not like we can't ever go on a second date."

"I'm not sure how easily I can get to Phoenix. That's one hell of a drive." He employed some playful sarcasm, but there was some hard truth behind the joke.

She offered him a bite of the chocolate crème brûlée. "Eat

this and be quiet." He decided it was best to do what the lady said. Besides, that particular dessert was possibly the best thing he'd ever tasted in his life.

"It occurs to me that I'm a senior. That means in less than a year, I go to college, and Richmond has several universities."

She leaned across the table and crooked a finger for him to meet her halfway. "How would you feel about dating a college girl?"

He answered her with a kiss.

# ACKNOWLEDGEMENTS

The desire to write a book hit me in high school, but it wasn't until I moved to Richmond, Virginia, that I gained the tools to get the job done right. This is a writer's town, home to one of the best writers conferences in the nation. David L. Robbins brought me into the inner workings of James River Writers, and I will always be grateful for the opportunities he gave me by doing that. JRW made Richmond my home.

I've connected with and befriended many writers here. Katharine and Shawna in the Ten Page Club, you both pushed me for many years to improve. Author Tiffany Trent provided important insights on the opening to this book. I also need to thank Kristi Austin for her thorough critique of the first draft. I don't know if Kristi will ever realize how much she kept my faith in this book alive with the declaration, "That book needs a home."

I also need to thank my parents and mother-in-law. They spent many hours with my son and daughter as I went to coffee houses and wine bars to raise this third, fictional child.

Most of all, I need to thank the woman who's been my first reader for almost a quarter century. So many writers don't have a spouse who can truly appreciate the art of the written word and the dark corners of imagination, but I got lucky. I married another writer. Sheri started me on the path to this book in one of my darkest moments with a simple question. "What is it you want to write?" You've now read the answer.